WARRIORS

LEGENDS OF
THE CLANS

WARRIORS

THE PROPHECIES BEGIN

THE NEW PROPHECY

POWER OF THREE

OMEN OF THE STARS

explore the **WARRIORS** world

ALSO BY ERIN HUNTER

SEEKERS

RETURN TO THE WILD

MANGA

SURVIVORS

WARRIORS

LEGENDS OF
THE CLANS

INCLUDES

Spottedleaf's Heart
Pinestar's Choice
Thunderstar's Echo

ERIN
HUNTER

HARPER
An Imprint of HarperCollinsPublishers

Legends of the Clans

Spottedleaf's Heart, Pinestar's Choice, Thunderstar's Echo

Series created by Working Partners Limited

Map art ©2017 by Dave Stevenson

Interior art ©2017 by Owen Richardson

www.harpercollinschildrens.com

ISBN 978-0-06-256087-2

18   19   20   CG/BRR   10   9   8   7   6   5

❖

First Edition

CONTENTS

WARRIORS

SPOTTEDLEAF'S HEART

Special thanks to Victoria Holmes

ALLEGIANCES

THUNDERCLAN

LEADER **SUNSTAR**—bright ginger tom with yellow eyes

DEPUTY **TAWNYSPOTS**—light gray tabby tom with amber eyes

MEDICINE CATS **GOOSEFEATHER**—speckled gray tom with pale blue eyes

FEATHERWHISKER—pale silvery tom with bright amber eyes

WARRIORS (toms and she-cats without kits)

STORMTAIL—blue-gray tom with blue eyes

ADDERFANG—mottled brown tabby tom with yellow eyes

HALFTAIL—big dark brown tabby tom with yellow eyes and part of his tail missing

SMALLEAR—gray tom with very small ears and amber eyes

FUZZYPELT—black tom with yellow eyes

WINDFLIGHT—gray tabby tom with pale green eyes

WHITE-EYE—pale gray she-cat, blind in one eye

POPPYDAWN—long-haired dark red she-cat with an extremely bushy tail and amber eyes

SPECKLETAIL—pale tabby she-cat with amber eyes

PATCHPELT—small black-and-white tom with amber eyes
  APPRENTICE, WHITEPAW

THRUSHPELT—sandy-gray tom with white flash on his chest and bright green eyes

DAPPLETAIL—tortoiseshell she-cat with a lovely dappled coat

BLUEFUR—thick-furred blue-gray she-cat with blue eyes

THISTLECLAW—gray-and-white tom with amber eyes
APPRENTICE, TIGERPAW

ROSETAIL—gray tabby she-cat with a bushy reddish tail

LIONHEART—golden tabby tom, green eyes

GOLDENFLOWER—pale ginger tabby she-cat with amber eyes

LEOPARDFOOT—black she-cat with green eyes

QUEENS (she-cats expecting or nursing kits)

ROBINWING—small brown she-cat with a ginger patch on her chest and amber eyes (mother to Brindlekit, a pale gray tabby she-kit, and Frostkit, a white she-kit with blue eyes)

SWIFTBREEZE—tabby-and-white she-cat with yellow eyes (mother to Spottedkit, a dark tortoiseshell she-kit; Willowkit, a pale gray she-kit with blue eyes; and Redkit, a small tortoiseshell tom with a ginger tail)

APPRENTICES (more than six moons old, in training to become warriors)

TIGERPAW—big dark brown tabby tom with unusually long front claws

WHITEPAW—pure white tom with yellow eyes

ELDERS (former warriors and queens, now retired)

WEEDWHISKER—pale orange tom with yellow eyes

MUMBLEFOOT—brown tom with amber eyes

LARKSONG—tortoiseshell she-cat with pale green eyes

HIGHSTONES

BARLEY'S FARM

FOURTREES

WINDCLAN CAMP

FALLS

CAT VIEW

SUNNINGROCKS

RIVER

RIVERCLAN CAMP

TREECUTPLACE

CARRIONPLACE

SHADOWCLAN
CAMP

THUNDERPATH

OWLTREE

GREAT
SYCAMORE

THUNDERCLAN
CAMP

SNAKEROCKS

SANDY
HOLLOW

TALLPINES

TWOLEGPLACE

DEVIL'S FINGERS
[disused mine]

WINDOVER FARM

NORTH ALLERTON ROAD

WINDOVER MOOR

DRUID'S HOLLOW

DRUID'S LEAP

TWOLEG VIEW

RIVER CHELL

MORGAN'S FARM CAMPSITE

MORGAN'S FARM

MORGAN'S LANE

NORTH ALLERTON
AMENITY TIP

WINDOVER ROAD

WHITE HART WOODS

CHELFORD FOREST

CHELFORD MILL

CHELFORD

KEY
To The
TERRAIN

DECIDUOUS WOODLAND

CONIFERS

MARSH

CLIFFS AND ROCKS

HIKING TRAILS

NORTH

CHAPTER ONE

❧

"*At my signal, unleash the force* of ThunderClan upon these rogues!" Spottedkit sank her claws into the tree stump and looked down at her loyal warriors. They stared up at her, huge-eyed, bristle-furred, ready to strike. Beyond them crouched the rogues, their tails flicking hungrily.

"ThunderClan forever!" Spottedkit yowled.

Below her, a dark tortoiseshell tom whirled around and sprang at the closest rogue.

"No, Redkit! That wasn't my signal!" Spottedkit jumped down from the stump and marched over to her littermate, who was trying to sink his teeth into the scruff of a pale tabby she-kit. "Leave Brindlekit alone!"

The she-kit shrugged Redkit onto the ground. He landed with an "oof!", then scrambled to his paws and glared at Spottedkit. "It sounded like a signal!"

"You didn't tell us what the signal would be," pointed out a white she-kit with eyes the color of the sky.

Spottedkit lashed her tail. "You've spoiled the game, Redkit! You can't be my deputy anymore."

"Can I be the deputy?" mewed a pale gray kit who had been

9

sitting in the shade of the tree stump.

"No, Willowkit, you're my medicine cat," Spottedkit told her.

"But I want to fight in the battle!" Willowkit protested.

A thick-furred white tom stood up from where he had been sitting on the other side of Brindlekit. "I'll be the medicine cat, if you like."

"It's not up to you, Whitepaw," Spottedkit mewed. "I'm the leader, I decide who does what."

Whitepaw scowled. "Well, I don't want to be a rogue. I'm a ThunderClan cat! You're so bossy, Spottedkit!" He padded over to Frostkit. "I'm going to be a warrior."

"But now we only have one rogue!" Spottedkit wailed. "That's not a proper battle!"

"I don't want to be a rogue either," mewed Brindlekit.

Redkit scored the dust with one tiny claw. "We don't want to play with you, Spottedkit. You're always telling us what to do!"

Spottedkit watched miserably as her denmates trotted across the clearing to a sun-warmed patch of sand, where they started batting around an old clump of moss.

"Is everything all right?"

Spottedkit turned to see her mother's tabby-and-white face. "Redkit says I'm too bossy."

Swiftbreeze bent her head and licked the fur on Spotted-kit's neck. Spottedkit snuggled a little closer, purring.

"Maybe you should let one of the others be in charge," Swiftbreeze suggested.

"But they said I could be Clan leader!" Spottedkit mewed.

"That means I have to look after every cat, doesn't it?"

"Well, the medicine cat has some responsibility, too," Swiftbreeze purred. "And no leader could do without their deputy. Think how Sunstar relies on Tawnyspots to organize the patrols."

"When I'm the leader of ThunderClan, I'll be in charge of all the patrols," Spottedkit announced. She curled up against her mother's belly and rested her chin on Swiftbreeze's hind paw. "I'm going to make Whitepaw my deputy. He's kind and smart, and he tells Tigerpaw to stop showing off whenever Thistleclaw teaches him a new way to fight."

Spottedkit felt her mother tense. "Thistleclaw shouldn't be teaching Tigerpaw so many battle moves, not when he's only been an apprentice for two moons. I'll ask Leopardfoot to have a word with him. She's Tigerpaw's mother; she won't want him getting hurt before he has a chance to do his final assessment."

"Leopardfoot doesn't mind, she said so. She says that Tigerpaw is Pinestar's son, so he has to be the best warrior in all the Clan." Spottedkit sometimes wondered how Tigerpaw felt, knowing that his father had left ThunderClan to become a kittypet. Sunstar was leader now, and he never let any cat tease Tigerpaw about his father. But cats still talked when Sunstar was out of earshot, and Spottedkit saw the dark brown tabby apprentice glaring at his Clanmates sometimes as if he blamed them for Pinestar abandoning him.

Spottedkit started following the scent of milk through her mother's belly fur. "Tigerpaw had better watch out. I'm going to be the best warrior ever, so there!"

Swiftbreeze shifted position so that she was lying more comfortably on the earth. "I don't doubt that for a moment, little one," she purred. "But before that happens, you must learn to play nicely with your denmates!"

There was a rustle of branches as cats pushed through the gorse tunnel. Spottedkit looked up over her mother's back, a droplet of milk clinging to her whiskers. "The hunting patrol is back!"

She scrambled to her paws and ran over to the fresh-kill pile where the warriors had lined up to deposit their kill. Tawny-spots was at the front, shoulders tensed under the weight of a full-grown squirrel. The deputy looked thin and his flanks heaved, as if he had run twice as far as the other warriors.

"Good catch!" Spottedkit mewed. The warrior nodded at her as he stepped back to let Tigerpaw's mentor, Thistleclaw, deposit his piece of prey. It was a thrush, its soft tawny feathers fluttering in the breeze. Thistleclaw noticed Spottedkit staring at the feathers. He pulled out a few with his front paw and offered them to her.

"Would you like these for your nest?" he meowed.

Spottedkit felt her pelt tingle. She wasn't sure if she was allowed to have first pick of feathers from the fresh-kill pile. Thistleclaw blinked encouragingly. "Go on, there's plenty for the elders."

Spottedkit stretched up and took the feathers in her mouth. They tickled her nose and she screwed up her eyes in an effort not to sneeze.

"Can I have some feathers, too?" Whitepaw ran over. "Patchpelt is out on border patrol, and I've finished collecting moss for Sunstar's nest." He looked up at his father with his head tilted to one side.

Whitepaw's mother, Snowfur, had died when he was still in the nursery. Spottedkit thought Thistleclaw seemed too young to have a son who was already an apprentice, but he spent time with Whitepaw every day, teaching him extra battle moves and telling him about the patrols. Spottedkit's father, Adderfang, said she was too small to learn anything yet, which wasn't fair *at all*. She was getting bigger all the time!

"Of course you can have some," purred Thistleclaw, scraping off another pawful from the breast of the thrush. He pushed them toward Whitepaw, who buried his muzzle in them. When he lifted his head, tiny feathers clung to his nose.

"Your warrior name should be Wingnose!" Spottedkit mewed. She dabbed some feathers onto Whitepaw's ears. "How many do you think you need before you can fly?"

Whitepaw reared up on his haunches and waved his front paws in the air. "More than that!" he declared.

Thistleclaw held out another clump of feathers. Spottedkit stuck them to Whitepaw's cheeks. "Try now!" she demanded.

A shadow loomed over her. "What's going on?"

Spottedkit spun around guiltily. Bluefur was glaring down at her, blue eyes blazing. "Why are you messing with those feathers?" she growled.

"We were only playing," Spottedkit explained. "We wanted to see if Whitepaw could fly!"

Bluefur looked at Whitepaw, who was trying to blow the last tiny feathers off his muzzle. "You're old enough to know better," she scolded. "Those feathers should be used for the elders' nests, not wasted in a silly game."

Whitepaw hung his head. "Sorry, Bluefur."

Spottedkit felt a stab of indignation. Just because Bluefur was Snowfur's sister didn't mean she could boss Whitepaw around. She started scraping the scattered feathers into a pile. "They can still be used for nests," she pointed out. "Should we take them over to the elders' den?"

"No, Spottedkit, that's an apprentice duty," Bluefur meowed.

"She was only trying to help," Thistleclaw put in. "And it was my fault they were playing with the feathers."

"You should know better, too," Bluefur muttered. She brushed past Thistleclaw and put the thrush back on the fresh-kill pile.

Thistleclaw caught Spottedkit's eye. "Oops," he whispered. Spottedkit tried to muffle her purr of amusement.

"Hey, Thistleclaw! I've been practicing that backward strike you showed me!" Tigerpaw came bounding across the clearing, his paws thudding on the earth. He launched himself into the air, landed on his forepaws, and flicked his hind legs out behind him. "Take that, ShadowClan mouse dung!" he hissed triumphantly.

"Why does Tigerpaw have to show off all the time?" Spottedkit muttered to Whitepaw, who shrugged.

Bluefur looked shocked. "That's a very advanced move!

You shouldn't be teaching him things like that, Thistleclaw."

Tigerpaw bounced on his toes. "Why not?" he argued. "Thistleclaw said I'm as strong as a warrior!"

The gray-and-white tom cuffed Tigerpaw lightly over his ear. "But you still have lots to learn! Did you finish checking the elders for ticks?"

Tigerpaw curled his lip. "That's the worst job in the world! It's not fair. Whitepaw got to go into the forest to fetch moss for Sunstar!"

Thistleclaw narrowed his eyes. "Does that mean you haven't done it? Go now, and then I'll take you out for some more training."

Tigerpaw scowled, but turned and stomped away toward the elders' den with his tail trailing on the ground.

Bluefur snorted. "You're too soft on him, Thistleclaw. He's lazy when it comes to doing anything that isn't learning to fight."

The gray-and-white tom met her gaze. "Are you trying to tell me how to train my apprentice, Bluefur?" There was a hint of warning in his voice.

Bluefur twitched her ears. "Just telling you what I've noticed," she meowed. She kinked her tail high over her back. "There's nothing wrong with wanting to fight, but Tigerpaw needs to learn that there's more to being a good warrior than defeating our enemies."

"I'm making sure he knows everything he needs to," Thistleclaw murmured. Spottedkit felt a thrill of excitement as she saw the warrior slide out his front claws until they pricked the earth. If Bluefur didn't watch out, she'd be fighting her own Clanmate!

The blue-gray she-cat held Thistleclaw's stare for a heartbeat longer, then turned and padded away. Spottedkit realized she had been holding her breath and let it out with a sigh.

"Thistleclaw's back!" There was a thrum of small paws as the other kits charged over to the fresh-kill pile. Brindlekit and Redkit hurled themselves onto Thistleclaw's shoulders, knocking him sideways. Willowkit and Frostkit pounced on his flank to pin him down. The gray-and-white warrior landed with a thud, sending a puff of dust into the air.

Thistleclaw's dark amber eyes were wide and startled, and his nostrils flared as if he was trying to draw breath. "Get off him!" Spottedkit ordered her denmates. "You've winded him!" The same thing had happened to her when she fell off the tree stump, and she knew it was a horrible feeling, waiting for the air to come back.

The kits scrambled off Thistleclaw, looking anxious. Spottedkit crouched beside the warrior's head and placed one paw gently on his shoulder. "Lie still," she mewed. "Try to take little breaths." She glanced over her shoulder. "Whitepaw, fetch Featherwhisker!"

The apprentice raced away to the ferns that hid the medicine cat's den. Thistleclaw blinked and took a rasping breath. "I'm okay," he croaked. He sat up and rubbed his chest with one paw. "Good attack, kits!"

"We're really sorry," Willowkit mewed, huge-eyed. "We didn't mean to hurt you!"

"No harm done," Thistleclaw replied, still sounding as if he had swallowed thorns. He looked down at Spottedkit. "Thank you for taking such good care of me," he murmured. "I don't think I'd have recovered without you!"

Spottedkit glowed from her nose to the tip of her tail. "Anytime!" she mewed.

Whitepaw returned with Featherwhisker. The medicine cat's thick silver fur trailed a scent cloud of herbs. "What's going on?" he demanded.

"We hurt Thistleclaw really badly!" Redkit announced.

"I thought he was dead!" squeaked Brindlekit.

"I'm fine," Thistleclaw purred. "Just a little rough play, that's all."

Featherwhisker mewed in amusement. "What kind of warrior gets knocked down by kits?" he teased before he trotted back to his den.

"One who teaches us the best battle moves!" Spottedkit mewed, and felt a burst of warmth as Thistleclaw blinked at her.

"You'll make a good little medicine cat one day!" he mewed.

"No way," Spottedkit told him. "I want to be a warrior like you!"

Thistleclaw bowed his head. "In that case, it will be an honor to fight alongside you, Spottedkit."

"I can't wait!" Spottedkit whispered.

CHAPTER TWO

"Spottedkit, you have reached the age of six moons, and it is time for you to be apprenticed." Spottedkit was trembling so much, she could hardly lift her head to look up at Sunstar. The leader's yellow eyes were warm as he gazed at her. "From this day on, until you receive your warrior name, you will be known as Spottedpaw. Your mentor will be Thrushpelt."

The rest of Sunstar's words were lost in a blur as Spottedpaw stared at the sandy gray tom who stepped up beside her. Thrushpelt bent his head to brush his muzzle against Spottedpaw's. He smelled of leaves and prey and the wild forest.

"Can we go outside the camp now?" Spottedpaw whispered.

Thrushpelt purred. "In a moment, little one."

Around them, their Clanmates' voices echoed through the ravine. "Redpaw! Willowpaw! Spottedpaw!"

Spottedpaw's littermates stood proudly beside her, their fur gleaming. Redpaw had been given grumpy Halftail as his mentor, and Willowpaw was paired with Poppydawn, who was a bit old but a brilliant hunter. Beyond them, Spottedpaw glimpsed the other apprentices: Frostpaw, Brindlepaw, and Whitepaw, who were shouting the new names the loudest, and

Tigerpaw, who was standing a little way off and not shouting anything. Instead he was glaring at the new apprentices as if they'd put brambles in his nest.

"Ignore him," Redpaw whispered in Spottedpaw's ear. "He's afraid we'll make him look bad when we learn everything faster than him!"

"Tigerpaw should be happy to have more apprentices," Willowpaw pointed out. "He and Whitepaw won't have to do all the duties now."

Halftail padded up to them. "Enough chatter," he ordered. "Are you ready to see our territory, Redpaw?"

"Absolutely!" squeaked Redpaw, bouncing on his toes. Then he looked embarrassed and mewed, "Of course, Halftail. Lead the way!"

The dark brown tom looked quizzically at him. "Well, I wasn't going to ask you to lead."

"We'll join you," said Thistleclaw, his tail twitching with amusement at the excited looks on the three new apprentices' faces. Tigerpaw glowered, but said nothing. Willowpaw widened her eyes at Spottedpaw and Spottedpaw purred back. She didn't care who came, she just wanted to see outside the ravine!

Green. So much green. Leaves, branches, trunks, ferns, grass . . . And so many scents! Thrushpelt tried to point out the differences between squirrel, mouse, blackbird, and pigeon, but even though Spottedpaw had encountered all of these on the fresh-kill pile, they smelled new and strange against the background of trees and undergrowth.

Tigerpaw bounded ahead, giving a running commentary: "This is treecutplace. Twolegs cut down the trees here. I don't know why."

Spottedpaw sniffed the pine-tinged air. The ground was soft and prickly with needles, and there was hardly any trace of prey. Her legs were aching and her paws stung. She hadn't realized the territory was so huge. How did the border patrols manage to get around so fast?

Thrushpelt stopped to renew a scent marker, and Thistleclaw slowed until he was walking alongside Spottedpaw. "How are you doing?" he meowed.

"Okay!" Spottedpaw puffed. "It's bigger than I thought."

Thistleclaw purred. "It won't seem so far once you've been on a few patrols. Can you see that fence over there?"

Spottedpaw peered between the trunks. The trees stopped beside a line of dark green grass, edged with a long stretch of pale wood. "Did ThunderClan make that?"

"No, Twolegs did. They live behind that fence in Twolegplace. Watch out for kittypets crossing the border. They're too fat and useless to steal any prey, but they like to cause trouble."

Spottedpaw let her hackles rise and sank her claws into the pine needles. "I'll chase them out!" she growled. "Sneaky trespassers! They need to learn that this is ThunderClan's territory, not theirs!"

Thistleclaw cuffed her gently over the ear. "You'll make an excellent warrior with that attitude."

"Not without learning how to hunt and defend herself,"

Thrushpelt put in, joining them at a trot. "You're looking tired, Spottedpaw. Do you want to go back?"

Spottedpaw lifted her head. "No way! Can I see the Thunderpath now?"

She noticed Thistleclaw exchange a glance with Thrushpelt over her head. "You'll have your paws full with this one," Thistleclaw commented.

Thrushpelt flicked the tip of his tail. "Nothing I can't handle," he meowed. "We'll finish patrolling the territory on our own, thanks. I don't want to keep Tigerpaw from his training."

Thistleclaw dipped his head. "No chance of that. Tigerpaw's the keenest apprentice I've ever seen!"

Wait until you see how keen I can be! Spottedpaw thought as she watched the two cats head back to the camp. *I'm going to work harder than any cat to become a warrior!*

"Thrushpelt, you and Spottedpaw can join Adderfang's hunting patrol with Thistleclaw and Tigerpaw." Tawnyspots nodded to the cats gathered in front of him. "I expect a full fresh-kill pile by sunhigh!"

Spottedpaw bounced on her toes. *Yes!* Now she could show Thistleclaw her hunter's crouch! She pressed her front paws into the ground and stretched out her back until her tail curled. Thrushpelt had made her practice her crouch over and over again for the last half-moon, and she was confident she could catch anything—even a badger—by now.

She followed her mentor through the gorse tunnel, screwing

up her eyes as a thorn sprang back at her. Thistleclaw was just behind her.

"I haven't seen you on a hunting patrol for a while," he commented as they scrambled up the ravine side by side.

"Thrushpelt wanted me to get my technique right first," Spottedpaw explained, puffing slightly.

"Your hunting skills looked good enough to me before your apprentice ceremony!" Thistleclaw meowed.

Spottedpaw felt warm under her fur. Before she could reply, Thrushpelt called to her. "Stick close to me, please. I'll tell you which scents are worth following."

Spottedpaw glanced at Thistleclaw and saw him roll his eyes. "I don't think there's anything wrong with your nose, either," the gray-and-white warrior whispered.

Swallowing a purr of laughter, Spottedpaw joined her mentor as he fell in behind Adderfang. She could hear Tigerpaw's heavy footsteps alongside Thistleclaw. If he kept stomping like that, all the prey would be in WindClan before they had a chance to get close!

They headed for the river through sun-warmed ferns that tickled Spottedpaw's back. Adderfang picked up the first scent, a powerful waft of river vole, which sent him bounding toward the gray bulk of Sunningrocks. Thrushpelt paused to sniff the air. "Pigeon over there," he hissed, nodding at a thicket bent double under the weight of starry white elder-flowers.

Spottedpaw started to move forward but Thrushpelt stopped her with his tail on her shoulder. "I'll take it," he told her, and stalked away, nose close to the ground.

Thistleclaw padded up to Spottedpaw. "I just saw a squirrel go up that trunk," he mewed, gesturing with his muzzle toward a pine tree. "Do you want to follow it?"

Spottedpaw blinked. "I . . . I haven't really practiced climbing trees yet. Only once, and Thrushpelt said I wasn't very good."

The gray-and-white warrior twitched one ear. "You'll be fine! Take it steady, make sure your claws have a good hold on the bark, and don't look down. Go on, I'll be here watching you."

Spottedpaw glanced around. Thrushpelt had vanished beneath the elderflower bush, and Tigerpaw was pushing his way into a clump of ferns. Thistleclaw gave her a gentle nudge. "You're not scared, are you?" he teased.

"Of course not!" Spottedpaw crouched down and sprang onto the lowest branch. It swayed under her weight and she scrambled up to the next one before she could change her mind. Something gray and fluffy whisked around the trunk above her, and she caught the faint scent of squirrel.

"That's it! You're nearly there!" Thistleclaw called from below. Spottedpaw risked a glance down, then wished she hadn't. The warrior looked tiny from up here, and the forest swam dizzyingly around her. She sank her hind claws more deeply into the branch and stretched up for the next one. It was out of reach by half a fox-length, so she would have to haul herself up the bare trunk.

Spottedpaw took a deep breath and wriggled her front paws

until her claws snagged into the bark. She pushed upward with her haunches and felt her hind paws scrabble in thin air. Before she could plant them on the trunk, a voice came from underneath the tree.

"What in the name of StarClan are you doing up there? Come back at once!"

Spottedpaw twisted her head to look down, which loosened her grip on the bark. There was a sharp tearing sensation in her front paws and suddenly she was bouncing down the tree, banging her shoulder against the lower branches. The grass zoomed up to meet her in a green blur. Then everything went black.

She opened her eyes to see Thrushpelt peering down at her. "Spottedpaw, are you all right?"

She tried to nod, but a searing pain in her shoulder made her gasp out loud.

"Where does it hurt?" demanded Adderfang, appearing beside Thrushpelt. Spottedpaw's father looked horrified.

Thistleclaw's face joined them. "That was quite a tumble!" he meowed.

Spottedpaw struggled to sit up and get some air into her chest. The forest whirled around her so she leaned back against the tree to wait for the dizziness to pass.

"Tigerpaw has gone to fetch Featherwhisker," Thrushpelt told her. "Keep still." He pushed a ball of moss soaked with water toward her. "Thistleclaw brought this from the river."

Spottedpaw bent down and sucked at the moss. The pain in her shoulder was like a bolt of lightning every time she moved. There was a strange roaring sound in her ears, and she felt sick. "Am I going to be okay?" she whimpered.

"You'll be fine," meowed a brisk voice. Featherwhisker's soft gray head pushed between the warriors, and he studied her with concern in his eyes. "How far did you fall?"

"She was trying to reach the third branch," mewed Thrush-pelt. He glared at Thistleclaw. "She should never have been up a tree in the first place. She's barely learned the hunting crouch!"

"Then you are training her too slowly," Thistleclaw retorted. "Tigerpaw was climbing trees after a quarter moon."

"This isn't the time for comparing training methods," Featherwhisker meowed as he gently pressed his paw along Spottedpaw's flank. "Come on, let's get this apprentice back to the camp."

With Adderfang taking almost all of her weight on her uninjured side, Spottedpaw hobbled along the path, trying not to whimper out loud. Swiftbreeze bounded over as Spotted-paw scrabbled through the gorse tunnel on her belly. "Great StarClan, what happened? Spottedpaw, are you all right?"

"Thistleclaw sent her up a tree after a squirrel," Adderfang meowed.

"It wasn't Thistleclaw's fault!" Spottedpaw protested.

"It was an accident," Featherwhisker mewed. "Let's get you into my den so we can find something to help with the pain."

Swiftbreeze took Adderfang's place and Spottedpaw breathed in her mother's scent. Every part of her body was aching, even her ears and her teeth. She staggered through the ferns and flopped onto the soft grass beside Featherwhisker's rock-cleft den. Goosefeather, the medicine cat who had trained Featherwhisker, was dozing in his nest. He briefly looked up at the new arrivals, then lay down again with a grunt.

Thrushpelt poked his face through the bracken. "I'll come and see how you are later, Spottedpaw. Don't worry about your duties; the other apprentices can take care of them. Just focus on getting better."

Spottedpaw blinked. "Thanks, Thrushpelt." She pressed her cheek into the grass and closed her eyes. She felt Swiftbreeze fussing around her, puffs of warm air coming from her muzzle as she sniffed along Spottedpaw's body. Featherwhisker emerged from his den trailing herby scents.

"Eat this," he urged, pressing something slimy and strong-smelling against Spottedpaw's mouth. Without opening her eyes, she swallowed it down. It tasted bitter but not unpleasant. "That's comfrey, to help with the swelling, and half a poppy seed to make you sleep." Featherwhisker ran his paw over Spottedpaw's head. "Lie still. You've taken a nasty knock today, but you'll feel better soon."

"Will she still be able to train?" Swiftbreeze asked.

Spottedpaw opened her eyes with a jolt. *I can't let an injury stop me from training!*

Featherwhisker rearranged Spottedpaw's wounded leg so that it was tucked under her more comfortably. "We need to give her a chance to recover first. I'm pretty sure nothing's broken, but let's wait and see how she gets on."

Spottedpaw fought against the waves of blackness that swelled behind her eyes, dragging her to sleep. *Oh StarClan, please let me get better! I promise I won't do anything stupid again.*

CHAPTER THREE

Spottedpaw raced through the trees, flinching as brambles whipped her muzzle. Her foreleg felt as if it were on fire but she knew she couldn't slow her pace or something terrible would happen. As she skidded past Snakerocks, she glanced down to see if the fox was still there. Yes, the creature was still clinging on, its jaws locked around her leg, the wound sending flames of agony shooting up to her shoulder. Spottedpaw wasn't quite sure how she was able to go so fast and drag the fox along with her, but the weight of the creature didn't seem to slow her down. However quickly she ran, she couldn't dislodge the thorn-sharp teeth that sank deep into her flesh. . . .

"Spottedpaw? Spottedpaw, wake up! You're having a bad dream!"

Spottedpaw blinked open her eyes to see Featherwhisker bending over her, his pale face creased with concern. "If you don't stop thrashing about, you won't have a nest left!" he mewed, straightening the shredded moss.

Spottedpaw tried to sit up and let out a yelp as her shoulder burned with pain. "Ow!" She flopped back and licked her stinging fur. She noticed that Goosefeather's nest was empty, and she felt a twinge of guilt. Had she driven him away with her troubled dreams?

Featherwhisker traced her leg with one paw. "I'm not surprised it's sore. You gave it a nasty wrench. Leave the trees to squirrels from now on!"

"But I have to get back to my training!" Spottedpaw wailed. "What if Thrushpelt gets another apprentice?"

The medicine cat rested his tail on her flank. "Stop panicking. Thrushpelt will wait for you to get better. You've only been here for three sunrises."

"But that's too long," Spottedpaw fretted. "I'm not learning anything! Can't I start walking today?"

"Not when you're in this much pain," Featherwhisker meowed. "But if you're really bored, I can find something for you to do."

"Like what?" Spottedpaw mewed suspiciously. "I'm not squeezing any dead mice to get out the bile!"

Featherwhisker purred with amusement. "Don't worry. I save that particular task for naughty apprentices! You could sort these herbs for me, though. Rosetail gathered tansy and marigold for me yesterday, but she let the leaves get muddled up, and I need to store them separately." He nudged a heap of strong-smelling greenery toward Spottedpaw. Her nose twitched and she leaned over the edge of her nest to study them more closely.

"Which one's which?" she asked.

Featherwhisker tugged out two stalks with a flick of his paw. "Tansy is the one with the smaller, feathery, pale green leaves, see? Marigold leaves are a similar shape, but bigger and a darker shade of green."

Spottedpaw nodded. She wriggled carefully onto her belly, leaving her injured foreleg cushioned on the moss.

"They smell totally different," she commented. "That's the easiest way to tell them apart."

Featherwhisker nodded. "Exactly." He was rolling dock leaves into tight wraps and stacking them neatly against one wall of his den. "Do you know what we use those herbs for?"

Spottedpaw paused to untangle some stalks that were knotted together. "You gave tansy to Whitepaw when he had a bellyache from eating too much mouse," she recalled. "But I've never seen you use marigold."

"Actually, you have," Featherwhisker corrected her. "Do you remember when Frostpaw got scratched in her eye by that stick?"

"That wasn't my fault!" Spottedpaw burst out. "I was just trying to see if it was long enough to reach Weedwhisker. Frostpaw ran into it without looking!"

Featherwhisker snorted. "I'm not sure poking Weedwhisker while he was trying to sleep was the best idea in the first place, Spottedpaw. Anyway, I used a poultice of marigold to clean Frostpaw's eye and keep away any infection."

"Infection is when a wound smells bad and doesn't heal, isn't it?" Spottedpaw checked.

"That's right. I go through a lot of marigold at this time of year, when leaves hide the brambles and warriors are more likely to get scratched. It's best to use fresh leaves, but dried ones can make a good enough poultice if you add water."

Spottedpaw puzzled over two very similar-looking stalks for a moment, then decided that one was a small piece of marigold and the other was definitely tansy. "It's amazing to think that one little leaf can do so much," she mewed. "I wonder how the first cats found out?"

"We have been blessed with some truly gifted medicine cats," Featherwhisker replied. "StarClan guided their paws and helped them to a store of knowledge that is so vast, I feel as if I have only glimpsed one little corner of it."

"But you know what all the herbs do, don't you?"

"All of the herbs that are found in ThunderClan territory, yes. But there are plants in other territories that are unfamiliar to me, which is why the medicine cats meet at each half-moon, to share any new discoveries and see if we can help with illnesses and injuries in the other Clans."

"Wow," breathed Spottedpaw. "Do you feel like StarClan? I mean, you have power over life and death!"

Featherwhisker twitched his ears. "Not as much as I'd like to, little one. We all lose cats that we have tried our hardest to save."

Spottedpaw flicked the last leaf onto the tansy pile and sat back in her nest. "Finished! Can I do something else now?"

The medicine cat looked around the narrow cave. "You could roll the rest of these dock leaves for me while I prepare a poultice for Mumblefoot's tick bite."

"Okay!" Spottedpaw leaned out of her nest and dragged the big shiny leaves toward her. It was a bit tricky to roll them up with one paw, but she figured out how to use her chin to keep the leaf tightly tucked in. On the other side of the den, Featherwhisker started chewing up some sharp-scented dark green leaves.

"Medicine cats have to heal any cat, don't they?" Spotted-paw mewed, her voice muffled because she was holding a dock leaf under her chin.

Featherwhisker spat out a clump of soggy greenery. "Well, our code only says that we must help kits from any Clan, but I don't know any medicine cat who would ignore a full-grown cat who was sick or injured."

"What about other animals?" asked Spottedpaw as she reached for the next leaf. "Would you help a mouse, or a bird?"

The silver cat purred with amusement. "Do you think I should try to resuscitate the fresh-kill pile? Warriors are trained to kill cleanly so that our prey doesn't suffer. We have to eat to survive; a medicine cat would not be helping his Clan if he tried to revive their fresh-kill."

"What about a fox, then? Or a badger?"

"Animals that treat us as prey can take care of themselves," Featherwhisker meowed firmly. "Have you finished rolling those leaves? You should have a rest."

Spottedpaw snuggled back into her nest. It was lined with thrush feathers, which reminded her of how Thistleclaw had gotten into trouble for giving her and Whitepaw feathers to play with. She wondered if Thistleclaw was worried about her. She didn't want him to blame himself because she fell out of that stupid tree.

"Hello? Are you receiving visitors?" A dark red face poked through the ferns.

Spottedpaw lifted her head. "Poppydawn! Of course, come in."

Willowpaw bounced behind her mentor, hardly visible behind a large young thrush. She dropped it on the ground beside Spottedpaw's nest. "I caught this for you!"

"Wow! Thanks, Willowpaw!" Spottedpaw leaned out to sniff the fresh-kill. Her shoulder brushed against the edge of the nest and she winced.

Willowpaw looked worried. "Does it still hurt?"

Spottedpaw nodded.

"When will you be able to start training again?" Willowpaw asked.

Featherwhisker padded over and rolled the thrush to the side of the den. "She needs a few more days off her paws."

"She's very young to suffer an injury like this," meowed Poppydawn. "Do you think she'll be okay?"

"Excuse me, I am right here!" Spottedpaw butted in. "I'm going to be fine, aren't I, Featherwhisker?"

Featherwhisker was taking care to tuck the thrush out of the way. "We'll see," he mewed without looking up.

Spottedpaw felt a flare of terror in her belly. Would her stupid accident prevent her from becoming a warrior? *I wish I'd never climbed that tree!*

After two more days, Spottedpaw no longer dreamed that her leg was being eaten by a fox, or woke in pain if she rolled over in her nest. When Featherwhisker left to fetch more marigold for Mumblefoot's tick bite, which was stubbornly refusing to heal, Spottedpaw decided to test how far she could walk. She'd been making her dirt in holes behind Featherwhisker's den but she was determined to go all the way outside the camp this time. Goosefeather had gone out, muttering about finding peace and quiet with the elders, so the medicine den was empty.

Gritting her teeth, Spottedpaw limped through the ferns and hobbled across the clearing. At first her paw throbbed when it touched the ground, but after several steps the pain became easier to bear and she found a way of rolling along that was almost comfortable.

"Hey! You're up!" Redpaw bounded over to her, his tail sticking straight up. He licked Spottedpaw's cheek, which almost unbalanced her.

"Careful!" she warned.

Swiftbreeze jumped up from where she had been basking outside the warriors' den. "Did Featherwhisker say you could leave your nest?" she fretted. "Where is he?" She looked around for the medicine cat.

"He's gathering herbs," Spottedpaw admitted. "But look! I'm fine!" She wobbled triumphantly in a small circle.

Sunstar entered the clearing at the head of a patrol. "Ah, good to see you back on your paws, Spottedpaw! We've missed you!"

Spottedpaw glowed with pleasure. Even the Clan leader wanted her to be training! "I'm feeling much better," she mewed. "I'll be able to go back to my duties tomorrow, I think."

"Not so fast," Sunstar purred. "Make sure you're completely healed first."

The rest of Sunstar's patrol spilled through the gorse tunnel. Tigerpaw roared in at top speed, then skidded to a halt by the fresh-kill pile. "I'm starving!" he declared. "Chasing off those kittypets was hard work, I can tell you!"

"Really?" mewed Weedwhisker from his basking place outside the elders' den. "A strong young apprentice like you, against some fat old kittypet?"

Tigerpaw puffed out his chest. "They were totally scared of me! You should have seen how fast they ran!"

A voice purred in Spottedpaw's ear. "Tigerpaw didn't look so brave when one of the kittypets stopped on top of the fence to hiss at him!"

Spottedpaw turned to see Thistleclaw standing beside her. His amber eyes were shining. "You must be feeling better," he commented. "It's great to see you again!"

"It's great to see you, too," Spottedpaw mewed, feeling hot to the tips of her ears. She wondered why Thistleclaw was looking at her so closely. Did she have moss on her muzzle?

"Can I eat now?" Tigerpaw demanded, bouncing on his toes beside the heap of prey. "Weedwhisker has already taken a shrew for himself and Mumblefoot, and Larksong doesn't want anything. My belly is *empty*!"

Thistleclaw nodded. "Go on, then. Don't fill yourself up too much, or you won't be up to battle training after sunhigh."

"I won't," Tigerpaw promised through a mouthful of squirrel.

Thistleclaw turned back to Spottedpaw. "What about you? Did you come out here to eat?"

Spottedpaw shook her head. "I wanted to test my leg. I think I'm ready to go back to training now."

Thistleclaw's eyes widened. "Wow, you really are determined, aren't you?"

"Of course! I don't want my littermates to be warriors before me!"

The gray-and-white warrior tilted his head on one side, studying her. "Would you like to go for a walk in the forest? If your leg feels okay, of course."

"I'd love to," Spottedpaw mewed. "But don't you want to have something to eat first?"

Thistleclaw shook his head. "I'm not hungry. Come on, let's go before Featherwhisker sends you back to your nest!"

With a mischievous purr, he led Spottedpaw through the gorse tunnel. He waited while she visited the dirtplace, then walked slowly beside her up the ravine, letting her rest on his shoulder for the steepest parts. His fur was warmed by the sun and his muscles felt strong and smooth beneath his skin. Spottedpaw could hardly breathe by the time they reached the top—and not just because she hadn't been out of her nest for so long.

They stopped in the shade of some brambles so that Spottedpaw could catch her breath. Thistleclaw dipped his head toward her, concerned. "Are you sure you're up to this? Featherwhisker will kill me if you come back in worse shape than before!"

Spottedpaw blinked. "I'm fine, honestly. It hardly hurts at all." She gave her shoulder a fast lick to ease the tingling. "I don't want to miss any more training," she confessed. "I'm worried that Sunstar will give Thrushpelt another apprentice if I stay in the medicine den too long."

"Sunstar wouldn't do that," Thistleclaw meowed. "Being a warrior is really important to you, isn't it?"

Spottedpaw pushed past the brambles and started walking along the path that led to Snakerocks. She guessed that Featherwhisker would have gone the other way because marigold grew beside the river. She didn't want the medicine cat to send her back to the camp.

"It's all I've ever wanted," she told Thistleclaw. "I want to be the best warrior ThunderClan has ever seen, then deputy and then Clan leader."

Thistleclaw purred with amusement, and Spottedpaw winced. Did that make her sound like a silly kit with fluff in her ears?

"There's nothing wrong with ambition," Thistleclaw mewed. "We should all want to serve our Clan as best we can."

They ducked under some bracken, and Spottedpaw noticed Thistleclaw flinch as the brittle fronds brushed his ear. "Are you hurt?" she asked.

Thistleclaw flicked the tip of his tail. "It's nothing," he

mewed, but Spottedpaw reared up on her hind legs to take a closer look. She was suddenly aware of how close their muzzles were, and how their warm breath was mingling in the still, leaf-scented air. Thistleclaw's ear had a long scratch running from base to tip, and his fur was sticky with dried blood.

"You've been clawed!" Spottedpaw gasped. "Was it one of the kittypets?"

"As if one of those mange-balls would get anywhere near me!" Thistleclaw scoffed. "I'm fine, forget about it." He stepped away and Spottedpaw almost lost her balance.

"I could put some marigold on it, if you like," she offered. "I've been helping Featherwhisker with his herbs, and I know how to use nearly all of them."

She thought Thistleclaw would be impressed, but he curled his lip. "Only the weak get injured in battle," he growled. "If you are strong enough and fast enough, the only blood shed will be the blood of your enemies!"

Spottedpaw blinked. "O-okay," she stammered.

Thistleclaw turned and took a pace back to her. He rested his chin on top of her head and she heard him sigh. "I'm sorry," he murmured. "I was just thinking about a fight that I lost—the one that gave me this scratch, actually. I won't be beaten next time, I promise!"

"I know you won't," Spottedpaw purred. She hardly dared to breathe because she didn't want Thistleclaw to move. Standing here, in the glade beside Snakerocks, with the warrior's scent wreathing around her and the pain in her shoulder little more than a dull ache, Spottedpaw thought she had never been happier. She could feel her heart pounding, and every blade of grass beneath her paws.

Nothing in the world will stop me from becoming a warrior alongside you, Thistleclaw, she thought.

CHAPTER FOUR

❦

Spottedpaw wrapped the last shred of cobweb around the twig and stowed it neatly in the cleft in the rock beside the piles of herbs. "All done!" she declared. "Your store is much tidier now, Featherwhisker. Try not to mess it up again!"

The silver-gray tom flicked her playfully with his tail. "Perhaps you should stay here to keep me in order," he suggested. "Goosefeather would be glad of the help!" He nodded to the elderly medicine cat, who was dozing in the sun.

Spottedpaw looked at Featherwhisker in alarm. "You don't mean that, do you? You said my shoulder was healed enough to go back to training."

Featherwhisker purred. "No, you're fit to train. But I've enjoyed having you here, Spottedpaw. If you ever change your mind about becoming a warrior, I'd be honored to have you as my apprentice."

"Never!" Spottedpaw meowed. The medicine cat blinked. "Sorry, I didn't mean to be rude. But I'm going to be a warrior."

Featherwhisker nodded. "Well, good luck, and if you see any catmint while you're on patrol, don't forget to pick some. Our stores are very low."

"Will do!" Spottedpaw trotted through the ferns, careful not to disturb Goosefeather, and emerged in the sun-dappled clearing. Thrushpelt was outside the warriors' den, his back arched in a stretch. Spottedpaw bounded over to him. "Featherwhisker said I can start training again!"

"That's excellent news," Thrushpelt meowed. "We'll do some hunting practice today, nothing too strenuous. I don't think you should go on patrol for a while."

"I'm fine, honestly. My shoulder still aches a bit, but Featherwhisker is happy for me to do as much as I can."

The sandy-gray warrior twitched his ears. "I'll be the judge of that."

He headed toward the gorse tunnel. Willowpaw and Redpaw were bundling through, dragging a squirrel between them.

"Wow!" mewed Spottedpaw. "Did you catch that?"

"Yup!" Willowpaw announced. "And yesterday I nearly caught a pigeon!"

Redpaw flicked her with his tail. "More like it nearly flew off with you!"

Spottedpaw felt a stab of envy. Her injury had put her far behind her littermates. She would have to train twice as hard—if Thrushpelt allowed her.

Thrushpelt beckoned to Spottedpaw with his tail and she trotted after him through the tunnel and up the ravine, stepping carefully to avoid jolting her shoulder. They plunged into the ferns, which were cool and damp after a recent fall of rain.

Spottedpaw breathed deeply, enjoying the freshness after the stuffy, still air inside Featherwhisker's den.

Thrushpelt stopped in a clear space and sat down, curling his tail around his haunches. "Let's start off with a hunting crouch, a sideways pounce, and some silent stalking."

Spottedpaw tucked her hind legs under her and balanced her weight over them. Her shoulder protested when she let her body slide backward but she kept her front paws resting lightly on the ground. When she sprang forward, she was careful to put more weight on her uninjured leg. She saw Thrushpelt narrow his eyes, watching for unsteadiness, but she kept her balance by sinking her claws into the dusty soil. Her mentor nodded. Spottedpaw relaxed, then gathered herself for the sideways pounce. She deliberately went toward her strong side but she still jarred her shoulder and let out a whimper.

"Take it easy," Thrushpelt murmured. "You're doing well."

Spottedpaw finished by stepping softly across the glade, lowering each paw onto the grass without making a sound. She had always enjoyed stalking. She might not be the fastest runner among the apprentices, or the strongest, but she could creep up on anything!

"Let's go see if there is an easy catch or two waiting for us," Thrushpelt meowed. "You obviously haven't forgotten any of your hunting skills." He stood up and let Spottedpaw take the lead. She headed toward treecutplace, knowing it would be easier to hunt without getting tangled up in undergrowth. She wasn't going to chase any squirrels up trees, though!

The pine trees were still and quiet, strongly scented from the rain. Spottedpaw and Thrushpelt padded across the bed of needles until the red dens of Twolegplace were visible between the trunks. Spottedpaw picked up a hint of something warm and furry—a rabbit or perhaps a vole—and bent her nose to the ground, following the trail.

A line of glossy-leaved bushes grew at the edge of the trees. The scent trail vanished among the branches. Spottedpaw wriggled underneath and cast around, but there was no trace of it. Suddenly she heard voices and froze.

"What are you doing here? This is ThunderClan territory!" That was Thistleclaw, but who was he talking to? Spottedpaw peered through the branches but could only see the swath of bright green grass running beside the Twolegplace fence.

Then Bluefur spoke: "Thistleclaw, he's only a kit. He's no threat." There was a hint of desperation in her voice. Spottedpaw crawled toward the edge of the bush, dragging her belly silently through the dust and leaf scraps. A tiny black kit was standing muzzle-deep in the grass, facing Thistleclaw and Tigerpaw. Bluefur stood behind Thistleclaw, her fur fluffed up.

"An intruder is an intruder, Bluefur!" Thistleclaw growled. "You've always been too soft on them." He looked at Tigerpaw, who was bouncing on his toes. "Here, let's put it to my apprentice. What do you think, Tigerpaw? How should we handle this?"

Tigerpaw's eyes gleamed. "I think the kittypet should be

taught a lesson. One it'll remember."

Spottedpaw felt her belly flip over. This was not going to end well.

"Now, hold on, there's no need for this . . ." Bluefur begged, lunging forward.

Thistleclaw spun to face her. "Shut up!"

At the same moment, Tigerpaw hurled himself at the kit. The tiny black cat flew across the ground and landed with a thud. Spottedpaw winced. Surely it would turn tail and flee now?

"Get up!" snarled Tigerpaw.

The kit scrabbled its paws in the dirt but before it could stand, Tigerpaw pounced on it and held it down. He raked its muzzle with bare claws, then slashed down its flank. Bright red lines of blood sprang onto the glossy black fur.

"Show it your teeth, Tigerpaw!" Thistleclaw urged.

The apprentice bit deep into the kit's shoulder. The kit let out a terrible screech and tried desperately to get away. Spottedpaw gathered her haunches beneath her, ready to spring out and rescue the helpless little cat. No kittypet deserved to be treated like this!

Before she could move, a blue-gray blur shot across the grass and Bluefur blocked Tigerpaw's path to the kit. "Stop, Tigerpaw!" she yowled. "That's enough! Warriors don't need to kill to win a battle, remember?"

Tigerpaw narrowed his eyes. The kit's blood dripped from his teeth and pooled on the dusty ground. "I was just defending our territory."

"And you've done that," Bluefur meowed more quietly. "This kit has learned its lesson."

Behind her, the kit stood up and stared in terror at Tigerpaw.

Tigerpaw glared back. "Yeah, you'll never forget me!" He took one step forward and the kit fled with a whimper, limping into the grass and vanishing under the nearest fence.

Bluefur let the fur rise along her spine. "If I *ever* see you do something like that again, I'll report you to Sunstar!"

Thistleclaw bared his teeth. "We were only defending ThunderClan from invaders."

"That so-called invader was a *kit*!" Bluefur pointed out.

"That's his problem," Thistleclaw mewed. He beckoned to Tigerpaw with his tail and stalked into the pine trees. The dappled shadows swallowed them up, leaving Bluefur alone, her pelt ruffled with anger.

Spottedpaw took a deep breath and backed out of the bush. She was shaking with horror at Tigerpaw's hostility toward the defenseless kit. If Bluefur hadn't stopped him, would he have *killed* that tiny kittypet? Spottedpaw pictured the deep scratch on Thistleclaw's ear, and wondered where it had come from. Had Tigerpaw caught him unawares during a mock battle? Was that why Thistleclaw had seemed so angry about his injury?

She padded through the slender pine trees, lost in whirling thoughts.

"Spottedpaw, is that you?" Thrushpelt stuck his head out from behind a tree. "Where did you go?"

"Oh, I . . . er . . . followed a scent trail back there." Spottedpaw gestured vaguely with her tail. "It didn't lead to any prey, though."

Thrushpelt snorted. "Well, I don't want to go back to the camp empty-pawed. Let's try nearer to Snakerocks."

He turned and trotted along a narrow path that led into the brambles. Spottedpaw followed more slowly, the screech of the terrified kittypet still echoing in her ears. She made an easy catch of an old, slow mouse, while Thrushpelt pounced on a blackbird that was wrestling a worm out of the ground. They carried their prey back to the camp, Spottedpaw trying hard not to limp under the weight of her fresh-kill. Her shoulder ached all the way from her toes to the tip of her ear.

Thrushpelt must have noticed, because he told her to take some prey for herself and find somewhere to rest. Spottedpaw dragged half a sparrow into the shade cast by the nursery bush. The brambles were a little overgrown and untidy because the nursery was currently empty; as soon as it was needed by an expecting queen, Fuzzypelt and Swiftbreeze would trim and weave the branches back into place, making a sheltered and watertight den.

"Mind if I join you?"

A shadow fell across Spottedpaw and she looked up to see Thistleclaw holding a baby vole in his mouth.

"Of course!" Spottedpaw shifted sideways to make room for him on the softest patch of grass.

They ate in silence for a while, Spottedpaw enjoying the feel of his warm flank against hers. But she couldn't shake her memories of Tigerpaw attacking the little kittypet, and Thistleclaw's encouragement.

"I . . . I saw what happened today," she began. "With the kittypet, and Tigerpaw."

Thistleclaw looked at her in surprise. "Really? I didn't see you there."

"I was stalking something." Spottedpaw felt hot underneath her fur. "Tigerpaw was kind of brutal, wasn't he? I mean, it was only a kit."

Thistleclaw's amber eyes narrowed. "Are we supposed to make allowances for different kinds of intruder? Should we welcome the kits, then change our minds when they are six moons old? Or twelve moons? Or elders?"

Spottedpaw twitched the tip of her tail. "I guess not. But Bluefur seemed pretty angry with how Tigerpaw reacted." As soon as she spoke, she wished she could take the words back. Thistleclaw's ears flattened and the fur on his neck spiked.

"Bluefur is not training my apprentice," he growled.

"I just think Bluefur did the right thing, stopping Tigerpaw. He was going to hurt that kit really badly, even though it was trying to run away!" Spottedpaw tried to swallow the lump of sparrow that seemed to be stuck halfway down. "Tigerpaw is so angry all the time. I . . . I think he's trying to prove to us that he's nothing like his father, that he'd never leave ThunderClan to become a kittypet."

Above her, Thistleclaw's nostrils flared and his amber eyes blazed. "Is there something wrong with wanting to be the best, the strongest, the most fearless in your Clan? Do you think we should all be medicine cats, mincing around with herbs and feathers and avoiding so much as a nip from a mouse?"

"No, of course not. I . . ."

"Tigerpaw has more courage than any apprentice I've ever known! I'm disappointed in you, Spottedpaw. I thought you were ambitious, too. Is Thrushpelt training you to be an 'okay' warrior? Just good enough to catch mice and renew scent markers?" There was a challenge in his voice, and Spottedpaw jumped up.

"Don't say that! Thrushpelt is a good mentor! I thought Tigerpaw crossed a line today, and I was glad when Bluefur stopped him. And I *am* ambitious! I just know there are worthier enemies than a helpless kit!"

Blazing with fury, Spottedpaw jumped up and raced across the clearing. She pushed through the gorse tunnel, not caring that thorns ripped at her fur. She charged up the ravine without knowing where she was going; she just wanted to be far away from Thistleclaw's scorn and disappointment.

She thrust blindly through the cool green ferns, past a startled patrol, until she felt warmth on her muzzle and a gentle breeze against her ears. She looked around. She had run all the way to the edge of the forest, and Sunningrocks loomed over her, gray and solid and echoing with the sound of the river just beyond. Spottedpaw scrambled up to her favorite basking place, halfway to the top with a clear view upriver to WindClan on the moor. She sat down and tried to empty her mind.

"Okay, I'm a squirrel-brained fool who doesn't deserve

your company," murmured a voice behind her. "But you left your sparrow, and I thought you might be hungry, so I'll just put it here. Then I'll leave you alone, I promise."

Spottedpaw turned to see Thistleclaw crouched at the edge of the flat rock. Her half-eaten fresh-kill lay beside him, and his ears were comically flattened like a scolded kit's. He looked up at her with huge eyes, then down again.

"I don't blame you for hating me," he mewed in a small voice. "You're twice the cat Tigerpaw will ever be. I could never be disappointed in you."

Spottedpaw purred. "I don't hate you, Thistleclaw. Come over here, you look as if you're about to fall off." She beckoned him with her tail, and he crawled toward her, his belly fur brushing the warm stone.

"I'm sorry," he mewed. "I was really rude to you. It won't happen again."

Spottedpaw touched his shoulder with her front paw. "I'm sorry too. I should never have doubted you. I know you have trained Tigerpaw to be the bravest, most loyal warrior that ThunderClan could wish for. It wasn't my place to judge him."

The pale-furred warrior blinked at her, his expression earnest. "But it was, Spottedpaw! I value your opinion, don't you know that? I want to know what you think about everything! Tigerpaw, Sunstar, Tawnyspots, StarClan, the fresh-kill pile, whether the elders should deal with their own ticks . . ."

He glanced sideways at her and Spottedpaw let out a purr of laughter. "Now you're being silly! But . . . thank you. That means a lot, to know that you think so much of me."

Thistleclaw leaned toward her until their cheeks brushed. "I think a very great deal of you, Spottedpaw. Wherever I am, in my nest, in the forest, patrolling the borders . . . you are always beside me."

Spottedpaw couldn't breathe. Her heart was beating so hard, she thought Thistleclaw must be able to hear it. This wasn't like a warrior talking to an apprentice about her ambitions; this was completely different. Thistleclaw was talking to her as if she was his equal. And she felt different, too. *Am I falling in love?*

"What about you?" Thistleclaw prompted softly. "Do you think about me too?"

Spottedpaw nodded. "Yes," she whispered. "But you're a warrior, and I'm only an apprentice. . . ."

"You won't be an apprentice forever! I've watched you train, and I know you'll pass your assessment with no trouble at all." Thistleclaw straightened up. "There is no harm in thinking about the future. *Our* future."

"Really?" Spottedpaw felt her heart flip over. *I must be dreaming!*

"Of course." Thistleclaw nodded solemnly. "Look around you. You believe in StarClan, don't you? We are surrounded by omens that tell us we should be together."

Spottedpaw stared at him. "Are . . . are you sure?"

Thistleclaw gestured with his tail. "Look at those two clouds, side by side. And those crows flying over the trees—how many of them are there? That's right, two! Down there beside the river, do you see those two dark stones? We're meant to be a pair, Spottedpaw. StarClan says so." He glanced at her, and there was a mischievous gleam in his eyes.

Spottedpaw cuffed him lightly with her paw. "Don't tease! Omens are very serious. I don't think Featherwhisker would see things the same way."

"Ah, Featherwhisker! Our mighty medicine cat!" Thistleclaw's voice took on a sharper tone. "We wouldn't want to contradict him, would we?"

"What do you mean? I think Featherwhisker has done an incredible thing, giving up his life to serve our Clan. He knows so much, yet he never acts as if he is better than the rest of us. I can't imagine a better medicine cat!"

Thistleclaw bristled. "You sound as if you like him more than me! If he's so precious, why don't you go hang out in the medicine den for a few more moons?"

"Don't be such a mouse-brain!" Spottedpaw forced her fur to lie flat and rested her tail on Thistleclaw's flank. "I want to be with you."

Thistleclaw's amber eyes burned into hers. "Prove it," he whispered.

Spottedpaw blinked. "What do you mean?"

"Prove how much I mean to you. Come with me tonight."

"Where? Are we going to cross the border?"

Thistleclaw twitched his tail. "You'll see. Go to your nest as usual, and I will fetch you. Tell no other cat that you'll be with me. Do you trust me?"

"Of course," Spottedpaw mewed.

"Then you have nothing to fear." The warrior sprang down

from the rock and vanished into the ferns, leaving nothing but a few quivering fronds to show where he had been.

Spottedpaw sat back on her haunches. Where in the name of StarClan was Thistleclaw planning to take her?

CHAPTER FIVE

❧

The sun had never set more slowly. Twitching with impatience, Spottedpaw watched the orange disc as it finally sank below the trees. Would it seem odd if she went to her nest now? The other apprentices were playing a complicated game of chase that seemed to involve circling the tree stump twice and jumping over one of the elders basking in the last dregs of warmth outside their den.

"Get off me, you ridiculous kit!" snapped Larksong, striking out with her foreleg as Willowpaw zoomed over her rump.

"Leave us alone," growled Mumblefoot.

Willowpaw yowled in triumph as she skidded around the tree stump and leaped on top. "I win!"

Spottedpaw trotted over to the elders. She felt bad for them, having their peace disturbed by her crazy denmates. "Don't worry, they'll be going to their nests soon," she mewed. She licked a patch of ruffled fur on Mumblefoot's shoulder, trying not to wrinkle her nose at his musty smell.

She lifted her head to find Goosefeather staring at her with his rheumy blue eyes. "Come closer," he rasped. Spottedpaw edged nearer as the old cat peered at her. "I know who you are," he muttered. "You're the one who loves foolishly."

Spottedpaw blinked. "What do you mean?"

Goosefeather turned away from her, wriggling to find a more comfortable place on the hard earth. "Your heart is blind, Spottedpaw," he murmured, so quietly she could hardly hear. "That's a lesson you will never learn."

"What are you talking about? What lesson?" Spottedpaw spoke sharply, feeling a jolt of panic rise inside her.

Goosefeather let out a faint snore and Spottedpaw resisted the urge to prod him awake.

"Ignore him, little one," rasped Mumblefoot. "He doesn't know what he's saying half the time. Most of us stopped listening to him moons ago."

Spottedpaw twitched her ears. Goosefeather was still a medicine cat. He knew things no ordinary cat could imagine. Had StarClan sent him a message about her?

She jumped as warm breath tickled the back of her neck. "You look sleepy," murmured a familiar voice. "Don't you think you should be heading to your nest?"

Spottedpaw looked up into Thistleclaw's warm amber eyes. "I was just going," she whispered.

"I'll see you later," he whispered back.

Spottedpaw padded over to the apprentices' den, waiting for some cat to ask why she was going to her nest so early. But no cat seemed to notice as she slipped through the branches into the shadowy, peaceful den. She curled into her nest and tucked her nose under her tail. Her heart was pounding and she didn't feel the tiniest bit sleepy, but she closed her eyes and forced herself to take slow and steady breaths, emptying her mind and letting it fill with swaths of green and black and soft, pale gray. . . .

There was a sharp crack, as if something had stepped on a twig. Spottedpaw looked around and felt a moment of terror as she realized she had no idea where she was. She was surrounded by huge tree trunks, the tops lost in drifting mist. It was night and the stars were hidden behind branches, yet there was a strange gray light that seemed to be coming from clumps of fungus that grew on the trees and beneath the limp, half-dead ferns. The air smelled of damp earth and rotten wood.

There was a rapid thud of paws and Thistleclaw bounded out of the undergrowth, his pelt slick from the mist. "You made it!"

Spottedpaw blinked in relief. She leaned close to inhale his scent, but somehow he didn't smell of anything; the stench of earth and woodrot was too strong. "Am I dreaming?" she whispered.

"Oh no," Thistleclaw meowed. His eyes were shining and his fur crackled with tension. "This is real. Follow me!"

He whirled around and bounded along a narrow path between the trees. Spottedpaw raced after him, trying not to slip on the cold, wet earth. Something slimy seeped between her pads and she wondered if she had time to stop and lick it off. But Thistleclaw kept running so she gathered her haunches under her and kept going. The trees loomed on either side, dark and somehow threatening, as if they were watching Spottedpaw with unseen eyes. Where was this place? It wasn't anywhere in ThunderClan territory, she knew that. Had they crossed the border into *ShadowClan*?

A tree root caught Spottedpaw's foot and she stumbled to her knees. "Help!" she gasped.

In a flash Thistleclaw was beside her, nosing her up to her paws.

"I'm scared," Spottedpaw confessed. "It's so dark and quiet here."

"You're safe with me, I promise," Thistleclaw murmured. He rested his muzzle briefly on top of her head, then took off again. "Come on, there's someone I want you to meet."

Up ahead Spottedpaw saw the bracken quiver and a tortoise-shell-and-white cat stepped onto the path. Her thick fur was ragged as if she hadn't groomed herself in moons, and scars crisscrossed her broad muzzle. She walked stiffly as if old wounds troubled her, but her amber eyes burned like fire.

"What is she doing here?" the cat snarled, glaring at Spottedpaw.

"This is Spottedpaw," Thistleclaw mewed. "She's with me. Spottedpaw, this is Mapleshade."

Spottedpaw stared at the she-cat, unable to speak. Her whole body was trembling with fear, and her paws seemed frozen to the ground. *It's only a cat!* she told herself.

"She doesn't say much, does she?" growled the ragged cat. "Good." She turned and stomped along the path. "Come on, you're late."

Thistleclaw trotted after her, his tail held high and his ears pricked. Spottedpaw finally unfroze her paws and stumbled after them. If this was ShadowClan, what were they doing here? Her belly flipped over. Was Thistleclaw a *traitor*?

The cats ahead of her stopped abruptly and Spottedpaw almost bumped into them. They had reached the edge of a clearing filled with scrubby grass and divided in half by a crumbling, half-rotten tree trunk. Mapleshade jumped on top of the trunk with more grace than Spottedpaw would have imagined.

"Who will fight first?" she yowled, her voice echoing around the trees. "Come on, you fox-hearted cowards!"

To Spottedpaw's astonishment, cats started creeping out of the bracken. Five or six of them, all different colors and sizes. She sniffed the air, trying to identify them by scent, but all she could smell was decaying wood and sodden leaves.

Mapleshade jerked her tail toward Thistleclaw. "You go first," she ordered. "Houndleap, you too."

A scrawny black cat slunk into the center of the clearing. Spottedpaw could see his ribs, and her instinct was to run off and catch him something to eat. Yet she hadn't smelled a single trace of prey.

Thistleclaw bounced forward to meet the black cat. "Any particular moves you'd like to see, Mapleshade?" he called.

The she-cat bared her teeth. "Ones that work," she hissed. "Nothing else matters."

Thistleclaw bowed his head. "Of course."

Spottedpaw blinked in surprise. Thistleclaw was acting

like a humble apprentice! What was this place? The more she saw, the less she thought they were in ShadowClan. Hound-leap looked like a WindClan cat, for starters, with his thin frame and hungry expression. There was a light brown tabby sitting beside the tree trunk that must have been a RiverClan cat, judging by her glossy fur and rounded belly. These cats were warriors, for sure, but where would they meet together like this? This definitely wasn't Fourtrees!

At a yowl from Mapleshade, Thistleclaw launched himself at the black cat. Houndleap thudded to the ground but wrig-gled free with a hiss and leaped onto Thistleclaw's back. In horror, Spottedpaw saw that the black cat's teeth were bared and his claws gleamed long and silver as he sank them into Thistleclaw's pelt. "Watch out!" she cried. Surely this was just a mock battle? There had been nothing to suggest that these cats were enemies.

Thistleclaw didn't seem to hear her. He flexed his broad shoulders and flicked Houndleap onto the grass. Spotted-paw winced as he curled his lip and bit down hard into the black cat's neck. Houndleap batted at Thistleclaw's belly with his hind paws, ripping the soft fur. Thistleclaw flinched and Houndleap reached up with his front paws, clawing at the ThunderClan warrior's eyes. Thistleclaw shoved him away, sending his opponent rolling over and over until he slammed into the fallen tree.

"No, stop!" cried Spottedpaw, but on the tree trunk Maple-shade paced excitedly, her tail fluffed up.

"That's it!" she screeched. "No mercy! I want this forest

running with blood! It's a shame you didn't fight like this when you were in WindClan, Houndleap!"

Spottedpaw stared at the black cat who had staggered to his feet and was glaring at Thistleclaw, flanks heaving and stained with blood. If Houndleap used to be in WindClan, did that mean he was somewhere else now? Somewhere with RiverClan cats as well? Somewhere like . . .

"Am I in *StarClan*?" Spottedpaw gasped. "But . . . how did I get here? Am I *dead*?"

"Of course you're not dead," grunted a black-and-white tom beside her. He turned toward Spottedpaw and she jumped when she realized that one half of his face was dreadfully scarred, with nothing but raw red skin where his eye used to be.

"Then why am I here?" Spottedpaw breathed.

The black-and-white cat shrugged. "Mapleshade brings cats here to train sometimes. Looks like she made a mistake with you, though." He let out a terrible rasping sound, and Spottedpaw realized he was shaking with laughter.

"I . . . I didn't imagine StarClan would be like this," Spottedpaw admitted. But the black-and-white cat was watching Thistleclaw and Houndleap grapple each other again, and didn't seem to hear.

In the clearing, Thistleclaw had pinned Houndleap down and was pummeling him with his front paws. To Spottedpaw's dismay, the black cat didn't even try to fight back. He lay there limply with blood trickling from one side of his mouth.

"Enough!" Mapleshade ordered. "Thistleclaw, you can

fight Rushtooth next." The tabby RiverClan cat stood up and dipped his head. Houndleap dragged himself to the edge of the clearing, not far from Spottedpaw. *He needs comfrey, marigold, and cobwebs,* she decided. Without waiting to ask Thistleclaw if she could leave, she whipped around and plunged into the bracken, mouth open to detect the scent of herbs.

Nothing. Not even a dock leaf. Spottedpaw cast about, running in a broad circle through the trees, searching for any sign of a stream where water-loving plants might grow, or a sandy bank that might catch the sun. The forest was the same everywhere: wilting ferns, mulchy grass, and those eerie glowing fungi. Spottedpaw ran back to the clearing, hoping she could do something with bracken to stanch the flow of blood, at least.

Houndleap was propped on his shoulder, licking the claw marks across his flank. In the clearing, Thistleclaw was thrashing on the ground with Rushtooth, more evenly matched in size and weight this time. Spottedpaw cast an anxious glance toward her Clanmate, checking that he wasn't scattering too much blood, then trotted over to the little black cat.

"I'm so sorry!" she burst out. "I've looked for herbs but I can't find any. I thought StarClan would have every kind of plant!"

Houndleap looked at her oddly. "StarClan? This is the Place of No Stars."

Spottedpaw sat down with a thud. "*What?* But . . . but . . . what is Thistleclaw doing here?"

"Becoming a better warrior," purred Thistleclaw, joining

her. Blood dripped from a scratch on his shoulder and one of his ears was torn at the tip, but his chest was puffed out and his eyes glowed with victory. Behind him, Rushtooth crouched below the tree trunk while Mapleshade told him what a sorry disgrace he was.

Spottedpaw stared at her Clanmate. "You have brought me to the Dark Forest," she whispered. "Cats are sent to this place because they are too evil to belong in StarClan. Why would you want to train here?"

Thistleclaw flicked one of his ears and a drop of blood struck Spottedpaw's muzzle. "Cats might think something is evil just because it follows different rules," he meowed. "You didn't see anything evil here tonight, did you? Just courage, skill, and strength—more than you'll ever see in one of your training sessions with Thrushpelt."

"No cat would fight like that unless they meant to kill," Spottedpaw protested. She could feel panic rising inside her. "That's against the warrior code. And to me, yes—that is evil."

She spun around and raced along the path, tripping and sliding on the muddy roots. She didn't know where she was going; she just knew she had to get away from that terrible clearing and those bloodstained cats. Faster and faster she ran, until the trees around her blurred and shadows rose up to drag her down into the dank, foul-smelling earth. . . .

CHAPTER SIX

❧

"Phew! Spottedpaw stinks!"

"Spottedpaw, wake up!" A paw prodded her in her side. "Where have you been? You're covered in mud and you smell like the bottom of a marsh!"

With a jump, Spottedpaw opened her eyes. The memory of fleeing through the Dark Forest filled her mind, and she was half-afraid that she was only dreaming that she was back in her nest, while still trapped in that awful place.

Then Redpaw's face appeared above her and she relaxed. "Did you go out last night? You need to clean yourself up before Thrushpelt sees you!"

Spottedpaw sat up. The moss in her nest squelched, and her belly fur was matted and filthy.

Willowpaw wrinkled her nose. "Did you fall in some fox dung? Be careful licking yourself clean. You might make yourself sick!"

Spottedpaw stood up and stretched, feeling her muscles ache as if she hadn't slept at all. Had she really been running through the Dark Forest all night? Was that where

Thistleclaw had suffered his battle wounds? She pushed past her littermates, wanting to find somewhere quiet in the forest to wipe her fur and try to forget about what she had seen.

"There you are!" Thrushpelt called as Spottedpaw pushed her way into the clearing. "Come on, Sunstar wants us to check the border by Fourtrees. The dawn patrol picked up some unfamiliar scent there, so we need to make sure we don't have any unwanted visitors." The sandy-gray warrior recoiled as Spottedpaw approached. "Great StarClan! What have you been doing? You're filthy!"

"I was on my way to clean up," Spottedpaw meowed.

"Good! Look, I don't have time to wait for you. I'll go with Adderfang instead and meet you after sunhigh for training." To Spottedpaw's relief, Thrushpelt didn't wait to find out where she had been to get so dirty. He bounded over to Adderfang and the two warriors vanished through the gorse tunnel.

Spottedpaw followed more slowly, wincing as the stony path up the side of the ravine stung her paws. How far had she run last night? She felt as sore and exhausted as if she'd circled ThunderClan's territory three times. As she reached the top, she heard a patrol approaching and ducked under some ferns to let them pass. The cats were laden with fresh-kill and Spottedpaw's belly rumbled, reminding her that she needed to eat. The last cat in the patrol was Thistleclaw. Spottedpaw held her breath, hoping he wouldn't notice her.

Too late. The gray-and-white warrior paused, sniffed, then

put down his catch—a young squirrel—and padded back to Spottedpaw's ferns. "Hey!" he whispered. "I know you're in there."

Spottedpaw stuck her head out. "I'm going to clean up," she mewed. "My fur is still covered in mud."

Thistleclaw nodded. "You'll learn to wipe yourself off before you come back next time." He glanced around. "Where's Thrushpelt?"

"On patrol with Adderfang." Spottedpaw's heart beat faster, as it always did when she was close to Thistleclaw. But she couldn't forget what she had seen last night. Why was he learning to fight from evil cats?

"So you're on your own?" Thistleclaw meowed. "Great! That means you can come training with me!" The warrior's eyes shone and Spottedpaw felt the whirl of questions fade inside her. *I trust him, don't I?*

Thistleclaw started to pad back to his squirrel. "I promised I'd take Tigerpaw and Whitepaw for some training. Patchpelt has a bellyache after eating a mouse that had maggots in it." He hissed. "What a bee-brain."

"I . . . er . . . yes, I'll come with you." Spottedpaw felt dazed. Perhaps concentrating on training would clear her head.

After retrieving his catch, Thistleclaw bounded down to the camp to fetch Tigerpaw and Whitepaw. Spottedpaw stayed among the dewy ferns, wiping her flanks against the fronds and scraping her muddy paws on the grass. Even if her pelt wasn't completely clean, she smelled green and forest-like instead of moldy and damp.

Tigerpaw scowled when she finally joined Thistleclaw and the apprentices at the top of the ravine. "What's she doing with us? She's only just become an apprentice!"

"It'll do you good to have a different training partner," Thistleclaw meowed. He blinked warmly at Spottedpaw over Tigerpaw's head. "Off you go! Last one to the sandy hollow has to do Weedwhisker's ticks!"

Spottedpaw lunged forward with Tigerpaw and Whitepaw, feeling their flanks press against hers as they raced down the narrow path. Tigerpaw pulled ahead, his long legs and broad shoulders eating up the ground. Spottedpaw and Whitepaw hurtled neck and neck toward the golden patch of sand, until Spottedpaw stumbled on a bramble and Whitepaw leaped into the hollow with a yowl of delight.

"Ha! You're on tick duty!" the white apprentice declared.

Panting, Spottedpaw trotted onto the sand. She was too winded to speak. Thistleclaw bounded up a moment later. "You all did well," he meowed. "Especially Spottedpaw, since she's younger than you two!"

Whitepaw rested his tail on Spottedpaw's shoulder. "Yes, you were much faster than I expected. Well done!"

Tigerpaw just glowered. "I told you she shouldn't be training with us."

Thistleclaw ignored him. "I want some one-on-one battle practice today, using everything I've taught you. Whitepaw, I'm sure Patchpelt has shown you the same moves. Spottedpaw, you can fight whoever wins this bout."

"This is going to be so easy," Tigerpaw gloated, striding

into the center of the hollow.

"Don't be so sure," growled Whitepaw. He bunched his hindquarters under him and leaped at the dark brown apprentice. Tigerpaw lost his grip on the slippery sand and Whitepaw managed to force him onto his side.

"Come on, Tigerpaw, you can't let him win that quickly!" Thistleclaw urged.

Tigerpaw responded by shoving Whitepaw backward and pummeling him with his front paws. As Whitepaw scrabbled to find his footing, sand flew up and hit Tigerpaw.

"Ow! My eye!" he screeched, stepping away from Whitepaw and rubbing his face with one paw. "I can't see!"

"Don't scratch it, you'll make it worse," Thistleclaw told him. "Try blinking it out."

"Does that mean I won?" asked Whitepaw. His coat was dusted with sand all the way to the ends of his whiskers, and his tail was fluffed out like a hedgehog.

Thistleclaw nodded. "All right, Spottedpaw. Show us what you can do."

Tigerpaw groused his way to the edge of the hollow and sat down, dramatically holding one paw over his closed eye. Spottedpaw faced Whitepaw, feeling the fur bristle along her spine. She had fought her littermates in mock battles before, but never an apprentice so close to becoming a warrior!

Whitepaw gave a tiny nod to reassure her, and Thistleclaw hissed, "Don't make it easy for her! Treat her as you would any opponent!"

In a spatter of sand, Whitepaw launched himself at

Spottedpaw, and she felt her paws sink deeper under the weight of him. She tried to wriggle free but she just became more stuck. Instead, she dropped to her belly, sending White-paw rolling away with an *oof* of surprise. As soon as the weight lifted from her shoulders, Spottedpaw pulled her legs free from the sand and spun around to leap onto the white apprentice. She took him by surprise and felt a thrill as he blinked in alarm and tried to scrabble away.

In a flash Thistleclaw was beside her, whispering encouragement. "Come on, Spottedpaw! You've got him now! Aim for his eyes, remember?"

Spottedpaw froze. She pictured Thistleclaw slashing at Houndleap's face, forcing the black cat to cower down in submission. *I could never fight like that!* Spottedpaw lunged sideways and let her front paws fall onto the sand with a thud.

"What are you doing?" screeched Thistleclaw. "Why have you stopped? You were about to win!"

Spottedpaw spun around and ran out of the hollow. Ferns lashed her muzzle and thorns clawed at her sides but she didn't stop running until she burst out on the bank of the river. The only sounds were the buzz of flies and the ragged sound of her breathing. She crunched down the stony shore and stared into the swift-flowing water. A dark tortoiseshell face stared back at her, with white-tipped ears and huge, startled eyes.

She was going to be a warrior: that meant she would always be ready to fight for her Clan. But that didn't mean she had to relish the feeling of claw against flesh, or try to prove her strength against her own Clanmates, or *enjoy* the thrill of battle the way that Tigerpaw and Thistleclaw seemed to. *What I have to do is talk to Thistleclaw about the Dark Forest.*

After rinsing her paws in the shallowest part of the river to clean away the last trace of Dark Forest scent, Spottedpaw pushed her way back into the undergrowth. She trotted down the ravine and marched over to Thistleclaw, who was talking to some warriors below Highrock.

He blinked at her in surprise when she appeared. "Spottedpaw, are you okay? I thought you might be hurt, the way you rushed off like that."

Thrushpelt narrowed his eyes. "What do you mean? You told me you'd taken her for a training session with Whitepaw and Tigerpaw. I trusted you to watch out for her."

Spottedpaw ignored him. "We need to talk, Thistleclaw."

"That sounds like an order!" Thistleclaw joked, glancing at the other warriors, who purred with amusement.

Spottedpaw didn't say a word, just trotted back across the clearing and headed up the ravine.

"What's this about?" Thistleclaw called, leaping after her. "You were brilliant against Whitepaw—before you ran off. You obviously learned a lot last night."

Spottedpaw stopped dead and spun to face him. "I learned that I don't enjoy fighting for its own sake! It's the Dark Forest, Thistleclaw! Why do you have to go there to train?"

Thistleclaw twitched the tip of his tail. "We can't talk here." He led her to a dense patch of brambles, and forced his way into the center, where gnarled branches as thick as a cat's tail had created an open space. Thistleclaw sat down, wincing slightly as he tucked his hind legs under him.

"You're hurt, aren't you?" Spottedpaw mewed. "Just like when your ear was clawed. Can't you see that those cats are dangerous?" Her mind filled with the image of Mapleshade crouched on the fallen tree, screeching at the warriors to fight harder, use their teeth, draw more blood.

"Not to me!" Thistleclaw's voice was low and passionate. "They're making me into the best warrior ThunderClan has ever known!"

"If you must be taught by dead cats, why not StarClan?" Spottedpaw begged. "At least they lived by the warrior code. The cats you fought last night have all done something evil. That's why they're in the Place of No Stars."

"But that doesn't mean I will be evil too! We are more than those who teach us, Spottedpaw. I want to learn everything I can from once-great warriors, but I am still responsible for making my own decisions. Do you doubt me that much?"

His eyes were hopeful, pleading, and Spottedpaw felt her pelt begin to lie flat. "No, I don't doubt you. But that doesn't mean I agree with your training in the Dark Forest."

"I'm not asking for your agreement," Thistleclaw meowed. "This is a part of who I am. I thought you would understand why I'm doing this. I just want to keep my Clan safe—to keep *you* safe. I would do anything for you, Spottedpaw."

Spottedpaw stared at him, her mind whirling. *How can I argue with that? I love you as much as you love me.*

Please don't let me down.

CHAPTER SEVEN

♣

Spottedpaw woke early from dreams filled with flashes of gray-and-white fur, Thistleclaw's sweet scent, and threatening shadows that loomed from the undergrowth. She stood up and tiptoed out of the den.

Outside, the sky was soft and milky like the underside of a dove's wing. Dew laced the grass, and Spottedpaw left neat wet footprints as she padded across the clearing. She could just make out the golden tabby shape of Lionheart sitting on the other side of the gorse, guarding the sleeping Clan.

"You're up early," commented Featherwhisker, stepping out of the ferns. He tipped his head to one side and studied her with his bright amber gaze. "Is something wrong, Spottedpaw?"

Spottedpaw looked down at her toes, studded with shining droplets of dew. There was no way she could tell him about Thistleclaw visiting the Dark Forest. That would bring all kinds of trouble, and after all, Thistleclaw hadn't done anything wrong, had he? For a moment Spottedpaw recalled Goosefeather's strange comment that she loved blindly and had a foolish heart. Was this what the old cat had been talking about?

"Spottedpaw, what is it?" Featherwhisker padded over and rested the tip of his tail on Spottedpaw's flank. "Are you sick?"

Spottedpaw shook her head. "No, I'm fine. I . . . I had some strange dreams, that's all."

"I heard that you ran off from battle training yesterday," Featherwhisker commented gently. "Tigerpaw gets too rough sometimes. He needs to remember to keep his claws sheathed when fighting his Clanmates."

"But we won't always be fighting our Clanmates, will we?" Spottedpaw argued. "One day I'll be fighting a real enemy, and I'll have to use my claws and my teeth and everything I've learned just to survive. . . ."

Featherwhisker looked concerned. "Warriors face many challenges, but the warrior code protects them, Spottedpaw. No cat should ever be killed, even in the heat of battle. We fight to defend our borders, not maim the cats on the other side."

"Some cats seem to enjoy fighting, whoever their opponent is," Spottedpaw mewed quietly.

"Battles are only a very small part of our lives," Featherwhisker went on. "A true warrior has more love in her heart than hatred. Love for her Clanmates, for the forest that shelters her, for the prey that feeds us all."

The brambles around the warriors' den rustled, and cats started gathering beneath the Highledge. Tawnyspots walked among them, choosing cats for the dawn patrol. Spottedpaw blinked in alarm as Stormtail emerged from the brambles. The warrior had lost weight, and he looked unsteady on his paws. The first thing he did was walk over to the heap of soaked moss outside the elders' den and drink deeply, as if he had not seen water for a moon.

Spottedpaw padded over to him. "Are you feeling all right, Stormtail?" she mewed.

Stormtail turned to look at her, his eyes bleary and ringed with sleep. "I'm fine," he rasped, but Spottedpaw noticed that his muzzle was dry and his breath smelled like crow-food.

"I don't think you are," she meowed. "Why don't you see Featherwhisker? I think you might be sick."

Stormtail lashed his tail. "Don't fuss. There's nothing wrong with me."

Bluefur overheard and came over. "My father knows if he is sick or not," she told Spottedpaw. "Leave him alone. The patrol is ready to go." She nodded to Stormtail, who followed her to the other warriors.

"I want you to head up past Snakerocks and then follow the border along the Thunderpath," Tawnyspots ordered. "We've chased off a couple of rogues there recently and I want to be sure they haven't come back. They didn't look dangerous but our territory is full of prey at the moment and they might see it as easy pickings. Speckletail, you take the lead."

The tabby she-cat nodded and trotted toward the gorse tunnel with the rest of the patrol bunched at her heels. Spottedpaw winced as Stormtail stumbled, but he gathered himself up and vanished into the gorse on Bluefur's heels. His flanks were so pinched and bony that Spottedpaw could see Bluefur's haunches clearly on either side of Stormtail's lean shape.

She watched as the gorse stopped quivering behind the cats, then turned and padded into the medicine den. Featherwhisker was sorting a pile of tansy leaves and the air smelled green and fragrant. The space seemed larger now that Goosefeather had finally agreed to move to the elders' den, and his ragged nest among the ferns had been cleared away.

"I think Stormtail is sick," Spottedpaw blurted out.

The medicine cat put down the leaf he was unfurling and looked at her. "What makes you say that?"

"He's not walking properly, his muzzle is dry, and his breath smells bad. And he drank nearly all the water from the elders' moss before he went on patrol. I don't know if he's eating, either. He's so thin!"

Featherwhisker's eyes darkened. "You're right. I'd noticed he was looking rather bony, but I assumed he'd had an upset stomach and not wanted to bother me. But if his muzzle is dry and he's that thirsty . . . He shouldn't have gone on patrol, that's for sure. Do you know where they were headed?"

"Up past Snakerocks to the Thunderpath."

"Right, I'll go after them and bring Stormtail back. Thanks for letting me know, Spottedpaw."

Featherwhisker was halfway through the ferns when there was a commotion in the clearing and a pale gray shape bundled into him.

"Whoa, White-eye!" Featherwhisker meowed. "What's the rush?"

The she-cat bounced back onto her haunches. "I've got a thorn in my eye!" she spat. "It caught me as I was coming out of the den, would you believe it?"

"Okay, let me take a look," Featherwhisker mewed, and he guided White-eye to the little space outside his den. The she-cat lurched beside him, letting out a little moan of fear. Spottedpaw felt her belly flip over. White-eye was already blind on one side, but it was her good eye that was closed and weeping from the thorn scratch.

Featherwhisker gently pried open her eyelid. "The thorn isn't there now, thank StarClan. Let me bathe it with some marigold and you should be fine."

White-eye sagged with relief. "I'm so scared of losing that one as well," she murmured.

The medicine cat stroked her shoulder with his tail. "I would be, too." He looked over White-eye's head at Spotted-paw. "Can you get Stormtail, please? I want to treat White-eye first."

"Of course!" Spottedpaw jumped up and pushed her way through the ferns.

Thrushpelt was washing his chest outside the warriors' den. "Hey, Spottedpaw!" he called. "You need to clean out the elders' den today, remember?"

"I'll do it later," Spottedpaw called back. "I have to do something for Featherwhisker first."

Thrushpelt narrowed his eyes. "You're not his apprentice."

"This is really important," Spottedpaw snapped. "Storm-tail's sick!"

She brushed past her mentor and hurtled through the gorse tunnel. As she plunged into the trees above the ravine, she flashed back to her dream of fighting for her life in a dense, shadowed forest, and for a moment her paws froze. Then she shook herself. She was in her own territory now, and there were no enemies here. Just a sick warrior who needed her help.

She raced along the path that led past Snakerocks and skidded to a halt at the edge of a thick swath of brambles. She could hear monsters rumbling along the Thunderpath on the other side. She swiveled her ears, trying to pick up the sound of the patrol. A crackle of twigs made her spin toward Twolegplace and struggle through the long grass around the edge of the brambles. She burst through a clump of dead bracken and came face-to-face with Thistleclaw.

"Spottedpaw! Are you looking for me?" he meowed.

She shook her head. "No, Stormtail. Is he with you?" She peered past him.

Bluefur was renewing a scent marker on a crooked oak tree. "What are you doing here, Spottedpaw? You're not on this patrol."

"I need to find Stormtail," Spottedpaw panted. "Featherwhisker sent me to get him." Out of the corner of her eye, she saw Thistleclaw's eyes darken.

"You're looking for Stormtail?" meowed Speckletail, joining them. She glanced over her shoulder. "I thought he was behind me, but he seems to have disappeared."

"He must have stopped to check the scent marker beside the Thunderpath," Bluefur mewed.

"Actually I've just done that one," mewed Rosetail, popping up from a clump of grass.

"Where's he gone?" muttered Speckletail.

"We have to find him!" Spottedpaw cried. She plunged past the warriors and followed the trail they had left, marked out by fresh scent and evidence of broken twigs and crushed grass. Behind her, she heard Speckletail ordering the rest of the patrol to spread out and look for their Clanmate. Spottedpaw paused at a spot where the trail seemed to separate and opened her muzzle wide to taste the air. The breeze carried the faintest tang of a rank, stale scent. Spottedpaw tensed. *That's Stormtail!*

She bounded toward the smell, flattening her ears to keep them out of the way of the brambles. "Stormtail! Are you there?" she yowled.

She stopped to listen, but there was only the alarmed *chack* of a blackbird startled from a holly bush. *Startled by what?* Spottedpaw wondered. She headed toward the bush, and at once the stale scent grew stronger. A blue-gray shape was slumped beneath the holly, as still as a boulder.

"I've found him!" Spottedpaw screeched. She raced over to Stormtail and pressed her cheek to his muzzle. She felt the faintest stir of air against her whiskers. *He's alive!* Bracken crackled as the rest of the patrol joined her.

"Great StarClan!" Speckletail swore. "Thistleclaw, Bluefur, get either side of Stormtail and prop him up. Rosetail, you take the weight of his haunches." The tabby she-cat looked around. "Spottedpaw, you carry his tail, make sure it doesn't catch on any thorns."

Spottedpaw nodded and picked up the warrior's heavy tail in her jaws. The other warriors clustered around him and boosted him to his paws. His head hung down and his eyes stayed closed, but at least he was breathing—ragged, gasping breaths that made his scrawny flanks heave.

It seemed to take a moon to get Stormtail back to the camp, with every root and tendril snagging his limp paws or clutching at his drooping muzzle. When they reached the top of the ravine, Speckletail ordered Spottedpaw to run ahead and let Featherwhisker know they were here. The medicine cat had already prepared a nest of soft moss, with more soaked moss close by for Stormtail to drink. The warriors eased the sick cat carefully through the ferns and laid him down in front of Featherwhisker, whose eyes darkened as he studied Stormtail's limp shape.

"He has the thirsting sickness," he murmured, and Spottedpaw pricked her ears, straining to hear from the back of the cluster of warriors. "I cannot cure it, but I can make him more comfortable." The medicine cat tucked Stormtail's legs under him and pushed the soaked moss against his muzzle. The warrior stirred and lapped feebly at the touch of water. Bluefur crouched beside him. "You're safe now," she whispered. "You're in Featherwhisker's den, and he's going to take care of you."

Spottedpaw felt a flash of indignation. No thanks to Bluefur, who had insisted Stormtail was well enough to go on the patrol!

"Leave us alone now," Featherwhisker mewed softly. He looked at Bluefur. "Don't worry. I will take good care of your father."

Spottedpaw followed the warriors into the clearing. Bluefur was standing alone beside the tree stump, her tail drooping. Spottedpaw marched up to her. "You shouldn't have forced Stormtail to join the patrol!" she meowed fiercely.

The she-cat looked startled. "I didn't force him!"

"You didn't listen to me either," Spottedpaw growled. "I told you he was sick."

"You're not a medicine cat!" Bluefur retorted. "Why should I have listened to you?" She stomped away, flicking her tail in disgust.

Thrushpelt padded over to Spottedpaw. "I hear you've been a bit of a hero," he meowed. "Stormtail will be very grateful when he's better." There was an edge to the warrior's tone that made Spottedpaw glance warily up at him. Thrushpelt nodded toward the gorse tunnel. "I think we need to talk."

In silence, Spottedpaw followed him out of the camp. Her legs ached from her frantic dash through the forest, and she was relieved when Thrushpelt led her to Sunningrocks and settled on a warm, flat rock. The sound of the river soothed her, and her eyelids began to feel heavy.

Thrushpelt sighed. "I have to ask you something, Spottedpaw."

Her heart started to pound. Did Thrushpelt know she had been to the Dark Forest?

The sandy-gray cat looked at her. "Is your heart truly set on becoming a warrior?" he mewed.

Spottedpaw flinched. "What do you mean?"

"You're a good cat, Spottedpaw, but you seem distracted in our training sessions, and lately you've been more interested in helping Featherwhisker."

Spottedpaw felt her pelt burn. "I'm sorry. I promise I'll train harder from now on."

Thrushpelt shook his head. "Spottedpaw, would you like to become Featherwhisker's apprentice instead?"

She stared at him in astonishment. "Wh-what?"

"Would you like to train as a medicine cat? I've seen how good you are at recognizing the herbs, and you probably saved Stormtail's life today. I know Featherwhisker has asked you before, and I want you to know that it would be okay. I like having you as my apprentice, but if your heart lies elsewhere, then I won't stand in your way."

Spottedpaw opened and closed her mouth like a fledgling waiting for food. "I-I don't know what to say," she stammered.

Her mentor tilted his head to one side. "Think about it," he urged. "But remember that if you do become a medicine cat, it would mean giving up more than just your warrior training. Very few cats can make the commitment that Featherwhisker has. I think you'd be a great medicine cat, but you have to want it with all your heart."

Spottedpaw blinked. How had Thrushpelt noticed so much, yet said nothing before now? Did he really believe she would be a good medicine cat? She shook her head. She had wanted to be a warrior since the day she was born. There was nothing more honorable than protecting your Clan, feeding your Clanmates, defending the borders. She had trained so hard alongside her littermates. They would stand side by side all their lives, fighting for ThunderClan.

And there was still Thistleclaw. . . .

She took a deep breath. "I appreciate what you're saying, Thrushpelt, I really do. But I want to be a warrior."

CHAPTER EIGHT
❧

Spottedpaw opened her eyes and saw greasy gray trunks looming around her, lit by a pale, unnatural glow. *It worked! I dreamed myself into the Place of No Stars!* With her heart pounding, Spottedpaw trotted along the narrow path between the dying bracken. This forest looked the same everywhere, so she couldn't tell if she had returned to the place she had been before.

She peered into the undergrowth. She had to find Thistleclaw and tell him that she had made the decision to be a warrior, not a medicine cat. And she wanted to give him one more chance to prove to her that he was learning valuable battle skills here, nothing more. . . .

Something black and slippery swooped overhead, and Spottedpaw ducked. She craned her neck to see where the flying thing went but it vanished into the shadowy branches. She padded on, her pelt crawling as rotten ferns clutched at her fur. Suddenly she heard crashing and a muffled screech, followed by a sickening thud.

She crept through the trees to the edge of a steep-sided hollow. Below her, Mapleshade watched a group of cats grappling with each other. Blood spattered the sandy ground, and

Mapleshade's eyes gleamed like pale stars. Spottedpaw winced as she recognized Thistleclaw's lean gray shape wrestling with a fox-colored she-cat whose ears were shredded to tattered stumps. White hairs on her muzzle suggested that she was older than the others, and her paws seemed to lose their grip too frequently on the slippery ground.

Spottedpaw waited for Thistleclaw to flip the she-cat onto her back and claim his victory, but he seemed to be playing with her as if she were a wounded bird, letting her scramble back to her paws after every blow. In horror, Spottedpaw realized that the she-cat wasn't fox-red at all, but a light brown tabby stained scarlet with blood. There was a deep wound on her flank and teeth marks along her spine. Spottedpaw sank her claws into the earth. Had Thistleclaw made those wounds?

For a moment the she-cat flickered against the ground, and Spottedpaw glimpsed sand and pools of blood through her fur. She blinked. Thistleclaw had one foot on the she-cat's neck now, pressing her down to the sand. The old cat's hind paws scrabbled to find a grip, but she was too weak. She started to sink to her belly.

Spottedpaw threw herself down the side of the hollow. "Stop, Thistleclaw! You're killing her!"

Thistleclaw looked up at her, blood dripping from his muzzle. "Get away from here!" he snarled.

Around him, the other cats stopped fighting and bristled, bloodstained and claw-scratched fur rising along their spines. Spottedpaw ignored them and threw herself at Thistleclaw, knocking him backward. She sprang to the side of the old cat and desperately pressed her paws against the wound on her flank, where blood was pulsing out relentlessly.

But it was getting harder to see the she-cat; her fur was fading against the bloodstained sand, and her body felt like mist beneath Spottedpaw's pads. Then she was pressing against nothing but the cold wet ground, and the old cat had vanished.

Spottedpaw stared at Thistleclaw in horror. "Where has she gone? What happened?"

There was a heavy thud of paw steps across the hollow and Mapleshade loomed above her, clouded in the stench of blood and crow-food. "This whiny little apprentice again, Thistleclaw?" she hissed. "Get rid of her, before I do." She turned and stalked toward the other cats, gathering them to her with a flick of her heavy white tail.

Spottedpaw was too furious to feel afraid. She stood up and faced her Clanmate, ignoring the stickiness beneath her paws. "I came to tell you that Thrushpelt asked me if I wanted to train as a medicine cat, and I said no!" she meowed. "How could I, if that meant losing you? But this place . . . this has done something terrible to you. You are not just training to be a loyal ThunderClan warrior. You're *murdering* helpless cats!"

"That cat wasn't helpless!" Thistleclaw spat. "She fought as hard as I did!"

"No, she didn't," Spottedpaw mewed. "She died." She looked around. "At least . . . she bled so much that she vanished. I cannot be with you if this is where you spend every night—if this is what you do here. If you truly love me, promise you will never come here again."

There was a flash of pain in Thistleclaw's eyes and Spottedpaw felt her heart leap with hope. Then he lifted his head. "This is my destiny, Spottedpaw. I am going to be the greatest warrior ThunderClan has ever known. I will be the next deputy, and the next leader of our Clan. Every cat in the forest will fear us! There will be no battle we cannot win! How can I possibly give that up?"

Spottedpaw felt a crack open up in her heart. "Being a warrior is not about destroying our rivals," she whispered. "It is about making our Clan strong and safe alongside the other cats in the forest. Please, Thistleclaw. I will give you everything."

Thistleclaw turned away from her so she couldn't see his face. "You don't get it, Spottedpaw," he meowed. "I can't turn away from my destiny. Nothing is more important than this. The rip of flesh beneath my claws, the taste of blood, the scent of my enemy's fear . . . I am hungry for all of it, and I will keep fighting until ThunderClan rules the entire forest!"

"Then you have made your choice," Spottedpaw told him, feeling as if she were falling into a deep, deep hole.

"There is no choice to make," Thistleclaw growled. "I have dedicated my whole life to becoming the greatest warrior ThunderClan has ever known. And if you won't help me, there is no place for you in my life."

"But what about the things you said to me before? What about love?"

"Love doesn't win battles!" Thistleclaw spat.

"You're wrong," Spottedpaw mewed quietly. "Love is stronger than everything." She turned and looked back over her shoulder. "Good-bye, Thistleclaw. May StarClan light your path, always." *Wherever your path leads,* she added silently.

As she padded out of the hollow, the forest faded around her and she was lying in her own nest, her fur smelling of the old she-cat's blood. There was a pain in her heart sharper than the bite of fox teeth. *I have loved foolishly, and my heart has been blind.*

She pictured going to Sunstar and Tawnyspots and telling them about Thistleclaw's visits to the Dark Forest. Would they even believe her? And what could they do? No cat could guard another in his sleep. There was no way to stop Thistleclaw from pursuing his murderous path; but there was something Spottedpaw could do to help her Clanmates.

The other nests in the den were empty and Spottedpaw guessed her denmates were on the dawn patrol. She pushed her way out through the brambles and almost collided with Stormtail, who was being propped up by Bluefur.

"I'm taking him to the dirtplace," Bluefur explained.

Stormtail focused his gaze on Spottedpaw. "Thank you," he rasped. "Featherwhisker says I would have died if you hadn't found me."

Spottedpaw dipped her head.

Stormtail shifted his weight from Bluefur's shoulder. "I'm not so feeble that my own daughter has to watch me make dirt," he grunted. He limped away.

Bluefur looked at Spottedpaw. "I'm sorry for what I said yesterday," she meowed. "I should have seen that Stormtail was sick."

Spottedpaw twitched her ears. "I made a lucky guess," she mewed with a shrug.

"No, you didn't. You're very smart, Spottedpaw. You always see so much."

Too much, thought Spottedpaw, picturing the old cat fading away in the Dark Forest.

Bluefur stared at the bushes that shielded the dirtplace. The leaves were still trembling from where Stormtail had pushed through. "I've lost my mother and my sister," she whispered. "I couldn't bear to lose my father as well."

There was so much sadness in her voice that Spottedpaw wanted to press her cheek against Bluefur's muzzle and promise she would never leave her. Instead, she meowed, "You are a ThunderClan warrior. You will never be alone."

Bluefur nodded. "You're right. Thank you, Spottedpaw. Take care of yourself. There are difficult times ahead for us, I can feel it."

Spottedpaw opened her mouth to ask what Bluefur meant. But Stormtail was emerging from the bushes and Bluefur trotted to meet him, her tail kinked high over her back. Spottedpaw watched the gray she-cat, wondering if her dreams were also filled with the sounds of screeching, clawing cats.

If Thistleclaw achieved his ambition to become Clan leader, so many blood-soaked battles lay ahead. There would be so many injures, so many lives lost. For what? A moment of victory, until the next time warrior was pitched against warrior?

These were not the kind of battles Spottedpaw had trained to fight. Her destiny lay on a different path.

She marched through the ferns to Featherwhisker's den. The medicine cat was at the mouth of the cleft in the rock, laying out some herbs to dry in the sun. He pricked his ears when he saw Spottedpaw.

"Can I help you?" he mewed.

"Yes," she replied. "I want to become your apprentice."

CHAPTER NINE

❧

"From this moment, you will be known as Tigerclaw. ThunderClan honors your courage and your skill at fighting, and we welcome you as a warrior. May StarClan light your path, always." Sunstar bowed his head to the dark tabby tom and stepped back. His paws left sharp black prints on the light dusting of snow, and his fur was speckled with white flakes.

"Tigerclaw! Whitestorm!" yowled the Clan.

Tigerclaw lifted his head and stared around at his Clanmates as they filled the ravine with the names of the new warriors. Beside him, Whitestorm's eyes shone.

"Snowfur would be so proud of him," Spottedpaw heard Bluefur meow.

"Not so many moons until you'll be watching your own kits become warriors," commented Poppydawn with a pointed glance at Bluefur's rounded belly, clearly visible under her thick fur.

"But will we know who the father is by then?" whispered Rosetail.

"Surely it's Thrushpelt?" hissed Fuzzypelt.

"I can't see who else it would be," Rosetail agreed, keeping her voice low. "But do you ever see the two of them together?"

Spottedpaw looked across the clearing at her former mentor. She knew he had always been fond of Bluefur, enough that she thought they might become mates. Spottedpaw felt a pang of regret that she had denied Thrushpelt the chance to watch her become a warrior. He had been a good mentor. But it would be a long time before Spottedpaw received her medicine cat name. There was so much to learn from Featherwhisker, more than could be fitted into six moons, or even a lifetime.

Her fur tingled, and she knew Thistleclaw was watching her. She stiffened, refusing to meet his gaze. Every cat knew he planned to become deputy after Tawnyspots. The gray tabby tom was well liked but it was no secret that he was becoming too frail to succeed Sunstar as leader. He would retire to the elders' den and Sunstar would choose another deputy before reaching his ninth life. Thistleclaw was the obvious choice, and he had already started to organize the patrols when Tawnyspots was too weak to leave his nest.

Only Spottedpaw knew what kind of leader Thistleclaw would be once he had clawed his way to power. Her heart had not turned to stone, however. It still hurt to look at him, especially when she glimpsed him being gentle or playful, and she recalled the cat she had once loved. But she had made her choice, and there was no turning back. *My heart is no longer foolish,* she told herself.

Paw steps crunched over the snow behind her, and Featherwhisker murmured, "Time to get back to the den, Spottedpaw.

I'd like you to empty the store completely so we can see what herbs we have to last us until the end of leaf-bare."

Shivering, Spottedpaw followed her mentor through the frost-nipped ferns. Every day seemed colder than the last, and the sky was a dull shade of yellow, promising more snow.

"Kits are always welcome," Featherwhisker meowed as they settled down in the shelter of the cave. "But great StarClan, couldn't White-eye and Bluefur have waited until newleaf? I don't know if I have enough milk thistle for another nursing queen."

White-eye had kitted two moons ago, when the days were still warmed by a generous leaf-fall sun. Mousekit and Runningkit had grown quickly, and were strong enough to see through the cold weather now. But Bluefur's kits would face a much tougher fight, and Spottedpaw had been gathering feathers from every bird on the fresh-kill pile to line the nest in the nursery.

"Don't worry, they'll have the whole Clan looking after them when they arrive," Featherwhisker purred as if he could see into Spottedpaw's thoughts. "ThunderClan never gives up its kits easily."

"Get your paws off!" Bluefur hissed as her belly rippled under Spottedpaw's forelegs.

Spottedpaw sprang back as if she had been bitten, almost colliding with Featherwhisker, who was crouched just behind her.

"Sorry," Bluefur grunted. "I just didn't expect it to hurt this much."

"Did I hurt you?" Spottedpaw mewed.

Featherwhisker touched her flank with the tip of his tail. "No. Queens can be a bit crabby when kitting." He glanced sideways at Bluefur. "Some are crabbier than others."

"You'd be crabby if you'd been kitting since dawn!" Bluefur retorted, then winced as another spasm wracked her body.

"Is she all right?" White-eye called anxiously from the other side of the nursery.

"She's fine," Spottedpaw replied. *Though it would be easier if there weren't so many cats in here!* Mousekit and Runningkit were staring huge-eyed from their nest, as if they couldn't believe they had joined the Clan the same way. Spottedpaw tried to shift in front of them so that Bluefur had more privacy.

"Here comes the first one," Featherwhisker announced from beside Bluefur's tail. "Spottedpaw, when it arrives, nip the kitting-sac with your teeth to release it."

A dark wet shape slithered onto the feathers and Spottedpaw craned her neck to break the delicate sac and release a tiny muzzle, already gulping for air.

"A tom!" Featherwhisker meowed.

Bluefur tried to sit up. "Is he okay?" she mewed weakly.

The little shape beside Spottedpaw's nose lay ominously still.

"Quick, Spottedpaw!" Featherwhisker ordered. "Lick him fiercely!"

Spottedpaw ran her tongue over the tiny creature as if she could pummel life into him.

"Is he breathing?" Bluefur wailed.

"He is now," Featherwhisker meowed. He nuzzled the kit into Bluefur's belly.

Bluefur curled around him and licked his head. "He's beautiful," she murmured.

"He truly is," Spottedpaw agreed, marveling at the miniature perfection of Bluefur's son.

There was another ripple across Bluefur's belly, and one more shape slid into the nest.

"A she-kit," Featherwhisker announced as he pushed the little cat to join her brother. He ran his paw over Bluefur's flank. "One more, I think."

Bluefur's eyes rolled with exhaustion. Spottedpaw bent down to her head. "You can do it!" she whispered. "You're being incredible!" She held Bluefur's gaze as the she-cat strained once more. "That's it!"

"Well done!" Featherwhisker cried. "Another she-kit! And all three look healthy and strong."

"You did it!" Spottedpaw mewed softly into Bluefur's ear. "Three perfect ThunderClan warriors! Or medicine cats," she added, earning a faint purr of amusement from the worn-out queen.

There was a rustle of branches and a sandy-gray head appeared through the wall of the nursery. "How is she?" Thrushpelt called.

"Bluefur's fine," Featherwhisker told him. "She had three

healthy kits. Two she-kits and a tom."

Thrushpelt clambered into the den and crouched down to rub his muzzle on Bluefur's ears. Spottedpaw wriggled back to let them speak alone. It looked like the she-cats of ThunderClan were right: Thrushpelt was the father of these kits. Yet they had never been affectionate in front of other cats the way that White-eye and Halftail or Robinwing and Patchpelt were.

"What are you going to call them?" White-eye asked, scrambling out of her nest to peer at the tiny bundles.

"The dark gray she-kit will be Mistykit," Bluefur purred. "And the gray tom, Stonekit."

"What about this one?" mewed Thrushpelt, touching the tiny gray-and-white kit with the tip of his tail.

"Mosskit," Bluefur meowed firmly.

Featherwhisker twitched his ears. "So you're not letting the father decide on any of the names?" he purred playfully. "You always were determined, Bluefur."

There was a light in his eyes beyond mere teasing, however. Spottedpaw felt her fur begin to tingle. Did Featherwhisker suspect that Bluefur was hiding something about these kits? Could there be a chance that Thrushpelt wasn't their father? But if not, who could it be? Which warrior in ThunderClan would want to keep a secret like that?

Spottedpaw forced her mind to stop chasing after wild imaginings. Right at this moment, nothing mattered more than these three perfect new Clanmates. She gazed down at them, feeling warm to the tips of her toes. *I will protect you with my life,* she vowed silently. *Whatever happens, I will be your medicine cat. It will be an honor to serve you.*

She let out a long purr. Being a medicine cat was better than she had ever imagined!

CHAPTER TEN

Spottedpaw stopped to catch her breath and wondered why she had ever wanted to be a medicine cat. Goosefeather had coughed himself hoarse and was demanding freshly soaked moss, which meant a slippery walk to a rivulet that had formed from recent rain near the top of the ravine. Spottedpaw had lost count of how many bundles of moss she had carried back from the tiny stream; she was close to telling all the elders to sit in the clearing with their mouths open next time it rained, to save her some time.

As she trudged back down the path, she saw Tawnyspots emerge from the dirtplace.

"Must have eaten a dodgy blackbird!" he mewed.

But Spottedpaw looked at his hollow flanks and the way each step made him flinch, and knew he was much sicker than that. Cats had started wondering how long he would be able to stay as deputy, and how soon Sunstar would appoint Thistleclaw instead. Spottedpaw braced her shoulders to push through the gorse and reminded herself to count out the herb supplies again, to see if there was any way of boosting them with the leaves that were available now.

"Spottedpaw! Did you bring me back a treat?" Mosskit bounced up on paws that seemed too big for her.

"And me! And me!" mewed Mistykit, trotting after her sister. Her stubby tail stuck straight up in the air and her dark gray fur was fluffed up around her ears. "Come on, Stonekit! Spottedpaw's brought us a treat!"

Spottedpaw put down the sodden lump of moss as the little cats bounced around her. Bluefur's kits were a moon old now, and growing fast in spite of the cold.

Stonekit stuck his nose into the moss and jumped back, shaking droplets from his muzzle. "Wet moss is a yucky treat!" he complained.

"That's because it's not meant for you," Spottedpaw meowed, picking up the moss before any more kits attacked it, and carrying it to the elders' den. Goosefeather was lying on his side in his nest, breathing laboriously. He started lapping at the moss at once, lashing his tail when Mumblefoot tried to crouch alongside to share it.

"I'll get some more," Spottedpaw promised wearily.

As she headed back across the clearing, she passed Thrushpelt, who was staggering under the weight of a plump squirrel.

"Good catch!" Spottedpaw called.

"Is that for us?" squeaked Mistykit, racing over to sniff at the squirrel. A piece of fur stuck to her muzzle and she sneezed.

"That's a real treat!" mewed Stonekit.

"Of course it's for you," Thrushpelt purred. "Is there any cat more important to feed than you?"

Mosskit shook her head. "I don't think so," she replied with a serious expression in her blue eyes. "The warrior code says kits and elders have to be fed first. And that's us!"

Bluefur padded over from the tree stump, where she had been talking to Rosetail. "Actually, I just fed them," she mewed to Thrushpelt. "You can put that squirrel on the fresh-kill pile."

"That's not fair!" wailed Mistykit. "Thrushpelt said he caught it for us!"

"I'm your mother," Bluefur meowed. "If I say you've had enough to eat, then you have."

Spottedpaw waited for Thrushpelt to remind Bluefur that he was their father, and if he wanted to catch fresh-kill for them, that was his right. But Thrushpelt said nothing, simply picked up the squirrel with a murmured apology to the kits and carried it away.

"That's not fair!" Stonekit pouted, turning his back on Bluefur.

"Life isn't fair," Bluefur retorted, but her attention was drifting away and her gaze was fixed on the gorse tunnel.

Thistleclaw was returning at the head of a border patrol, with Tigerclaw bouncing beside him. Their pelts were fluffed up and Tigerclaw's muzzle bore signs of claw marks.

"Those kittypets won't be coming back into ThunderClan territory again!" Thistleclaw declared. "Tigerclaw will be picking their fur from his claws for the next moon!"

Sunstar pricked his ears from where he sat beneath Highledge. "More intruders?" he asked. "I renewed the scent markers beside Twolegplace yesterday. I can't believe those kittypets have crossed them already!"

"Don't worry," Thistleclaw assured him. "Our borders are safe now."

The rest of his patrol entered the clearing, and Spottedpaw noticed that Fuzzypelt was limping. She went over to the black warrior and asked if he was okay.

Fuzzypelt twitched his ears. "It's nothing. Just a splinter."

"Let me have a look." Spottedpaw steered him to the edge of the clearing and bent down to study his paw. Sure enough, a shard of wood was stuck in the soft part of his pad. "I can get this out, but it might sting a bit," she mewed. Before Fuzzypelt could object, she gripped the tip of the splinter in her teeth and tugged it free.

"Ow!" Fuzzypelt jumped backward, but then tested his paw on the ground and nodded. "Much better. Thanks, Spottedpaw."

Spottedpaw was studying the splinter. It was very pale and straight, and had a strong, distinctive smell. This hadn't come from a tree or a fallen branch. "Where did you get this?" she meowed.

Fuzzypelt shrugged. "I don't know, somewhere in the forest, I guess." He sounded evasive, and when Spottedpaw looked up at him, he wouldn't meet her eye.

"I recognize this scent," she murmured. "You got this splinter from a Twoleg fence, didn't you? Did Thistleclaw lead a patrol into Twolegplace *looking* for kittypets?" She felt cold beneath her pelt.

Fuzzypelt's yellow eyes filled with confusion. "He said we weren't to say anything. Those kittypets need to be taught a lesson! They keep crossing our borders!"

"But they didn't cross them today," Spottedpaw pointed out. "Not since Sunstar renewed the scent markers. Thistleclaw should not have gone into Twoleg territory."

"No harm done," Fuzzypelt mewed uneasily.

"I wonder if the kittypet whose fur is underneath Tigerclaw's claws would agree."

Fuzzypelt backed away, looking relieved when Thistleclaw summoned him to the fresh-kill pile.

"My warriors need to eat!" the gray-and-white warrior declared.

"They are not his warriors," growled a voice beside Spottedpaw.

She jumped, and turned to see Bluefur beside her, scowling at Thistleclaw. "He took that patrol into Twolegplace, didn't he?" the gray she-cat hissed. "That was not his decision to make!"

"Are you going to tell Sunstar?" Spottedpaw asked.

Bluefur lashed her tail. "What would be the point? Ever since our victory in the battle with RiverClan, which Thistleclaw claims he fought single-pawed, Sunstar listens to everything he says. You know he's taken over organizing all the patrols now?"

Spottedpaw meowed, "We're going to have to get used to him being in charge. Sunstar is bound to make him our next deputy."

Bluefur's eyes darkened. "Not if I can help it," she rasped, and Spottedpaw flinched.

She gestured with her tail to where Stonekit, Mosskit, and Mistykit were playing pounce with a dead leaf. "Thistleclaw can't be that important to you," she urged. "You have three other lives to think about now!"

To her astonishment, Bluefur's eyes clouded with sorrow. "I love them so much," she murmured. "But I love my Clan, too. I could never wish they hadn't been born, but why now? What if my Clan needs me more than they do?"

Spottedpaw froze. Had Bluefur intended for her to hear that? The queen sounded so desperate, so lonely, but Spottedpaw couldn't bring herself to ask what she meant. Instead, she mewed, "You are not alone, Bluefur. Thrushpelt will always help you to care for your kits."

The queen looked at her, though her gaze seemed focused on something beyond Spottedpaw. "I cannot ask more of him than I already have."

But he's their father! The words stuck in Spottedpaw's throat. Was Bluefur about to tell her that wasn't true?

Bluefur sighed. "Love can lead a cat so far astray that it becomes too late to turn back," she whispered.

Spottedpaw thought of how she had fallen for Thistleclaw, how her foolish heart had been blind to his cruelty and his ambition until she watched him kill a cat in the Dark Forest. "It's never too late!" she blurted out. "You can always change the path you follow!"

Bluefur stared at her kits, who had finished demolishing the dead leaf and were now stalking the tip of Mumblefoot's tail. "I have a decision to make," she mewed softly. "But I am filled with too much love, and too much fear."

"What do you mean?" Spottedpaw pressed. "Can I help?"

The queen shook her head. "No. This is something I must do alone."

She padded away, not to her kits but to the gorse tunnel. Spottedpaw watched her leave, her belly heavy with dread. Bluefur sounded as if she was about to choose between life and death, she had been so serious. What was she going to do?

A full, gleaming moon hung over the trees, turning the snow-covered ground silver. The air in the camp crackled with tension as warriors circled, ready to set off for the Gathering. Spottedpaw was staying behind to watch over Tawnyspots, who had weakened so much that Featherwhisker ordered him to sleep in the medicine den. She stood among the ferns at the edge of the clearing, watching her mentor talk quietly to Sunstar.

"Spottedpaw, can I ask you a favor?" It was Bluefur, her eyes huge and anxious. Her breath hung in a cloud around her muzzle.

"Of course. Are the kits all right?"

"They're fine. I wore them out today with a game of hide-and-seek, so they should sleep till dawn." Bluefur shifted her paws. "I . . . I want to go to the Gathering tonight. Please, will you check on my kits while I'm away? White-eye said she'd watch them but she has her paws full with Runningkit and Mousekit."

Spottedpaw blinked. A nursing queen never went to Gatherings, not when her kits still needed her. But there was something desperate in Bluefur's gaze that made her nod. "Yes, I'll keep an eye on them," she meowed.

Bluefur blinked warmly at her. "Thank you, Spottedpaw. I'll remember this." She trotted away and her blue-gray pelt merged with the other warriors as they headed into the gorse.

Spottedpaw made sure that Tawnyspots was comfortable and gave him another mint leaf to chew. Mercifully she had found a fresh plant near the river that had been sheltered from the worst of the snow. The leaves would ease Tawnyspots's bellyache, though Spottedpaw knew there was little more that she and Featherwhisker could do to help him.

When Tawnyspots had finished his leaf and was dozing with his chin propped on the edge of his nest, Spottedpaw trotted over to the nursery. Her paws crunched in the snow, and the bitter cold stung her pads. She poked her head through the brambles and was relieved to see that all the kits, and White-eye, were fast asleep, tiny snores filling the air. The nursery was warm and milk-scented, and for a moment Spottedpaw was tempted to creep in and curl up among the kits. But she wouldn't sleep tonight, at least not until Featherwhisker returned. She was the sole medicine cat in the Clan, and all the cats here were in her charge. Puffing out her fur, Spottedpaw headed back to her den to wait out the night.

The cats returned just before dawn, quiet and hunched from the cold. Spottedpaw nodded to them as they trooped into the clearing and headed for their dens. Bluefur stopped beside her. Her eyes were clear, and she seemed much calmer now.

"Have you decided what to do?" Spottedpaw asked.

Bluefur nodded. "I have made my choice." She walked away without saying anything, and Spottedpaw wondered if she would ever know what that decision had been.

Spottedpaw opened her eyes with a start. What was that noise? The sky was filled with stars, hazy in the bitter cold. More snow had fallen since the Gathering, and all around the medicine den the ferns were flattened under the weight of its icy white pelt. Spottedpaw sat up. Was Tawnyspots stirring in his nest? She craned her neck to see, but the deputy seemed to be lying still, breathing loudly but steadily.

The noise came again, a soft rustle and the tiniest murmur. Spottedpaw stepped out of her nest and crept past Featherwhisker and Tawnyspots, thanking StarClan that she hadn't forgotten how to stalk like a warrior. The clearing was still and silent, every sound muffled by the snow. Spottedpaw padded over to the nursery and listened, but only soft snores came from inside. What had disturbed her?

She turned toward the gorse tunnel. Stormtail was on guard tonight, back to warrior duties now that Featherwhisker had found herbs to help with his thirsting sickness. Spottedpaw decided to check that he was okay in the bitter cold. She pushed through the frosty gorse, shivering as icy thorns brushed the back of her neck. Stormtail jumped when she appeared, then let out a purr.

"I was almost dozing off!" he told her. "It's so quiet out here."

"Better than a ShadowClan invasion," Spottedpaw joked. Suddenly she spotted movement behind Stormtail, halfway up the ravine. Was it a cat? Why weren't they using the regular path? She peered closer.

Great StarClan, it's Bluefur and the kits!

What could possibly be happening? Spottedpaw pictured the desperation in Bluefur's eyes when she talked about her kits, and the decision she had to make. Should she tell Stormtail? He would take Bluefur straight back to the camp. *Do I trust Bluefur enough to let her go?* Spottedpaw had no doubt that Bluefur loved her kits. *Whatever she's doing, she won't let any harm come to them.*

In the shadows, Bluefur slipped and a twig cracked. Stormtail pricked his ears and began to turn around.

"What's that?" Spottedpaw pointed with her tail to the other side of the ravine.

Stormtail jumped to his paws and stared into the bushes. "Where?"

Behind her, Spottedpaw heard a tiny rustling sound. *Had Bluefur taken her kits out of sight yet?* She didn't dare to turn around.

"Just by that tall tree," Spottedpaw mewed. She walked over to Stormtail and pretended to peer more closely. "I'm sure I saw something move there. Maybe a fox?"

"I'll check it out," Stormtail growled. He padded away, his pelt bristling along his spine.

Spottedpaw stayed where she was, watching Stormtail prowl into the undergrowth. She was desperate to follow Bluefur and find out where she was going, but she couldn't risk Stormtail seeing her go up the ravine.

The warrior returned, his pelt ruffled from the brambles. "No trace of any scent," he reported.

"I'm sure I saw something," Spottedpaw persisted. "It was heading farther along the ravine. Why don't you check that way, and I'll go up to the top and see if I can spot anything?"

Stormtail nodded and headed back the way he had come. Spottedpaw raced up the path, her feet slipping in the snow. More flakes were falling, making Spottedpaw blink and shake her head. She strained to spot any signs of a trail in the darkness. Which way had they gone?

In the shelter of some brambles, she spotted a faint trail of paw prints, some large and some so tiny she could hardly make them out. It looked as if they had taken the path that led to Sunningrocks. Spottedpaw took a deep breath and started walking through the bracken, lifting each paw high out of the snow and shaking it to get some feeling into her toes. Ice clumped against her belly fur, and her ears stung with cold. *I hope the kits are all right!*

The night closed silently around her, and Spottedpaw wondered if she had lost them. She pushed her way into a clump of ferns, trying to find some shelter. Then she heard voices up ahead, low and urgent. Spottedpaw peeked through the stalks and made out two bulky shapes on the shore of the frozen river.

One of them turned toward her and she shrank back out of sight. This was Bluefur's secret to keep. The larger shape started to make its way down the shore with a cluster of tiny shadows stumbling beside it. Spottedpaw gasped. *Was Bluefur giving her kits away? Why would she do that?*

She could think of only one reason: so that Bluefur could leave the nursery and take over as Clan deputy instead of Thistleclaw. This was a measure of how much she loved her Clanmates, and how much she feared Thistleclaw, even without seeing him in the Dark Forest.

Spottedpaw sighed. *Thistleclaw has changed both our destinies, Bluefur. You will never realize how much you and I have in common.*

"StarClan, please keep Bluefur's kits safe. Let them grow bold and strong, and above all else, loved," Spottedpaw prayed as she crouched among the bracken.

The air stirred around her and a warm, half-familiar scent drifted into her muzzle. Spottedpaw narrowed her eyes and saw the faintest white-furred shape slip through the stalks in front of her.

We will do our best, a voice breathed inside her mind. *Thank you for trusting my sister, Spottedpaw.*

"Snowfur?" Spottedpaw whispered. "Is that you?" But the ferns around her were still and silent, and the pale shape had vanished into the falling snow.

Bluefur and I will do our best, too, Spottedpaw vowed. *I will never be foolish or blind again. Thistleclaw has shown me where my destiny truly lies. From now on, my heart belongs to my Clan.*

WARRIORS

PINESTAR'S
CHOICE

For Susi Plattner—Clanmate, friend, and Warriors expert

Special thanks to Victoria Holmes

ALLEGIANCES

THUNDERCLAN

LEADER   OAKSTAR—sturdy brown tom with amber eyes

DEPUTY   DOEFEATHER—pale fawn-and-white she-cat with amber eyes
APPRENTICE, DAISYPAW

MEDICINE CAT   CLOUDBERRY—long-furred white she-cat with yellow eyes

WARRIORS   (toms and she-cats without kits)

MISTPELT—thick-furred gray she-cat with green eyes
APPRENTICE, PINEPAW

NETTLEBREEZE—ginger tom
APPRENTICE, FLASHPAW

SWEETBRIAR—light brown tabby she-cat with white paws

MUMBLEFOOT—brown tom with amber eyes

FLAMENOSE—ginger tom with amber eyes

LARKSONG—tortoiseshell she-cat, pale green eyes

ROOKTAIL—black tom with blue eyes

WINDFLIGHT—gray tabby tom with pale green eyes

HAREPOUNCE—light brown she-cat with yellow eyes

SQUIRRELWHISKER—brown tabby she-cat with amber eyes
APPRENTICE, LITTLEPAW

HOLLYPELT—black she-cat with green eyes

RAINFUR—speckled ginger-and-white she-cat with amber eyes

STAGLEAP—gray tabby tom with amber eyes

FALLOWSONG—light brown she-cat

DAPPLETAIL—tortoiseshell she-cat with a lovely dappled coat

APPRENTICES (more than six moons old, in training to become warriors)

FLASHPAW—dark ginger she-cat with a white muzzle

DAISYPAW—gray-and-white she-cat with yellow eyes

PINEPAW—red-brown tom with green eyes

LITTLEPAW—black-and-white tom with blue eyes

ELDERS (former warriors and queens, now retired)

DEERDAPPLE—silver-and-black tabby she-cat

SEEDPELT—gray she-cat

BLOOMHEART—gray tabby tom

THRUSHTALON—light brown tabby tom

CAT VIEW

HIGHSTONES

BARLEY'S FARM

FOURTREES

WINDCLAN CAMP

FALLS

SUNNINGROCKS

RIVER

RIVERCLAN CAMP

TREECUTPLACE

CARRIONPLACE

SHADOWCLAN
CAMP

THUNDERPATH

OWLTREE

GREAT
SYCAMORE

THUNDERCLAN
CAMP

SNAKEROCKS

SANDY
HOLLOW

TALLPINES

TWOLEGPLACE

KEY
To The
CLANS

THUNDERCLAN

RIVERCLAN

SHADOWCLAN

WINDCLAN

STARCLAN

NORTH

DEVIL'S FINGERS
[disused mine]

WINDOVER FARM

NORTH ALLERTON ROAD

DRUID'S
HOLLOW

WINDOVER MOOR

DRUID'S
LEAP

TWOLEG VIEW

RIVER CHEILL

MORGAN'S FARM
CAMPSITE

MORGAN'S
FARM

MORGAN'S LANE

NORTH ALLERTON
AMENITY TIP

WINDOVER ROAD

WHITE HART WOODS

CHELFORD FOREST

CHELFORD MILL

CHELFORD

KEY To The TERRAIN

DECIDUOUS WOODLAND

CONIFERS

MARSH

CLIFFS AND ROCKS

HIKING TRAILS

NORTH

CHAPTER ONE
❧

"And this, young Pinepaw, is Twolegplace!" Mistpelt pointed with her tail to the tall wooden fence that ran along the edge of the trees.

Pinepaw tipped back his head to look at the top of the fence. It stretched away on either side of him, all the way to the ends of the forest. "Did the Twolegs build the fence to keep us out?" he asked.

Mistpelt purred with amusement. "We're not that scary! I think they wanted to mark their border, just as we mark ours, but they're too lazy to send out patrols. Just like any other Clan border, you must remember that we are not welcome on the other side." The warrior's eyes gleamed, startlingly green against her pale gray fur. "That's not to say we can't have a poke around over there when we wish, though. It's nothing like the forest, that's for sure!"

She started to pad away along the edge of the trees, her belly fur brushing the long grass. The scents of greenleaf hung heavy in the air and the breeze tasted of pollen and sap.

Pinepaw stayed where he was, trying to imagine what could be so different on the other side of the fence. Were the trees a different color? What sort of dens did Twolegs live in? He spotted a small hole in the fence, just at the level of his ears. He crept up to it and peered through.

A huge yellow eye glared back at him. Pinepaw squealed and leaped backward. There was a mad scrabble of claws and a deafening rattle of wood as Mistpelt hurtled up the fence and balanced on the top, arching her back and screeching.

"Leave my apprentice alone, you mangy furball! Too frightened to come over here and face us, aren't you? Go back to your Twolegs, fox-brain!"

She jumped down again and nodded to Pinepaw. "Nothing but a fat old kittypet," she meowed, sounding rather out of breath. She dipped her head to lick the fur on her chest. "You'll chase them off yourself next time."

Pinepaw glanced nervously back at the hole. Was the kittypet still watching him? He was sure he'd have bad dreams about monstrous eyes peering through holes for the rest of his life. He kept close to Mistpelt's flank as she padded away, resisting the urge to glance back and see if they were being tracked.

"I don't mind if I never see a kittypet again," he muttered.

Mistpelt purred. "Oh you will, but they won't frighten you. Their teeth and claws are as blunt as stones, and they're all scared of their own shadow!" She nodded toward a thick swath of brambles that blocked their path. "Beyond that is the Thunderpath. Can you hear it?"

Pinepaw paused to listen to the steady growl of monsters rumbling past. They didn't seem as alarming as the kittypet because he knew they never left the hard black stone. The biggest danger here was encountering trespassing warriors from ShadowClan, who lived on the other side. Mistpelt led him into the prickly brambles and Pinepaw peeked out at the blurred shapes of monsters rushing past. A stench-filled, warm wind buffeted his fur and he shrank back, trying not to gag.

"We won't go any closer than this," Mistpelt warned. "You'll learn how to cross the Thunderpath when you go to the Moonstone, but that won't be for a while."

Pinepaw felt a prickle of excitement beneath his fur. His whole life seemed to be rolling out before him, as clearly as if he were gazing down at it from the top of a tree. This was only his first day as an apprentice, and already he had encountered kittypets and monsters! He wondered if they would come across the other apprentices, who were all out training with their mentors. Pinepaw was used to being alone, as he didn't have any littermates, but he was looking forward to training with the others, and trying out for real the battle moves he had attempted as a kit.

He followed his mentor along the territory border, a few tail-lengths from the rumbling Thunderpath. The gritty scent of the monsters clung to every leaf and blade of grass, and Pinepaw wasn't looking forward to cleaning it off his fur later. Ahead of him, Mistpelt halted abruptly, her ears pricked. Pinepaw could see flashes of bright orange between the trees, and throaty Twoleg bellows cut through the growl of monsters.

"We'll have to go around them," Mistpelt whispered. "I don't think they'd be interested in us, but let's not take any risks." She crouched down and crawled into the bracken, away from the Thunderpath and the cluster of Twolegs who stood at the edge. Pinepaw hung back, trying to peer through the trunks to see what they were doing. They all had shiny orange pelts and hard white heads that reflected the sun. Two of them were standing in a muddy hole at the edge of the Thunderpath, and another was prodding the ground with a stick.

"Come on!" Mistpelt hissed in Pinepaw's ear, making him jump. He'd been so busy watching the Twolegs, he hadn't heard his mentor return. "What are you waiting for?"

"I was trying to see what they're up to," Pinepaw whispered back.

"Curious apprentices get their noses bitten," Mistpelt teased. "Oakstar sent a patrol out here last night. It looks like the Twolegs are digging a tunnel under the Thunderpath, where it gets very boggy."

"Cool!" breathed Pinepaw.

His mentor looked at him. "Hardly. We don't want to make it easy for ShadowClan to wander into our territory, do we?" Her tone was dry, and Pinepaw ducked his head, feeling foolish.

They pushed through the bracken and headed away from the Thunderpath. Pinepaw's legs were aching and his pads were stinging from thorns and stones. He had never walked so far in his life! He didn't know how patrols managed to go all around the territory every single day. The noise of the

Thunderpath faded away, and soon Pinepaw could hear the gentle splash of running water.

The river! He had heard so much about it and tried so hard to picture it. He burst out of the ferns and stood on the shore. *It's like a watery Thunderpath,* he thought, feeling slightly disappointed. From the way the elders talked about it, the river seemed like a terrible place, waiting to suck young cats under the surface. The fact that RiverClan warriors liked to swim just made them more sinister and terrifying.

Mistpelt padded past him over the crunchy stones. "Come dip your paws!" she called as she stepped delicately into the water.

Pinepaw backed away, imagining the water lapping hungrily at his belly, dragging him off his feet. "I'm okay, thanks," he mewed. He stared across the river to the willow trees on the other side. Their leaves shimmered gray and silver in the breeze, and the reeds beneath them whispered. Were they being watched by RiverClan cats? Pinepaw shuddered. He didn't want to meet any of those fish-breaths today. Not before he'd learned how to fight properly.

Mistpelt returned, shaking droplets from each paw in turn. "Let's head back," she meowed.

"Really? I've seen the whole territory?" Pinepaw asked.

Mistpelt purred. "Well, most of the borders. We'll leave everywhere else for another day." She ducked into the ferns and picked up a tiny path, strongly scented with rabbit and something else, sharp and bitter. "That's fox," Mistpelt commented, noticing Pinepaw wrinkle his nose.

Pinepaw blinked. "Is it near?" he squeaked.

"No, this is an old scent." Mistpelt picked up speed as the path widened, and suddenly Pinepaw realized he had seen these trees before, and smelled these exact scents . . . and there was the path at the top of the ravine that led down into ThunderClan's camp. *Home!*

He followed his mentor down the stony path and pushed his way through the gorse into the clearing. Before he could catch his breath, a brown tabby she-cat with green eyes was nuzzling him, licking the fur on his back and purring.

"Well, what do you think?" Sweetbriar demanded. Before Pinepaw could reply, she turned to Mistpelt. "Was he good? Did he listen to you?"

Pinepaw wriggled free. "Of course I did!" he mewed. His mother was so embarrassing.

Mistpelt nodded. "He was a perfect apprentice."

"Of course he was," rumbled Oakstar, coming to join them. His dark brown fur gleamed in the sun, and his eyes were warm as he gazed at Pinepaw. "My son is going to be the finest warrior this Clan has ever known!"

Pinepaw straightened up. "I'll try!" he promised.

"You must listen to everything Mistpelt tells you about training for battle. I want you to be ready to fight those mangy RiverClan cats!" Oakstar meowed. "They will not take another son from me!"

Pinepaw watched his father's eyes cloud with sorrow. He had never known his half brother Birchface; he just knew that Birchface had died in a battle with RiverClan.

A cream-and-white she-cat joined them. "He might fight ShadowClan warriors before then," she warned. "Those Two-legs will finish the tunnel soon, and ShadowClan will have direct access to our territory."

Oakstar nodded. "You're right, Doefeather, but I think they'll turn back if we renew the scent markers there every day. Can you make sure the dawn patrols do that, please?"

Doefeather nodded. "Of course."

There was a crackle of gorse and Flashpaw, Daisypaw, and Littlepaw burst into the camp, closely followed by their mentors.

"We just had a great battle practice!" Daisypaw mewed. Her gray-and-white fur was sticking up along her spine and there was a piece of bracken hanging from one ear.

Doefeather studied her. "You look as if you lost," she pointed out.

"She did," Daisypaw's sister, Flashpaw, declared. "Littlepaw and me nearly squashed her!"

"Not necessarily a move to take into battle," commented Littlepaw's mentor, Squirrelwhisker. She nodded to Doefeather. "Your apprentice fought well, though. Very brave, even when the other two joined against her."

Doefeather purred. "I'm glad to hear it. Thanks for taking her."

Flashpaw's mentor, Nettlebreeze, was drinking water from some soaked moss at the side of the clearing. Swallowing, he turned to Pinepaw. "How was your first walk around the territory?"

"Amazing!" Pinepaw mewed. "I saw a kittypet and some Twolegs!"

"Ooh, scary," teased Daisypaw.

"He did very well," Mistpelt meowed. "In fact, I think he can join your practice tomorrow to help Daisypaw out. What do you think, Squirrelwhisker?"

The brown tabby warrior dipped her head. "We'd be honored to have you with us, Pinepaw and Mistpelt."

Pinepaw bounced on his toes. Being an apprentice was the best thing ever!

Crack! A twig snapped beneath Pinepaw's foot and he stopped dead, holding his breath. Ahead of him, the blackbird was still pecking in the leaf mulch. He let out a sigh of relief. Out of the corner of his eye, he saw Flashpaw mouth, *Lucky!* at him, and Pinepaw nodded. Just a few more steps and he'd be within pouncing range.

He had been an apprentice for almost one moon, and this was his fourth hunting patrol. He had caught something on every single patrol so far, and he wasn't going to let that change now! He eased his weight onto his front paws and gathered his haunches beneath him in the hunter's crouch.

"Sssshhhh!"

Pinepaw looked around. Who said that? Flashpaw had vanished and he seemed to be alone among the ferns.

"Get off my tail!" hissed a different voice. "Do you want to let the whole of ThunderClan know we're here?"

Pinepaw froze. That wasn't one of his Clanmates. Were

they being *invaded*? He sniffed the air. This close to the Thunderpath, the scent of leaves and prey was mostly smothered by the stench of monsters, but today there was something else, the faintest hint of a cat scent that he hadn't smelled before. . . .

His pelt bristling along his spine, he prowled toward the bush where he had heard the voices. He had forgotten about the blackbird. It flew up with a squawk, and there was a flurry of movement among the brambles. Pinepaw glimpsed flashes of brown, gray, and orange fur, and the glint of unsheathed claws. He had lost his chance to creep up on them now.

"Intruders!" he yowled, spinning around and racing toward where he had left the rest of his patrol. "Come quick!"

Doefeather leaped out in front of him, her fur standing on end. A splash of blood on her muzzle showed she had just made a successful catch. "Where?" she demanded.

Pinepaw nodded over his shoulder. "In those brambles," he panted.

"Wait here," the deputy told him. She bounded toward the bush, letting out a screech. "ThunderClan warriors, to me!"

The undergrowth around Pinepaw came alive as Mistpelt, Squirrelwhisker, Daisypaw, and Littlepaw burst out. Mistpelt paused beside Pinepaw. "What's going on?"

"We're being invaded!" Pinepaw told her.

Squirrelwhisker sniffed the air and bared her teeth. "A ShadowClan patrol has come through that wretched tunnel! Come on, let's chase them back where they came from!"

As she raced away with Littlepaw at her heels, Mistpelt mewed, "Pinepaw, go to the camp for more warriors!" Then she disappeared after her Clanmates.

Pinepaw was about to plunge into the bracken toward the camp when something struck him. He was sure he had only seen three or four cats among the brambles. That meant they were already outnumbered by the ThunderClan patrol. Rather than waste time by fetching more cats, why didn't he join the others and give chase now, before the intruders got too far into the forest?

Whirling around, he set off after his mentor. A volley of yowls and hisses told him that the invaders had been confronted. Pinepaw launched himself through a dense thicket of elder and scrambled out on the other side. In a small clearing, the rest of his patrol faced four ShadowClan warriors. Their heads were lowered and their tails lashed from side to side. Pinepaw gaped at the moment, struck by how lean and strong the ShadowClan cats looked, how calm and ready for battle.

Then he looked at his own Clanmates, standing their ground with their fur bristling. He knew which side he wanted to fight on! He bounded over to stand beside Mistpelt, who hissed, "I told you to fetch help!"

"That would take too long. I can be of more use here!" Pinepaw whispered back. He sank his claws into the damp earth and ran through every battle move in his head.

Littlepaw touched him with the tip of his tail. "Fight alongside me," he murmured. "We'll cause more trouble if we stick together!"

Pinepaw nodded and shifted closer to the black-and-white tom.

"You want us to leave?" sneered one of the ShadowClan warriors, an orange-and-gray she-cat with mean amber eyes. "You'll have to make us!"

"We will!" Doefeather retorted. She sprang at the intruder, clearing the gap with a single stride. At once the other ShadowClan cats rushed forward and the ThunderClan cats leaped to meet them.

Pinepaw and Littlepaw threw themselves at a light brown tom with a distinctive snaggletooth. Pinepaw clung onto the warrior's neck while Littlepaw nipped his ears. The cat flung himself to the ground, dislodging Littlepaw, but Pinepaw held on, sinking his claws into the warrior's fur. When the cat tried to roll over and crush him, Pinepaw sprang sideways, then jumped back onto the warrior's shoulders as he scrambled to his paws.

"Nice move!" Littlepaw panted, ducking around to bite the ShadowClan cat's tail. The warrior let out a yowl and staggered. Pinepaw took the opportunity to cuff his broad head, and the cat sank to his knees.

On the other side of the clearing, Mistpelt was snarling at a dark gray tom. Blood dripped from the she-cat's ear, but her eyes were fierce as she lashed out at the intruder. He tried to step back but was blocked by a bramble; trapped, he could only duck as Mistpelt rained blows on his head.

"Go, Mistpelt!" yowled Pinepaw.

The orange-and-gray cat rolled away from Doefeather and stood up. "ShadowClan warriors, retreat!" she growled.

The fourth intruder, a gray-and-white she-cat, snapped at

Daisypaw's ears once more, and got clouted by Squirrelwhisker in return. Pinepaw braced himself for another attack, but the orange-and-gray warrior hissed, and as one, the Shadow-Clan warriors turned and sprinted away. Doefeather charged after them and the rest of the patrol fell in behind. In spite of his scratches and bruised paws, Pinepaw felt himself fly over the ground. *We won!*

They chased the intruders all the way to the tunnel under the Thunderpath, then stopped just beyond the churned-up earth and watched them flounder back into the damp-smelling hole.

"And stay out!" Doefeather screeched.

There was a rustle of bracken on the far side of the Thunderpath as the ShadowClan cats emerged, then silence. Even the Thunderpath was empty and quiet, save for the panting of the ThunderClan warriors.

Mistpelt nudged Pinepaw, and he looked up at her. "You fought well, youngster," she mewed. "Your father will be very proud."

Pinepaw felt his pelt grow hot with pride.

Doefeather nodded. "Good decision to stay with us," she grunted. "Brave, too. We'll make a leader of you yet, Pinepaw. Just wait and see."

CHAPTER TWO

"But Mapleshade hadn't finished her revenge. She wasn't going to rest until she had tortured every cat that she blamed for the death of her kits! She came back to ThunderClan looking for one cat in particular: poor, helpless Frecklewish." Nettlebreeze lowered his voice and Pinepaw shivered. He had heard this story many times, all the apprentices had, but that didn't stop them from begging Nettlebreeze to tell them the tale again.

"Tell us what happened when she found her!" begged Daisypaw, her yellow eyes huge. The skirmish with ShadowClan warriors had left her with a deep bite on her foreleg, so she had been staying in the medicine cat's den for the last few days, but she would be back in training soon.

Nettlebreeze crouched down and let the fur rise along his spine. "Mapleshade found her, all right, patrolling by Snakerocks. Mapleshade forced her into a pile of stones where snakes were hiding, and one of them spat venom right in Frecklewish's eye!"

He paused, screwing up his own eyes to show what Frecklewish would have looked like.

"Bloomheart found her," Nettlebreeze went on, his voice

growing husky with grief. "But there was nothing he could do. ThunderClan had no medicine cat then, because Mapleshade had killed Ravenwing without an apprentice to take over. Frecklewish died a few sunrises later, when the poison took hold of her from the inside." He shook his head. "Perhaps that was a sign of mercy from StarClan. If she had survived, she would have been blind and driven mad by the horrors she had seen. If Mapleshade is not in the Place of No Stars, there is no justice!"

"No justice!" echoed the apprentices faintly, shaking their heads.

"Nettlebreeze, are you telling them about Mapleshade again?" Fallowsong pushed her way into the apprentices' den, shaking raindrops from her fur. "For StarClan's sake, stop! You keep giving them bad dreams!"

"No, he doesn't," Littlepaw protested.

Fallowsong tipped her head on one side. "My nest is just the other side of the den wall," she pointed out. "I can hear you! Okay, Doefeather has sent most of your mentors to renew the border marks by the tunnel, so she has asked us to take you on a hunting patrol. We'll try not to stumble across any intruders this time, okay?"

Pinepaw scrambled to his feet and followed the others out of the den. The rain had eased to a fine drizzle that clung to his fur and tickled his eyelashes. He blinked, then broke into a run so that he didn't have to linger under the dripping gorse.

Fallowsong and Nettlebreeze took them to the pine trees near treecutplace. It was silent and shadowy under the brittle branches, and the cats didn't say a word as they spread out, looking for prey. Pinepaw watched the other apprentices cover the needle-strewn ground and decided to head closer to Twolegplace in the hope of finding something in the long grass at the edge of the trees. He had patrolled along the fence several times now and never stopped to peek through the hole again. He wasn't afraid of a lazy kittypet, he told himself. He just didn't see any need to cross their path.

As he approached the edge of the forest, he saw the sharply pointed red roofs of the Twoleg dens. There was a chatter of high-pitched Twoleg voices, abruptly cut off by a thud, then a monster began rumbling, loud at first but fainter as it rolled away. Pinepaw swerved around a dripping dock leaf, letting the scents of the forest fill his muzzle. There was definitely a hint of prey—rabbit, possibly—and something else, mustier and almost hidden beneath the scent of rain-soaked leaves.

A fallen tree lay ahead, the ground around it sandy and bare of grass where the roots had disturbed the earth. Pinepaw crept toward it, pinpointing the scents to the roots that reached into the air above a deep, sandy hole. The air began to taste warm and furry. *This is going to be a great catch!* Pinepaw thought gleefully.

Suddenly there was an explosion from the trees beside him and a deafening screech of barking. Pinepaw spun around to see a fox snarling at the edge of the grass. Her russet-colored hackles were raised and drool dripped from her teeth. Behind him, he heard the faintest of yaps from beneath the roots of the tree, and his heart sank. He hadn't been following the scent of prey. He had picked up the trail of some fox cubs!

The mother fox took a step closer, and now Pinepaw could smell her breath, meaty and hot and foul. Her eyes gleamed with fury and hunger. Pinepaw scanned the gap between the fox and the tree trunk. Could he make a run for it before she caught him? His heart pounded so hard that he couldn't think clearly, and his legs trembled until it was an effort to stand upright.

The fox leaned forward, ready to strike. Pinepaw closed his eyes and braced himself. He knew he wasn't fast enough to run away. He would have to hope that he could somehow fight his way out.

Just as the fox was about to leap, there was a thunder of paws along the fallen tree. A ginger-and-white shape flew down to land in front of Pinepaw. It was a cat, her fur fluffed up and her tail bristling.

"Get away from him!" the cat hissed. She lashed out with one forepaw, and sharp claws glinted briefly in the air. "Leave him alone!"

To Pinepaw's astonishment, the fox lowered its muzzle and took a step back. Its ears flicked as if it was trying to work out what this fierce cat was saying.

"Get onto the fence," the cat muttered to Pinepaw out of the side of her mouth. "Go on, *now*!"

Pinepaw turned and jumped onto the fallen tree. Without looking back, he raced along the trunk and leaped from there onto the Twoleg fence. It wobbled under his weight and for a moment he thought he would fall down into the grass to be snapped up by the fox . . . but then he dug in with his claws and found his balance and stood triumphantly on top of the fence. The ginger-and-white cat joined while the fox barked in frustration below.

"Ha!" jeered Pinepaw. "Can't catch me!"

The ginger-and-white cat looked at him with cool blue eyes. "And you did what, exactly, to save yourself?" she meowed. "You would have been fed to those cubs if I hadn't turned up in time."

"You don't know that," Pinepaw argued, feeling his fur grow hot. "I'm a ThunderClan warrior! I know how to fight!"

"You should also know not to come between a fox and her cubs," mewed the she-cat. "Clearly they aren't training warriors properly these days."

"Are you from another Clan?" Pinepaw asked, staring at her glossy fur.

The she-cat rolled her eyes. "What, and chase prey all over the place to catch my dinner every day? Don't be ridiculous. I live here." She nodded to the Twoleg den behind them.

Pinepaw gaped. "You're . . . you're a *kittypet*! But kittypets don't know how to fight!"

The she-cat blinked. "You might have noticed that I didn't fight that fox. I just scared it long enough to let you get away. We're not all cowards, you know." She stood up and kinked her tail over her back. "Especially if we have kits. Like that fox, we'd do anything to protect our young." She padded lightly along the top of the fence. "Now, go back to your territory, and stay away from foxes! I won't always be here to save you."

She jumped down onto the bright green square of grass below the fence. Without looking back, she trotted to the Twoleg den and vanished through a little gap in the wall. Pinepaw studied the stretch of ground between the fence and the trees. There was no sign of the mother fox; he guessed it had gone into its den under the fallen tree. He leaped down, holding his breath when the fence rattled under his hind paws. He crouched in the long grass for a moment, but there was no movement, no fresh fox scent carried to him on the breeze, so he darted across the open ground to the safety of the pine trees.

His second encounter with a kittypet had been even more startling than the first. And much as he hated to admit it—and he certainly wasn't going to tell Mistpelt or his denmates what had happened—he owed his life to that bold she-cat. Too late, he realized he hadn't thanked her. *And I'll probably never see her again,* he thought as he trotted through the trees toward the sound of his patrol.

CHAPTER THREE

❧

Pinepaw clenched his teeth and tried not to gag as he dabbed the moss soaked in mouse bile onto Seedpelt's gray pelt. The stench made Pinepaw's eyes water, but the elder didn't seem to notice. Seedpelt grunted as the bile sank into the skin around the fat tick on her belly, and wriggled farther onto her back so that Pinepaw could apply the moss again.

Pinepaw wondered how long he could hold his breath before he keeled over. He couldn't believe he had been an apprentice for nearly six moons, yet he still had to do the most disgusting jobs. If only there were younger apprentices to take over tick duties! He pressed down a little harder, and with the faintest pop, the tick jerked free from Seedpelt's skin. Pinepaw knocked it to the ground and squashed it firmly.

"Thanks," Seedpelt mewed, sitting up and licking the speck of blood left behind on her belly. "That feels much better."

Pinepaw scooped up the moss with the dead tick inside it and headed toward the dirtplace tunnel. He was almost among the brambles when there was a thud of paws behind him as several cats burst into the clearing. Pinepaw dropped the bundle of moss and whirled around.

Mumblefoot stood in the center of the camp, his thick-furred brown flanks heaving. The rest of the border patrol crowded behind him, all breathless. "Kittypets!" Mumblefoot burst out.

Several cats around the clearing jumped to their paws. "Where? Here? Are we being attacked?"

Oakstar and Doefeather emerged from the leader's den beneath Highrock. "What's going on?" Oakstar demanded.

"Not here," Mumblefoot panted. "But inside our territory, on this side of the fence."

"I picked up their scent under the pine trees," Windflight put in. "Farther in than they've ever come before."

"They could be planning an invasion!" Hollypelt meowed, her black fur fluffed up and speckled with bits of fern from her race through the forest.

Littlepaw and Daisypaw joined Pinepaw. "Do you think kittypets would really be dumb enough to attack us?" whispered Littlepaw.

"I wish they would!" mewed Daisypaw, unsheathing her front claws. "I'd love to show them just how hard we fight!"

"I don't think we're in any great danger," Oakstar meowed. "But we do need to remind those furballs that they aren't welcome in our territory. It's a sign that they're getting much too bold if they're coming all the way into treecutplace." He looked around the clearing. "I think we should send a patrol into Twolegplace tonight to show them that we won't tolerate this. What do you think, Doefeather?"

The Clan deputy nodded. "That's an excellent idea." She

gestured with her tail to warriors dotted around the clearing. "I'll lead it, and I want Rooktail, Harepounce, Mistpelt, and Squirrelwhisker to join me. We'll take our apprentices, too."

"What about me?" called Flashpaw. "You didn't choose Nettlebreeze."

"I think my days of chasing around Twolegplace are over," grunted his mentor. "But you can join the patrol if you wish."

"I'll keep an eye on her," Rooktail offered, and Nettlebreeze nodded his thanks.

"We'll leave at sunset," Doefeather decided. "Warriors, take something from the fresh-kill pile and get some rest. Those of you who won't be coming with me, please take over hunting duties for the rest of the day."

There were quiet murmurs as the cats dispersed around the camp. Pinepaw joined the other apprentices at the end of the queue for the fresh-kill pile, behind the warriors.

"I'm too excited to eat!" Daisypaw confessed.

"But we'll need our strength," Littlepaw pointed out solemnly.

Pinepaw said nothing. He was eager to go over the fence and explore Twolegplace, but he wasn't convinced that the kittypets were such a terrible threat. If they were really as lazy and well fed as his Clanmates said, surely they weren't interested in stealing ThunderClan's prey? And he couldn't believe they'd find their way right to the camp, hidden in the ravine among bushes and trees.

Then he thought of the fierce kittypet who had chased away the fox all those moons ago, and he reminded himself that he shouldn't underestimate any cat, not even those who lived with Twolegs.

The patrol set out toward Sunningrocks as the last rays of sun glowed above the trees. A three-quarter moon was already high in the pale sky, ready to cast enough silver light for the warriors to see clearly once they were outside familiar territory. Pinepaw felt his heart race as he pushed through the gorse with his denmates and scampered up to the top of the ravine. What would be waiting for them in Twolegplace?

"We're not out to cause damage," Doefeather warned over her shoulder as she led them at a brisk walk through the ferns. "Our plan is to find as many kittypets as we can and give them a good scare—claw their fur if they fight back, but there's no need to shed blood unnecessarily. They just need to learn to respect the Clan cats, and stay out of our territory!"

The warriors around her nodded. "I'm happy to teach them a lesson they won't forget," muttered Harepounce, her light brown fur turning pale gray in the dusk.

Pinepaw had been out of the camp at night before—his journey to see the Moonstone had begun long before dawn, and they had been halfway across WindClan's territory before the sun rose—but this was the first time he had set out to defend his Clan from enemies. He was surprised it was quiet even with so many cats walking together; hardly a pine needle cracked underpaw, and even the whispers stopped as they approached the edge of the trees.

Doefeather stopped below the fence and the warriors circled her. "I'll take the lead," the deputy whispered, her voice hardly louder than the breeze. "If I spot a kittypet, I'll let you know. We'll separate into groups to issue each warning. No need for all of us to terrorize one cat!"

There was a purr of amusement through the patrol, but Pinepaw was aware of tension crackling through the air like lightning. He flexed his legs in turn, preparing his muscles for battle moves, if only to strike fear into the too-bold kittypets.

Suddenly Doefeather was vanishing over the fence, her paws hardly seeming to touch the wood as she leaped to the top and disappeared down the other side. The patrol streamed after her and the fence creaked ominously under the weight of so many cats. Pinepaw jumped down to the short, soft grass and felt the others land around him, hardly visible in the shadows beneath a heavily scented tree. Doefeather trotted into the moonlight cast on the grass and the rest of the cats followed in silence, ears pricked and muzzles open to taste the air. They rounded the edge of the silent Twoleg den and entered a narrow gap between red stone walls, too high to jump up on. Doefeather picked up speed and they burst out onto a little Thunderpath, lined with sleeping monsters.

A pair of yellow eyes gleamed on the far side of the Thunderpath. Doefeather jerked her muzzle. "Rooktail, Harepounce, Flashpaw, off you go."

The three cats bounded across the hard black stone and Pinepaw heard a thrum of paws as the kittypet tried to run away. Rooktail let out a screech and the warriors sped up, hurtling around a corner with the kittypet yowling just ahead of them.

Doefeather nodded in satisfaction. "Come on," she ordered the rest of the patrol. They followed the Thunderpath between the Twoleg dens, keeping to the shadows cast by the motionless monsters. Pinepaw felt his pelt crawl at being so close to the stinking silver beasts, and he prayed to StarClan that none of them suddenly woke up.

The soft rumble of a mew drifted on the warm air, and Doefeather froze, her tail up in warning. Pinepaw strained his ears and picked up the sounds of two cats talking quietly beyond a low gray wall. Doefeather pointed to him and Mistpelt. "You can take those. Squirrelwhisker, you go with them. Daisypaw and Littlepaw, stay with me."

Mistpelt nodded and set off toward the wall at a run. Pinepaw followed with Squirrelwhisker at his heels. *Watch out, kittypets! Here comes ThunderClan!*

They bounded over the wall and crouched down among the shadows. Two shapes were outlined in moonlight on the far side of a stretch of pale stones. "We'll make too much noise if we approach them directly," Mistpelt whispered. "Get back on the wall and see if we can follow it around."

They jumped onto the wall and padded along it, crouching low to avoid making too large a silhouette. Pinepaw concentrated on keeping his balance low and steady, even though his heart was pounding hard enough to make him out of breath. They passed a deep shadow between the wall and a much smaller den made of wood. Mistpelt hesitated, pricking her ears.

"I think I hear something down here. Pinepaw, check it out."

Pinepaw gulped. *On my own?* Then he told himself that he was very nearly a warrior, and if Mistpelt trusted him, he wasn't going to argue. As the others continued along the wall, he sprang down into the shadow. It was almost pitch black down here, and he blinked hard to force his eyes to adjust. A pair of eyes shone out of the darkness and the scent of several cats reached Pinepaw, making his fur stand on end. He crouched down, ready to leap at the kittypets and give them a demonstration of how ThunderClan warriors were brave and ready to fight.

Before he could move, a paw lashed out at him, almost taking off his whiskers. Pinepaw found himself face-to-face with a furious she-cat, her teeth bared and her claws glinting in the moonlight.

"It's you!" he gasped. This was the cat who had faced down the mother fox. In all of Twolegplace, Pinepaw had found her—this time as an enemy.

"Get away from here!" the she-cat snarled.

Pinepaw bristled. "Don't tell me what to do, kittypet! I'm a ThunderClan cat!"

"Is that supposed to scare me?" hissed the she-cat.

Pinepaw braced himself for a full strike with his front paws. Then he caught a different scent, one that he had smelled a long time ago, soft and milky and filled with tender memories. *There are kits here!*

He looked at the she-cat and saw the same fury that had been in the eyes of the fox. This cat was frightened of nothing, not when she had her kits to protect. And did she really deserve to be attacked, after she had saved his life? Pinepaw took a step back and forced his fur to lie down.

"It's okay," he mewed. "Your babies are safe. I'm not going to hurt them."

"I wasn't going to let you," growled the she-cat.

"I know you weren't," Pinepaw mewed hastily. He didn't want this cat to think she needed to prove a point.

Beyond the walls that sheltered them, the air was split with yowls and screeches and thudding paws as the ThunderClan cats rousted and startled kittypets.

The she-cat's eyes grew huge. "What's going on?"

Pinepaw glanced over his shoulder. "I . . . er . . . we came to teach a lesson to the kittypets who've been straying into our territory."

"A lesson in what? That we aren't safe in our own homes?"

"No, that you're not welcome in ours."

The she-cat harrumphed. "Well, it wasn't me. I've got more than enough to deal with here."

As she spoke, three tiny faces peeked out from behind her. Above them, a sharp white light flicked on, and Pinepaw found himself staring at a ginger tom with the greenest eyes he had ever seen. He flinched at the sudden brightness. "What's that?"

The she-cat shrugged. "My housefolk put a light on so I

can find my way back at night." She curled her tail around the kits. "Come on, little ones. It's time for bed." She started to usher the kits past Pinepaw. "Are you going to chase me into my house?" she teased.

Pinepaw shook his head. Suddenly there was a yowl above him, and a scrabble of paws.

"Pinepaw? Are you down there?" Mistpelt was standing on top of the wall, unable to see Pinepaw and the kittypets in the tiny gap.

The she-cat's eyes stretched wide and her tail folded more closely around her kits. Pinepaw gave a tiny shake of his head. *I won't bring them to you,* he promised silently.

"Just coming!" he called up to his mentor. "There's nothing down here." He stepped back and let the she-cat move into the shadow with her kits. She broke into a trot, her babies scampering behind her. Just before they vanished around the corner of their den, the ginger tom looked back at Pinepaw.

"Thank you!" mewed the tiny cat, and Pinepaw nodded.

"Are you stuck in something?" Mistpelt bellowed. "Where are you?"

Pinepaw whisked around and jumped up onto the wall. "I'm here, everything's fine," he panted.

Mistpelt twitched the tip of her tail. "While you've been hiding down there, the rest of us have chased off that pair of chattering kittypets. Doefeather is waiting for us on the Thunderpath, come on."

Pinepaw followed his mentor at a run along the wall and joined the rest of the patrol in a patch of shadow cast by a huge, straight-backed monster. Doefeather looked around at her Clanmates and nodded. "A highly successful mission," she declared with a purr. "Those kittypets have learned we won't stand for trespassing!" She set off along the side of the den, following the path that led back to the fence. "Come on, let's go tell Oakstar that our boundary is safe once more!"

The sun scorched Pinepaw's red-brown pelt as he stood beneath Highrock with his head bowed. Oakstar stood over him, less than a mouse-length taller than Pinepaw at his shoulder. Pinepaw thought back to the days when his father had seemed to loom over him, bigger than a badger. *I'm becoming more like him all the time,* he thought. *Perhaps I will follow in his paw steps one day and lead our Clan.*

"The raid on Twolegplace was a success," Oakstar declared, purrs rumbling in his chest. "It is easy to dismiss our kittypet neighbors as a flea-bite nuisance, rather than a real threat. But they are as capable of stealing our prey as any cat, and if we do not tolerate other Clans setting foot across our borders, we should not allow kittypets to trespass either." He looked down at Pinepaw. "I am especially proud of the way my son acted during the raid. Mistpelt told me he worked alone, with all the bravery of a full warrior."

Pinepaw tried not to squirm. How could he explain that he didn't actually fight any kittypets; rather, he let them know he would leave them in peace as long as they didn't try to interfere with the invasion.

Oakstar bent his head and touched his muzzle lightly to

Pinepaw's ear. "From this moment, you will be known as Pineheart," he announced. "ThunderClan honors your courage in the invasion of Twolegplace, and your sense of strategy when under attack. May StarClan light your path, always." He touched his muzzle to the top of Pineheart's head and murmured, "I am so proud of you, my son."

"Pineheart! Pineheart!"

Pineheart lifted his head to listen to his Clanmates as they cheered his new name. His future unrolled before him like a shining sunlit path. He had never felt more fortunate than at this moment, knowing how lucky he was to have been born in the forest, the son of a great leader, with the life of a warrior stretching ahead. No cat was more committed to his Clan, more grateful to StarClan, or more certain that his dying breath would be dedicated to keeping his territory and his Clanmates safe.

Chapter Four

Pineheart strode through the gorse tunnel and carried the dead squirrel across the clearing. Around him, the trees clattered their empty leaf-bare branches, and a cold wind lifted the fur along his spine. But there were tiny green buds appearing on the trees, and the mornings no longer dawned with frost that made clouds of the cats' breath as they set out on patrol.

Pineheart thought he would never be happier to see the end of leaf-bare. He had been forced to watch his Clanmates starve around him as first floods then snow destroyed what little prey there was. Goosefeather's idea of burying fresh-kill to preserve it had failed dismally when rain turned the clearing to mud and rotted the food before the cats could take a single mouthful. As the deputy of ThunderClan, Pineheart had felt painfully helpless, and as terrified as a kit.

Now Pineheart was aware of cats watching him and murmuring, the voices growing louder as the rest of his patrol entered the camp laden with prey. *Look! Feast your eyes, then your bellies!* Pineheart thought, unable to speak with his jaws full of fresh-kill. *The hungry moons have passed!*

He heard Larksong warning her kits to take tiny mouthfuls.

"Don't rush, or you'll give yourself bellyache. Flamenose caught this squirrel just for you! You must thank your father when you have finished eating."

Cloudberry took a piece of prey over to Mistpelt. "Your belly has been empty for so long, too much food will make you ill," the medicine cat told the only surviving elder. "Why don't we share this mouse that Mumblefoot brought?"

Mistpelt grunted in agreement, and Pineheart felt a pang of sorrow for his former mentor. She had watched her denmate Nettlebreeze starve to death, along with many others in the long, harsh leaf-bare. Pineheart knew his bones stuck out as much as his Clanmates', and all the cats had added more moss to their nests because lying down was so uncomfortable.

But the weather had turned at last. The snow was melting so fast that every tree in the forest dripped like rainclouds. The air felt warmer, and there was a faint scent of greenness in the brittle undergrowth. Today was the first properly successful hunting patrol Pineheart had led since the previous leaf-fall, with every cat making a catch. The fresh-kill pile had returned, and he listened to his Clanmates' paws squelching in the mud as they crowded around to take their share.

Pineheart didn't add his squirrel to the pile. Instead he carried it straight to Highrock and brushed past the brambles to duck inside the leader's den. He may have grown scrawny, but he was still one of the tallest cats in ThunderClan, and his ears brushed the roof of Doestar's cave.

"Fresh squirrel, just for you!" he declared, setting it down in front of the cream-and-white she-cat. Curled in her nest, she blinked at him with clouded, unfocused eyes.

Cloudberry's apprentice, Goosefeather, stood up. "Look what Pineheart brought!" he meowed. He nudged Doestar with one paw. "Come on, don't you want to try it?"

Doestar turned her head away. "Put it on the fresh-kill pile," she rasped.

Pineheart crouched beside her. "There is plenty of food to feed the Clan," he told her. "I caught this for you."

The leader shifted so that she was looking up at Pineheart. "The fresh-kill pile is full?"

Pineheart nodded. "Every cat on my patrol caught something. New-leaf is here, Doestar! Everything is going to be okay." He pushed the squirrel closer and Doestar bent to take a bite. Goosefeather met Pineheart's gaze over the leader's head, and nodded in satisfaction.

Pineheart left Doestar eating and backed out of the cave. In the clearing, his Clanmates had gathered in little groups to share the fresh-kill. The pile had vanished, but Pineheart forced down the jolt of alarm in his belly. *We will catch more tomorrow,* he told himself. *And the day after, and the day after that. ThunderClan does not have to starve anymore.*

Mumblefoot padded alongside him and brushed his tail against Pineheart's flank. "We did well today," the old warrior murmured. "Thank StarClan that they have spared us."

"Not all of us," Pineheart mewed, looking through the leafless branches to the mounds of earth halfway up the ravine, beyond the walls of the camp. As well as Nettlebreeze, they had lost Harepounce, Stagleap, Hollypelt, and Flashnose; all starved to death in the bitter rains and endless, preyless leaf-bare moons.

A scuffle beside the apprentices' den dragged Pineheart back to the present. Rabbitpaw and Moonpaw were squabbling over the ears of a rabbit. Pineheart trotted over and placed his paw on the contested scraps. Before the great hunger, prey ears would have been buried in the dirtplace or used as playthings for kits. Long moons of starvation had turned them into highly prized treats.

"Two ears, two of you," he declared, pushing a scrap of skin and fur toward each apprentice. "And we are not starving anymore. There is plenty for every cat!"

The young cats blinked up at him, a faint spark of hope in their eyes. Moonpaw's silver-gray pelt hung loosely over her ribs, and her tail was dirty and matted.

"No chores for the rest of the day," Pineheart announced. "Stay here and clean yourselves up. We are warriors of ThunderClan, not homeless rogues."

As he turned away, he saw Cloudberry watching him. The medicine cat was so frail that Pineheart could hardly believe she had survived the hunger. Somehow she had clung to life, eating bark and dry leaves with the rest of the Clan when prey had vanished altogether. And here she was, still caring for them all, still fussing over her Clanmates as if they were her kits.

Pineheart stopped alongside the medicine cat. "Is Doestar all right?" he asked quietly.

Cloudberry blinked. "She is weak, like all of us."

"That's not an answer," Pineheart meowed. "I'm her deputy. I need to know if she is going to lose a life."

Cloudberry sighed. "This is her last life, and she knows it. She refuses to tell me how she is feeling, but I think she is more ill than any cat realizes. Prepare to say good-bye, Pineheart. StarClan will gather her to them soon."

Pineheart stared at the cat in alarm. "Her last life already? I . . . I had lost count." He shook his head miserably. "She can't leave us! I still have so much to learn before I become leader."

"You'll be fine," Cloudberry meowed. "You are a brave and skillful warrior, just like your father was. ThunderClan deserves to be led by a cat like you." She touched Pineheart's flank with the tip of her tail. "Have faith."

She limped away, her tail dragging in the mud. Pineheart headed back to the den below Highrock. Grief weighed in his belly like a stone, and he fought down the wave of panic that threatened to overwhelm him. He couldn't become leader yet! It was too soon!

Doestar was dozing, but she stirred when Pineheart settled down beside her. "Pineheart?" she whispered. "Is that you?"

"Yes," Pineheart replied. "Is there anything I can get you?"

"Ah, no," sighed Doestar. She wriggled deeper into her nest, which was lined with glossy black rook feathers. "Deerpaw was here just now. Did you see her?"

Pineheart froze. Deerpaw was Doestar's littermate, who had died during her apprenticeship. Had she come to take her sister to StarClan? "I don't see her now," he mewed carefully.

"Good," Doestar grunted. "She was bugging me to go

somewhere, but I don't feel like leaving my nest today. Maybe tomorrow I'll go with her."

Please don't! Pineheart thought. *I'm not ready to become leader! Stay until the Clan is fit and strong again!*

"The apprentices hunted well today," he meowed, changing the subject. "Heronpaw caught a pigeon all by himself."

Doestar let out a creaky purr. "He was always fast, even as a kit."

Pineheart felt a flash of relief that his leader had returned to the present.

"I shall make them all warriors tomorrow," Doestar announced abruptly. "They have served their Clan well through the hungry moons, and we all deserve to celebrate our survival." She sat up, her eyes clearer now, looking more like her old self.

Pineheart dipped his head. "That's an excellent idea," he purred.

The she-cat reached out and rested her paw on Pineheart's foreleg. "I am so pleased that you will take care of Thunder-Clan after me," she mewed. "It was an honor to serve your father, and I am only sorry that I won't be here to watch you lead the Clan as well."

"But that won't be for a long time. . . ." Pineheart started to object, but Doestar silenced him by gently pricking his leg with her claws.

"We've known each other too long to tell lies now," she meowed. "I have reached my ninth life sooner than I expected, but ThunderClan will be safe with you. All of the Clans suffered this leaf-bare, but this only means they will want to prove their strength as soon as the warm weather returns. You must guard the borders fiercely, do you understand? Especially Sunningrocks. Your father never trusted RiverClan, remember." Her eyes blazed in the dusky light.

"I promise we will not lose Sunningrocks," Pineheart told her. "ThunderClan will be as strong as it ever was, even if we have to fight all of our enemies in turn to prove it." His heart started to pound and he unsheathed his claws into the hard earth floor of the den as he imagined leading his Clanmates into battle to defend their territory and their honor.

Suddenly he realized that Doestar had slumped down into her nest, and her breath was coming in ragged gasps. "Doestar? Doestar, are you okay?" The she-cat stirred but didn't sit up.

Cloudberry entered the den behind Pineheart. She was carrying a bundle of soaked moss, which she set down beside the leader's nest. "She's okay, just tired," the medicine cat mewed. "Leave her be, now."

Pineheart backed out of the den, unable to take his eyes from Doestar. *Please don't leave me yet! ThunderClan still needs you!*

CHAPTER FIVE

♣

Pineheart stared at Doestar's body, slumped in the middle of the clearing. Cloudberry lay beside her, almost as still and silent as the dead leader. She had forbidden any other cat to come close, frightened that the sickness that had taken Doestar so swiftly at the end might be infectious. Pineheart thought back to the last conversation he had had with Doestar, two sunrises ago. Had she known Deerpaw would come for her again so soon? At least she had been strong enough to hold naming ceremonies for Moonflower, Poppydawn, Heronwing, and Rabbitleap yesterday. ThunderClan's newest warriors crouched at the edge of the clearing now, their heads bowed in sorrow.

Cloudberry was speaking quietly to Goosefeather. Pineheart padded over to them, his paws feeling like stone. It was clear from Cloudberry's hunched shoulders and dull, glazed expression that Goosefeather would be taking him to the Moonstone. "Shall we go?" Pineheart mewed. He looked back at Doestar again. "I never thought this would happen so soon. I don't know if I'll be half the leader she was."

"Doestar will watch over you from StarClan," meowed Goosefeather. "You'll be fine."

Pineheart felt a flare of hope in his chest. He had had little to do with Goosefeather, never imagining they would be leading the Clan together so soon. "Really? Have you had a vision?"

Goosefeather nodded, but didn't say anything more. "Come, we have a long journey ahead of us," he meowed, and headed for the gorse tunnel.

Pineheart had traveled to the Moonstone before, but this time it felt very different. The cavern beneath the ground was as cold as ice, and the Moonstone glittered so brightly that it hurt his eyes. He screwed them up, and when he opened them he was standing in a sunlit forest, his fur lifted by a prey-scented breeze and the sound of birdsong in his ears. Goosefeather stood a little way off, his gray pelt dappled with shade.

"You came!" cried Doestar, trotting over the grass to meet him. The white patches on her pelt gleamed, and she looked strong and full-fed once more.

Pineheart dipped his head. "Of course," he murmured. Hardly daring to move, he looked out of the corner of his eye and saw more cats stepping from the trees. *This is it!* he thought. *I am becoming the leader of ThunderClan!*

"I give you a life for survival, for rebuilding your strength after great hardship," Doestar announced, resting her chin on his bowed head. A great force flowed through him, dazzled with sunlight, bursting with green leaves and rustling prey and the deafening noise of forest life.

Then Doestar stepped back, and another cat approached.

Pineheart felt his heart lift with joy at the sight of the broad-shouldered, glossy brown tom. Oakstar purred loudly. "I always knew you would be leader one day," he meowed. "I give you a life for judgment, for knowing which path to follow, however hard it seems." This time the force was sharper, more painful, stiffening Pineheart's limbs and making him yelp. Then it passed, and his legs stopped trembling.

He was overjoyed to see his former Clanmates Hollypelt, Harepounce, and Stagleap once more. "We miss you so much!" he blurted out.

The StarClan cats nodded, their eyes filled with stars. They gave him lives for courage and loyalty, for knowing when to fight and when to choose peace.

Next came Pearnose, an ancient ThunderClan medicine cat. His life was dedicated to trusting the wisdom of the leader's closest companion in protecting his Clanmates; Pineheart glanced at Goosefeather, watching from the trees, and nodded.

Two more lives came from cats so old that they were almost invisible against the soft green grass. A dark brown she-cat, Hawkfoot of WindClan, gave Pineheart the strength of a nursing queen when defending her young. As this life burned through his limbs, Pineheart thought of the kittypet in Twolegplace who had been ready to face all the warriors from the forest to protect her babies. Then an orange cat with huge paws and amber eyes approached.

"I am Thunderstar," he murmured, so quietly that Pineheart could hardly hear. "Every leader faces difficult choices. And yours will be the most difficult of all. Know that whatever decision you make, you will have to carry it for the rest of your life. If you can do that, then it will be the right one."

This life was different from the others, churning, toppling, dizzying, so that Pineheart felt as if he was being tumbled over and over, suspended in the air. When he felt his paws firmly on the ground again, he opened his eyes.

A long-legged gray tom with pale blue eyes stood in front of him. "My name is Morningstar," he rasped. "I give you a life for compassion for weaker cats, in your own Clan and others. Now go back to your Clan, Pinestar. Lead them well."

The ninth life blazed through Pinestar like icy fire, leaving him clearheaded and strangely calm. He looked around. The clearing was empty apart from Goosefeather, who was watching him closely.

"I received my nine lives!" Pinestar whispered.

The medicine cat said nothing. Pinestar felt a sudden longing to ask Goosefeather what his vision had been: Was ThunderClan going to rule the forest once more after the great hunger? What battles lay ahead, and which could be avoided? But Goosefeather was already walking away into the shadows beneath the trees, and Pinestar could do nothing more but hurry to catch up.

"You don't have to go out on patrol now that you're our leader," teased a soft voice.

Pinestar paused just before entering the tunnel of gorse. Squirrelwhisker was lying outside the elders' den, warming her belly fur in the sun.

"Mumblefoot sent out two hunting patrols, and the border patrol has only just returned," she went on. "Do you think they might have missed something?"

Pinestar shook his head. "I just felt like stretching my legs, that's all." He had been leader for less than a quarter-moon and already he was feeling restless. He had less to do now than when he had been a warrior! Mumblefoot was proving an excellent choice as deputy, in spite of a few muttered comments about his age. Pinestar trusted him completely to organize the different patrols and duties, and he was well respected by the other cats. Pinestar knew he could join in with a patrol if he wanted, but he didn't want his warriors to think he was interfering or trying to take on too many responsibilities at once.

"You're welcome to come with me, Squirrelwhisker," he meowed, but the elder shook her head.

"I was a warrior only a few sunrises ago," she pointed out. "Let me enjoy the chance to lie in the sun, knowing that some other cat will catch my food!"

Pinestar purred with amusement and ducked into the gorse. He leaped up the ravine and plunged into the forest, losing himself to the scents of new growth and prey and soft, damp earth. New-leaf had fallen upon the forest almost overnight, and it was becoming hard to remember the empty, hungry days.

The sound of a patrol by Snakerocks prompted Pinestar to swerve toward the treecutplace. He didn't want to be disturbed, not yet. He trotted over the needle-strewn earth below the pine trees and emerged from the trees into slanting rays of sunlight. The long wooden fence that edged Twoleg-place felt warm as Pinestar settled himself against it, ready for a doze in blissful quiet before heading back to the camp.

He was just drifting off when the fence behind him rattled, and there was a sound of scrabbling paws above his head. He opened one eye and looked up to see a ginger cat staring down at him.

"What are you doing down there?" mewed the tom.

"Trying to sleep," grunted Pinestar.

The fence creaked against his back as the cat jumped down into the long grass. Pinestar sat up.

"Are you one of the wild cats?" asked the tom. His fur was thick and shiny, striped in several shades of orange, and his eyes were a startling light green. In fact, there was some-thing about them that stirred one of Pinestar's long-forgotten memories.

"I'm from ThunderClan, yes," mewed Pinestar. He decided not to mention that he was the leader of the Clan. He had a feeling this kittypet wouldn't be impressed. Though his mother might be . . .

The tom was studying him closely with his head tilted to one side. "I think I've seen you before," he announced at last.

"You're right." Pinestar was astonished that the cat remem-bered him, since he couldn't have been more than a half-moon old when they met. "You were with your mother when Thun-derClan came into Twolegplace."

The kittypet wrinkled his nose. "What's Twolegplace?"

Pinestar nodded toward the fence. "Over there, where you live."

"That's weird." The tom rubbed his nose with a paw where a long strand of grass had tickled him. Then he looked at Pinestar, his eyes glinting with curiosity. "How come you're talking to me? Are you supposed to chase me back over the fence and claw my ears to frighten me? That's what the other cats say you do."

Pinestar couldn't help feeling a glow of pride at his Clanmates' fearsome reputation. "I don't think you are a threat to ThunderClan," he meowed.

The young cat looked indignant. "I could be! You don't know how good I am at catching mice and birds and squirrels!"

"Well, are you? Good at catching mice?"

The kittypet sat down with a thump. "Not really. But I did scare some rabbits once! They were inside a cage, and I sat on top of it all day until I got hungry. Then I had to go home."

Pinestar tried to hide his amused purr at the thought of getting hungry within paw's reach of some rabbits.

"My name's Jake," the kittypet mewed. He stood up and bobbed his head.

"I'm Pinestar," replied Pinestar.

"Cool name," purred Jake. "My mother is named Crystal, and my littermates are Ferris and Whiskers, but I don't know where they live now."

"I remember your mother well," meowed Pinestar. "She saved my life once, did you know that?"

"Really? How?" Jake's eyes stretched wide.

"I got between a mother fox and her cubs when I was just an apprentice. Your mother scared the fox just enough for me to get away."

"She's really brave," Jake mewed proudly. "She doesn't see so well now, and she has to eat special food which tastes disgusting. But she still scratches the dog if it gets too close!"

Pinestar purred. "I can imagine her doing that." He stood up and flexed each leg in turn. "I must go back to the camp. Nice meeting you, Jake."

"And you!" meowed the kittypet. "I'll tell my friends that wild cats aren't nearly as fierce as they think!"

"Some of us are," Pinestar warned. "You certainly shouldn't wander into the forest. You keep to your territory, and we'll keep to ours, okay?"

"We'll see about that!" called Jake as he scrambled back up the fence. "See you again, Pinestar!" He vanished over the top with a whisk of his ginger tail.

Pinestar shook his head. Kittypets were such strange creatures! All the strengths and skills of a Clan cat, but not remotely aware of what they could do. How could they lead such boring lives? What did they even do all day?

But he had enjoyed talking to Jake. It made a change from discussing patrols or borders or where to find the best source of prey. Perhaps he would see him again, just to pass the time. Shaking a loose blade of grass from his pelt, Pinestar turned away from the fence and trotted into the trees.

CHAPTER SIX

Pinestar wrenched himself free from the WindClan warrior and felt his pelt rip. The black WindClan tom staggered sideways on his twisted paw but quickly recovered his balance and sprang at Pinestar again, teeth bared. Pinestar whirled to face him and reared up on his hind legs to strike at the cat with his front paws. He rained down blows, screwing up his eyes against the blood that spattered his muzzle and belly. The WindClan tom—Pinestar thought it was Deadfoot but in the scrum he could barely distinguish his own Clanmates—let out a yowl and streaked away, ears flattened.

Pinestar paused and looked around. He was halfway up the side of the hollow that sheltered WindClan's camp. The shallow dip was alive with writhing cats and the air echoed with screeching. Just below him, Stormtail and Dapple-tail were fighting side by side against three WindClan cats, bravely holding their ground. On the far side of the camp, Swiftbreeze was dragging Leopardpaw to safety. The apprentice had a deep wound along her flank, and Pinestar could see Featherwhisker waiting for her just behind a boulder on the edge of the hollow.

This was not supposed to happen! Goosefeather said we could destroy WindClan's supply of herbs to weaken them, but that no blood would be shed. How did I ever imagine that WindClan would allow us to attack their medicine stores?

There was a flash of movement outside the WindClan medicine den and Pinestar watched Moonflower and Stonepelt slip inside.

We've done it! Pinestar thought with relief. *I will call my Clan to retreat.*

But before he could open his mouth, two WindClan cats followed the ThunderClan warriors into the den. A heartbeat later, the WindClan medicine cat, Hawkheart, streaked across the blood-soaked clearing and crouched at the entrance, his tail lashing as if he was waiting for prey.

"Oh StarClan, no," Pinestar whispered.

There was a terrible howl from inside the medicine cat's den and Stonepelt scrambled out, blood pouring from a fresh wound on his shoulder. A WindClan warrior snarled at his heels. Then came Moonflower, her blue-gray fur stained green with herb juice. The second WindClan cat was chasing her, but he fell back as Hawkheart lunged at Moonflower, hurling the she-cat off her paws.

Pinestar bunched his hindquarters beneath him, ready to spring down and help his Clanmate, but Hawkheart was already springing onto Moonflower and sinking his teeth into her neck. Moonflower struggled free and clouted Hawkheart's muzzle with her paw. Hawkheart shrugged her off as if she were nothing more than a fly. He snatched the

ThunderClan she-cat by the throat and threw her across the grass. She landed with a wet thud, and lay still.

"Noooooooo!" A tiny wail pierced the air, and with a sinking heart, Pinestar stared across the camp to Bluepaw, Moonflower's daughter, who was watching in horror from the top of the hollow. She had only been made an apprentice two sunrises ago. *And now she is in the thick of battle, with her mother dying in front of her. Is this what StarClan had wanted when they spoke to Goosefeather about the WindClan herbs?*

"ThunderClan, retreat!" Pinestar tipped back his head and yowled the order to the vast empty sky.

The clearing below fell silent, with only the howling rain and wind to remind Pinestar that he was still alive, still in this terrible place filled with blood and pain . . . and now death. Heatherstar padded up the slope to meet him. Her blue eyes were filled with rage.

"This attack was unjust," she growled. "StarClan would never have let you win. Take your wounded and leave."

I am so, so sorry. Pinestar knew there was nothing he could say. He dipped his head and turned away to join his Clanmates, who were gathering at the entrance to the camp. Each warrior stood with glazed eyes and drooping tail, blood staining their battered pelts. Behind them, the WindClan cats melted away, vanishing into their dens. One shape remained in the clearing, her fur flattened by the pelting rain. Pinestar watched numbly as Bluepaw stumbled over to her mother's body and crouched beside it.

"Moonflower! Moonflower! It's me, Bluepaw!"

But Moonflower didn't respond. Pinestar couldn't bear it any longer. He padded across the muddy, scarlet-streaked grass and looked down at the apprentice. "Bluepaw," he prompted gently.

The little she-cat stared at him. "Why won't she get up?"

"She's dead, Bluepaw."

"She can't be." Bluepaw put her tiny paws on Moonflower's sodden flank and shook her. "She can't be dead. We were fighting warriors, not rogues or loners. Warriors don't kill without reason!"

How can I tell her that she is right? That the warrior code has been broken, and her mother is gone? We started this battle. This is all my fault.

"She tried to destroy our medicine supply," came a low growl. Hawkheart had left his den and was crouched a fox-length away. "That was reason enough."

"But StarClan *told* us to do it!" Bluepaw mewed. Her huge blue eyes burned into Pinestar's. "We had no choice. They told us to, didn't they? Goosefeather said so."

Hawkheart let out a harsh huffing sound. "You risked so much on the word of Goosefeather?" He lashed his tail and stalked away, hunched against the rain.

"What does he mean?" Bluepaw whispered. She turned back to Moonflower and shoved her with her muzzle. The dead cat rocked limply in the shallow puddle that had formed around her. "Wake up!" Bluepaw pleaded. "It was all a mistake. You don't have to be dead."

Swiftbreeze stepped forward and pulled Bluepaw gently away. Pinestar bent down and picked up Moonflower by her scruff. He winced as her weight dragged on muscles already sore from fighting, but he forced himself to lift her clear of the puddle and carry her across the clearing to the rest of the ThunderClan warriors. He would take her all the way home for a warrior's burial, then face the fury of his Clanmates as they realized he had led them into a terrible defeat.

"Was it really bad?" Jake asked. His green eyes were full of sympathy.

Pinestar nodded. "I thought Swiftbreeze was going to kill Goosefeather, she was so angry that Moonflower had died."

"At least she blamed the right cat," Jake commented. "It was Goosefeather who told you to attack WindClan, after all."

"But I am the Clan leader!" Pinestar protested. He shifted his haunches so that he was sitting more comfortably on the short, soft grass. They had met behind Jake's Twoleg den, in the shade of a bush with long, trailing branches and pale green leaves. "It was my decision to lead them into battle."

Jake reached up and licked the cut on Pinestar's ear. The blood had dried and was tugging at his fur. "You told me that a leader has to trust his medicine cat," he murmured. "You may be leader, but you are still bound by the warrior code."

Pinestar pictured Goosefeather, his gray hair ragged, his blue eyes glazed and wild. "I . . . I don't know if I can trust him anymore," he admitted, each word wrenched from his belly. "His prophecies are so strange now, and I've seen him watching me as if he knows something that I don't. I'm scared that he has seen an omen about me which he isn't sharing."

"Perhaps an omen telling him that you won't always listen to his nonsense?" purred Jake. He finished with Pinestar's ear and started to knead the ThunderClan leader's flanks with his paws, purring softly.

Pinestar stretched out flat and rested his cheek on the ground. It had been so easy for Pinestar to slip into the habit of visiting Jake every moon, then every half-moon, to talk about nothing much at all, to lie in the sun on the Twoleg-groomed grass, to watch birds fluttering without feeling the need to stalk them.

Jake was curious about life in the Clans, but not to the point of wanting to go over the fence into the forest. He was no threat to ThunderClan, even though he knew the deputy and medicine cat by name, knew where the weakest parts of the border were, and how Pinestar was concerned about the safety of new apprentices. Pinestar had mentioned a WindClan warrior, Talltail, from time to time, and the first question Jake had asked Pinestar today was whether he had seen the long-tailed black-and-white tom in the battle. Pinestar had assured him that Talltail had not been injured, as far as he knew.

Jake was not a Clanmate, but a friend. And Pinestar valued him as much as any of his warriors.

"I cannot ignore my medicine cat," Pinestar meowed now, twisting so that Jake could give some attention to his other shoulder. "I cannot do anything but watch my Clanmates die," he added quietly.

Jake paused and rested his muzzle on Pinestar's back. "I wish there was something I could do to help you."

"Ah, you help me plenty," mewed Pinestar, sitting up. "There is no other cat I can talk to like this."

"What about Leopardpaw?" Jake teased. "You've mentioned her often enough."

"She's a good apprentice," Pinestar meowed a little defensively. "I'm going to make her a warrior soon. She was wounded in the battle, but she's going to be okay, thank StarClan."

Jake studied him with his head tilted on one side. "You care too much, Pinestar. You can't save every one of your Clanmates from the dangers of the life you lead."

"I wish I could," whispered Pinestar, lying down and resting his head on his paws.

"Hey, Jake, I didn't know you had a visitor!"

Pinestar lifted his head as a small brown tabby jumped down from the wall and trotted across the grass.

"I'm Shanty," she mewed.

"This is Pinestar," meowed Jake, standing up to touch muzzles with the she-cat.

Shanty tipped her head on one side and wrinkled her nose. "You're not a kittypet."

"No, I'm a Clan cat," mewed Pinestar. "I live in the forest."

"With the wild cats? Cool!" Shanty settled down beside them and curled her tail over her paws. She narrowed her eyes at Pinestar. "You look kind of battered. Are you okay?"

Pinestar twitched his ear. "I'm fine," he murmured.

Shanty turned to Jake. "Did you hear about Tyr? His Twolegs left his door locked all night and he had to sleep in the shed!"

"Whoa! Tyr would *not* have liked that!" Jake snorted. "He's a pedigree Burmese," he explained to Pinestar.

"And never stops reminding us!" Shanty added with a sniff.

Pinestar knew he couldn't tell a Burmese from a badger. He tried not to lean closer to sniff Shanty's fur. The tabby was definitely a she-cat, but she smelled different from any Clan queen. Pinestar liked that she wasn't afraid of him, or even particularly curious about life in the forest. On this side of the fence, Pinestar wanted to be treated like any other cat. A friend, not a strange and fearsome enemy. He trusted Jake as much as he did his Clanmates—and more than some of them.

Perhaps Shanty would become a friend, too. He settled back onto his belly and closed his eyes. The battle with WindClan, his injured Clanmates, the humiliation of defeat, all seemed a long way away as he listened to Shanty and Jake chatter about cats he didn't know, and had no responsibility for.

CHAPTER SEVEN

"You've made the right choice there," Smallear commented, flicking a midge off his pelt with his tail.

"Hmm? What?" Pinestar lifted his head. The sandy ground was warm beneath his shoulder, and he had been dozing off after a long hunting patrol.

Smallear gestured toward a mottled black she-cat who was nibbling on a starling outside the warriors' den. "Leopardfoot, I mean," he meowed. There was a glint in his eye. "Cats are starting to talk, you know."

"I didn't think you were one for listening to gossip," Pinestar retorted. His fur felt hot. He did like Leopardfoot, and he had been spending time with her recently, but he didn't want to make a statement to the entire Clan about it.

Smallear pricked his ears. "Then the rumors aren't true? We won't be hearing the patter of tiny paws in the nursery anytime soon?"

Pinestar stretched out and rolled over. "New kits are always a blessing," he murmured, closing his eyes. He didn't want to have this conversation with one of his warriors. Just because he was Clan leader, he wasn't allowed any kind of private life? He told himself that he was feeling prickly because of Smallear's curiosity—and not because he was waiting until the clearing was quiet enough for him to slip out and visit the Twolegplace again.

He opened his eyes a slit and watched Bluepaw and Snowpaw carefully dividing a squirrel between them. They deserved to be made warriors soon. They had been so brave since watching their mother die in the battle with WindClan. Pinestar shut his eyes and tried to ignore the wave of pain that swept through him. So many more battles since that day, so many vigils for fallen Clanmates . . .

He had fought alongside his warriors every time, plunging himself into the thickest action, losing more lives than he could keep count of. In fact, Goosefeather had reminded him recently that he had only two left, and had told him to take more care. Inside his mind, Pinestar shrugged. He had more lives to lay down than his Clanmates; why should he treat himself with any more care? Sunfall would make an excellent leader in his place; there would always be more Clan leaders, more battles to be fought and lives to be lost.

"Hey, Smallear!" Sweetpaw was calling to him from the tunnel of gorse. "You promised to take me battle training after sunhigh!" The white patches on the little cat's pelt gleamed in the sun, and her tiny ears were pricked.

Smallear heaved himself to his paws. "StarClan save me from overenthusiastic apprentices," he muttered, and Pinestar purred with amusement. For a moment he wondered if Leopardfoot would have his kits, and if she did, would he take one of them as his own apprentice.

And teach my own son or daughter how to attack and wound and frighten our enemies, for the sake of these invisible walls we have built around our home? Could I really do that, knowing I might have to watch them die in battle one day?

The clearing fell silent as cats headed out for patrols or training, or to take advantage of the cool forest while the sun was at its height. Pinestar stood up and walked over to the entrance. No cat called after him to ask where he was going, or whether he had any orders. He ducked through the gorse tunnel, raced up the side of the ravine, and plunged into the trees. He took a less direct route so that he avoided a hunting patrol led by Sunfall, entering treecutplace close to the Thunderpath instead. He trotted through the long grass at the foot of the wooden fence, enjoying the feeling of cool stalks brushing his belly fur.

When he drew level with a stunted pine tree that had a broken branch trailing on the ground, he scrambled up the fence and dropped down on the other side. There were no kittypets living here, but Pinestar had seen a pink-faced Twoleg watching him through one of the openings in the side of the den. He crossed the grass in two bounds, then leaped over the wall and ran along a narrow stone path. Nothing about this place resembled his home in the forest—not the scents in the air, the hard red dens, the rumble of monsters and shriek of young Twolegs—and yet it felt safe and familiar to Pinestar now. He avoided kittypets he hadn't met yet, and he knew which dens had noisy dogs, but there was nothing here that frightened him. Monsters weren't interested in him as long as he stayed out of their way; even Twolegs ignored him, except for the time he had stopped to make dirt beneath a bush and been chased off with a low yowl and waving pink paws.

He crossed over an empty Thunderpath and headed for a low, glossy-leaved hedge. As he passed, a small brown head popped out. "Pinestar!"

He stopped and looked back. "Hello, Shanty. Is this where you live?"

Shanty stepped out of the hedge. "Yes. Would you like to come and look around?"

Pinestar glanced along the Thunderpath. "I was on my way to see Jake."

"He's mooning over Quince today." Shanty tipped her head on one side. "She lives by the main road. Have you met her?"

Pinestar shrugged. "I don't think so."

"I'm sure you'd like her," Shanty mewed dryly. "All the toms seem to." She turned back to the hedge.

"Wait!" Pinestar called. "I . . . I'd love to see where you live, if that's okay."

He squeezed into the hedge behind her and wriggled through the branches. The grass surrounding this den was soft and short and dazzlingly green like the rest of the grass in Twolegplace. There was a small round pool in the middle of the space with a spray of water splashing into it. Shanty beckoned to Pinestar with her tail and trotted over to the edge of the pool.

Following more cautiously so that he dodged the flying

droplets, Pinestar crouched down and peered in. Two bright orange shapes glided just below the surface.

"Fish!" Pinestar exclaimed. "Can you catch them?"

Shanty shook her head. "I tried once, but I fell in. My housefolk had to rescue me."

Pinestar reached out with one paw and dabbed at the water. With a flash of gold, the fish vanished among some thick green plants. "You need to make sure RiverClan doesn't find these," Pinestar joked.

But Shanty was already trotting away toward the side of the Twoleg den. Pinestar ran after her, his wet paw cool against the grass. They plunged into a welcome stretch of shade, then out into the sun again behind the den. The grass here stretched farther, still short and soft and bright, bright green. A clump of silver birch trees stood at the far end, casting dappled shade onto a heap of logs with ferns growing over them. Pinestar padded over and sniffed at the cool fronds.

Behind him, Shanty mewed, "I don't like it over here. It's too cold."

Pinestar arched his back and brushed against one of the drooping ferns. "I think it's peaceful," he murmured. He could hear a faint monster grumbling far away, and two sparrows quarreling on the other side of the fence that surrounded Shanty's territory. But the ferns blotted out most of the sound, and the birch leaves rustled in the breeze, reminding Pinestar of the forest.

There was a noise close by and Pinestar jumped. An opening had appeared in the side of the den and a Twoleg was coming out. Pinestar shrank back against the logs. Had it spotted him? Shanty ran across the grass and stretched up to rub her head against the Twoleg's front paw. Pinestar forced his pelt to lie flat. This must be one of her housefolk. From the tone of the Twoleg's voice, he was pretty sure it was a female. She had brown skin and black fur on her head, and although her white teeth were bared, she was making soothing sounds.

Shanty called to Pinestar, "Come on over. I think she'll like you."

Pinestar took two steps toward the Twoleg, then stopped. He could feel his heart pounding, and his mouth felt dry. The Twoleg stopped petting Shanty and crouched down on its haunches, staring at Pinestar. Now he could see that her eyes were a shade darker than her skin, and her long straight fur was as glossy as a RiverClan pelt. She reached her front paw toward Pinestar and made a noise a bit like a dove, low and cooing.

Pinestar took another step. He kept his ears pricked and his tail low. He was a ThunderClan warrior; he didn't want to frighten the Twoleg into running away. *Which one of us is the most scared?* he wondered.

Shanty bounced on her paws. "Let her stroke you!" she mewed. "She won't hurt you, I promise!"

Suddenly the Twoleg was right in front of him and Pinestar froze. He felt a warm, naked paw rest on his head. With a hiss, he ducked away. *Too close!*

Shanty twitched her tail. "I thought warriors were braver than that!"

The Twoleg leaned toward him again, making more cooing sounds. Pinestar forced himself to stay still. The Twoleg put her paw lightly on his head and brushed it along his fur, all the way to his tail. Pinestar blinked. It felt odd, but not unpleasant, like a very large, dry tongue licking him. The Twoleg stroked him again, then tickled him under his chin. Pinestar stepped away. That wasn't so pleasant, and made him feel too vulnerable.

Shanty came over and stood beside him, her flank warm and fluffy against his pelt. "You're being really brave," she purred, with a hint of teasing in her voice. "She's nice, isn't she?"

The Twoleg stood up suddenly and Pinestar leaped backward. There was a low, gruff sound and another Twoleg appeared in the entrance to the den. This one was taller, with darker skin and a more powerful scent. Pinestar guessed it was a male. The female Twoleg pointed at Pinestar and yowled something. Pinestar flattened his ears. The territory was starting to feel small and crowded.

Shanty nudged him. "It's okay. That's my other housefolk. He can be a bit loud but he's safe, I promise."

Pinestar backed toward the ferns. "I think I've made enough new friends today," he mewed, trying to sound light-hearted.

Shanty nodded. "I'm impressed." Pinestar glanced at her, but she sounded sincere. "I wouldn't go into the forest and hang out with the wild cats," she went on.

"You'd be safe if you were with me," Pinestar mewed,

though in his mind he couldn't begin to imagine a time when he would introduce Shanty to his Clanmates. "You can trust my warriors."

"And you can trust my housefolk," Shanty replied. They had reached the ferns and were sitting at the foot of a sun-warmed log, their pelts lightly dappled with shade. "All my life, they have treated me kindly, fed me, sheltered me, given me space to play in."

"Did your mother live with them?" Pinestar asked.

"No. I was born somewhere else, but I can't really remember anything about it. I know I had littermates, but I don't know where they are now."

Pinestar was shocked. "Aren't you worried about them?"

"Why should I be?" Shanty shrugged. "If they have found housefolk like mine, then I know they are safe and happy."

"But . . . but aren't you bored?" Pinestar blurted out. All the questions he had wanted to ask Jake came tumbling out. "What do you do all day? You don't have to patrol your territory, or catch your food, or train any apprentices, or practice for battle. . . ."

Shanty stared at him, her amber eyes huge. "Why would I want to live like that? You make it sound as if every day is a struggle to survive." She gestured around her with her tail. "There is no cat here that I want to fight. I don't want to worry about where my next meal is coming from. I am not a prisoner in my territory; I can visit my friends, just as they can visit me." She sniffed. "Some are more welcome than others, but Quince is okay when she hasn't got a tom hanging around her."

Pinestar lifted his muzzle. "What do you do to earn this life? Where is your loyalty, your courage, your honor? How do you know if you have lived your life well if you cannot judge it against the warrior code?" His fur prickled, and he heard a note of desperation in his voice. *Do I want Shanty to prove to me that my life is worth more than hers?*

The brown she-cat blinked. "I have loyalty and honor too. Look around you, Pinestar. What is keeping me here? I could climb that fence and be gone in a heartbeat. But I love my housefolk. I *honor* them. They feed me and care for me because they value me. They enjoy my company, they want to keep me safe, and they are afraid if I go away for too long." She stood up and glared at him, as fierce as any warrior. "Isn't this the same way you feel about your Clanmates, Pinestar? Just because I don't look the same as my housefolk, don't speak with the same words or eat the same food, doesn't mean that we are not a Clan too. They are not my enemies. Not everything is predator or prey!"

She sat down, panting. "Sorry," she murmured. "I think you hit a nerve."

Pinestar reached out with his tail and stroked her flank. "I'm the one who should say sorry," he mewed. "When I became leader of ThunderClan, a cat named Oakstar gave me a life for judgment. I should have learned to use it more wisely by now."

Shanty looked up at him, confusion in her eyes. Pinestar rested his muzzle on the top of her head. "I judged you too quickly," he explained. "You and all the kittypets. Forgive me."

He felt the she-cat's purr, rumbling through his body like far-off thunder. "You're all right," Shanty meowed. "I always heard wild cats were a bit dumb."

Pinestar grunted. "But our claws are still sharper than yours!" he teased. He closed his eyes and shifted his weight so that he was lying beside Shanty. Patchy sunlight warmed his fur, and the scent of ferns filled his nose as he drifted into sleep.

Pinestar stood beneath Fourtrees, looking around. The hollow was empty and above, the sky was spattered with stars but no full moon. This wasn't a Gathering, so what had brought him here?

"I did," mewed a voice. A fawn-and-white she-cat stepped out from behind the Great Rock.

"Doestar!" Pinestar gasped. He trotted to meet his former leader, rubbing his head along her cheek.

Doestar stepped back and studied him. "Your time as leader hasn't been easy," she commented, nodding to the scars on his muzzle. "I am sorry I could not leave ThunderClan in peace."

Pinestar twitched the tip of his tail. "None of the battles were your fault. This is a difficult time for all the Clans. If RiverClan would give up its claim to Sunningrocks, everything would be easier."

"For cats who can swim, a river is no kind of boundary," Doestar pointed out. "Your battle for those rocks is not over yet."

"And lose more lives for the sake of warming our pelts on a heap of stones?" Pinestar growled. "I can't wait."

The she-cat blinked. "Those are not the words of a warrior. Where is your pride, Pinestar? Your promise to keep the boundaries of our territory safe?"

Pinestar flattened his ears. "I have not forgotten," he mewed. "I will do everything to defend our Clan, of course."

Doestar paced around him. "You will have even more reason to protect your Clan soon." Her amber eyes gleamed in the starlight. "You are going to be a father. Leopardfoot is expecting your kits!"

"What?" Pinestar stared at her. "Are you sure?"

The she-cat nodded. Then her gaze darkened. "But you must be careful, Pinestar. One of your kits, a tom, has a shadow over his destiny."

"What do you mean?" Pinestar demanded, letting his claws slide out and prick the earth. "What kind of shadow?"

Doestar turned away. "The worst kind," she murmured. "He will be born with the power to destroy ThunderClan."

"You can't possibly know that! One kit, against a whole Clan? Don't be ridiculous!" His heart was beating faster and his fur stood on end. *What threat could one tiny cat offer to a Clan full of warriors?*

The StarClan cat faced him again. "Listen to me, Pinestar. No cat knows your son's destiny yet; only the possibilities he will be born with. It is up to you to teach him honor, loyalty, compassion—everything given to you for your nine lives. This cat will have the power to be a great leader, if you guide his paw steps well."

Pinestar opened his mouth to ask more questions, but the starlight in Doestar's fur was dazzling him and he screwed up his eyes against the brightness. Something was digging into his back. Was it the Great Rock?

"Wake up, Pinestar. You're having a bad dream."

Shanty was prodding him in the ribs. Pinestar opened his eyes to see her anxious brown face against pale green fern fronds.

"I have to go back to my Clan," he mewed, sitting up. "I . . . I shouldn't be here."

Shanty looked puzzled. "What do you mean?"

Pinestar scrambled to his paws. "You wouldn't understand," he muttered. His pelt burned with shame and anger. Couldn't he escape his duties for just one day?

Before he could race off, Shanty pressed her cheek against his shoulder. "Come back anytime," she mewed. "You will always be welcome here, friend."

Pinestar started running across the grass. The peace he had found with Shanty had been shattered. The needs of his Clan were dragging him back to the forest, back to blood and conflict and the desperate struggle to survive. And now there was a new threat, one he had created himself, which he already felt powerless to stop.

How am I going to protect my Clan from an unborn kit?

CHAPTER EIGHT

Pinestar padded through the bracken, ignoring a brittle frond that tickled his ear. He had taken to pushing through the thickest undergrowth on his way to and from Twolegplace, avoiding the tiny paths where he might encounter a border or hunting patrol. A quarter moon ago, Lionpaw had seen him talking to Jake's housefolk and Pinestar had lied to explain himself, telling the apprentice that he had only pretended to befriend the Twoleg in order to find out more about the kittypets.

Pinestar's fur prickled. He couldn't let his Clanmates find out about his friends outside the territory. They would never understand that it was cats like Jake and Shanty who kept him calm and focused, who listened to fears he couldn't share with his warriors.

Today, Shanty had reassured him that he was doing the right thing by holding back from yet another attack on Riv-erClan, even though the mangy fish-eaters had set their border marks around Sunningrocks again. Pinestar knew his warriors were unhappy, and were waiting for him to give the command to attack their neighbors. Shanty had agreed that he couldn't risk injuries or death so close to leaf-fall, when the warriors should be concentrating on hunting and building up their strength for the cold weather. She shrugged off Pinestar's fear that his Clanmates thought he was too fox-hearted to defend their territory.

"They must know you are only trying to protect them from getting hurt," she mewed impatiently.

The only thing he hadn't confided to the kittypets was Doestar's warning about his unborn kit. That was something Pinestar couldn't begin to deal with until his son had arrived.

He was sitting beside the fresh-kill pile with Patchpelt when Sunfall's border patrol returned. To Pinestar's relief, none of his warriors bore any signs of a skirmish. His fur pricked when he saw Bluefur studying him intently, as if she was trying to detect traces of Twolegplace on him.

Suddenly Featherwhisker appeared from the nursery. The medicine cat's silver fur was ruffled and his eyes were wide with alarm. "Leopardfoot's kits are coming!" he announced.

"So early?" Swiftbreeze gasped. "They're not due for half a moon!"

"Is she okay?" Patchpelt called.

Featherwhisker ignored them. "Pinestar!" he meowed. "Will you stay with her while I fetch supplies?"

Pinestar stared at him in dismay. *No! This can't be happening! I'm not ready!* "I think it's best if I leave it to you and Goosefeather," he mewed, his pelt burning under the gazes of Bluefur and Swiftbreeze, who were looking at him as if he'd grown an extra head.

"*I'll* sit with her!" huffed Swiftbreeze, pushing her way into the nursery.

Pinestar sagged with relief. Leopardfoot would be much better off with her mother to care for her. But his respite was short-lived. Behind him, Goosefeather had started sifting through the fresh-kill pile, scowling and muttering to himself. Pinestar's heart started to pound. *Was he looking for omens to mark the birth of the new kits?*

The day dragged on. Goosefeather stopped fiddling with the fresh-kill pile and limped out of the camp. Patrols returned and excitement spread through the Clan about the kits. Featherwhisker sent Bluefur for herbs, and the waiting cats tensed as if braced for bad news. But nothing came from the nursery, only the sound of Leopardfoot groaning and soft murmurs of encouragement from Featherwhisker and Swiftbreeze. Pinestar looked impatiently at his gathered warriors, who were acting as if a tree was about to come crashing down on their heads. Kits were born all the time! Why was today any different?

"We must eat," he told them. "Starving ourselves won't make these kits come any quicker."

He caught Bluefur glaring at him and turned away. Too wound up to eat, he stalked past the fresh-kill pile and headed into his den beneath Highrock. He knew his Clanmates were judging him for being cold and uncaring toward the mother of his kits. But nothing would make him share Doestar's warning. How could he possibly tell them that his own son was going to be the greatest threat the Clan would ever face?

Outside, he heard excited voices. Then Bluefur announced, "Two she-cats and a tom."

He is here. The cat that will destroy us all.

In the midst of his Clan, which had just swelled by three, Pinestar had never felt more frightened or more alone.

The night was starless and unseen brambles clutched at his paws as Pinestar ran blindly through the forest. He knew he should be with Leopardfoot, with their newborn kits, watching over them as proudly and fiercely as Oakstar had once watched over him. But how could he?

These kits should never have been born!

Even as the thought slipped through his mind, Pinestar recoiled in horror. He had stared across the clearing at the nursery as dusk fell, the simple clump of tightly woven brambles changed by shadows into a dark and thorn-pierced trap. His paws had refused to carry him one step closer, as if he had turned to stone where he sat. Gradually the clearing emptied and the camp fell silent as his Clanmates settled down to sleep. Pinestar stood up, stretching out each stiff limb, then headed toward the gorse. Guilt and shame dragged at his pelt. But he would not, *could* not, enter the nursery.

There was only one place he could find comfort now, far from the Clans, far from the weight of the terrible prophecy about his own son. He leaped over the wooden fence and streaked along the hard stone paths. A couple of kittypets sprang out of his way with angry hisses, but Pinestar ignored them. He raced around the corner of a Twoleg den and skidded to a halt at the edge of the little Thunderpath.

Shanty was sitting on the other side, talking to a fat gray tom. She jumped up when she saw Pinestar, her fur bristling.

"What are you doing here at this time? Is everything all right?"

Beside her, the gray tom slipped into the shadows and disappeared.

"Leopardfoot's kits have come!" Pinestar called.

He saw Shanty's eyes widen. "That's . . . that's good news, isn't it?"

"No," meowed Pinestar. "It is the end of my Clan." All his sorrow, all his self-loathing, all his fears came crashing down on him, and he sank to the ground with a moan.

Shanty gasped and sprang toward him. At that moment, a pair of glaring white eyes appeared at the end of the Thunderpath. With a roar, the monster launched itself toward the little brown cat. She stopped dead in the middle of the Thunderpath, frozen in horror.

"Shanty!" Pinestar yowled. He threw himself toward her, his paws skidding on the black stone. He was less than a mouse-length from her when the monster struck them both, slamming Pinestar so hard that he flew into the air and tumbled over and over before he crashed to the ground with a thud.

Suddenly his eyes were dazzled by silver light and he felt cats close around him, sniffing his pelt, urging him to lie still, promising that all would be well. Pinestar had been here before. He was losing another life. He let his body sink into the ground, felt the searing pain ebb out of his muscles, and waited for his mind to clear.

A cat leaned over him, musty breath warm against his ear. "The time to choose is near, Pinestar," rasped an ancient voice. "Only you can decide."

Thunderstar? Pinestar struggled to sit up and looked around. He was alone at the edge of the Thunderpath. The monster had gone and everywhere was silent. In the center of the Thunderpath, a small brown heap lay very still. Pinestar climbed stiffly to his paws, his pelt lifting in dismay.

"Shanty!" he whispered. He padded over to her, each paw carrying the weight of Sunningrocks. The little brown shape didn't move. Pinestar pushed his muzzle into her fur, trying to feel a heartbeat or a stir of breath. "Shanty, wake up!" Surely the monster had hit him harder? The loss of his life didn't matter, as long as Shanty had escaped. *She can't be dead! Not now, when I need her more than ever!*

There was a thud from the Twoleg den behind the hedge, and a beam of light slanted through the dense leaves. Pinestar heard rapid paw steps and he looked up to see Shanty's housefolk rush out, their mouths open wide. Pinestar backed away from Shanty's body.

"I'm sorry," he mewed. "I tried to save her but I was too slow."

The female Twoleg dropped to her knees and bent over the dead cat. A howling sound rose into the air. The male Twoleg patted her and made gruff noises as he wiped at his face with a hairless brown paw. Pinestar felt his heart crack. He wanted to tell them that he shared their grief, that he had loved Shanty too, she had been his dearest friend, closer to him even than his Clanmates. . . . But he knew that he couldn't make them understand him, even though he felt the same pain as they did. They would sit vigil for Shanty tonight, not him.

The Twoleg walls blurred around him as Pinestar padded away.

He walked in the forest until dawn, then sat beneath a tree and watched the sun rise. *A day that Shanty will not see.* He felt hollow and cut loose, as if his paws weren't quite touching the ground. He knew he wouldn't find Shanty in StarClan, however much he dreamed. That was not where kittypets went at the end of their lives. *Wherever you are, I hope you are warm and safe, and can see me.* The thought that Shanty might have vanished into nothingness was too much for Pinestar to bear. He had felt alone before; now he felt as if he were teetering at the edge of a shadowy chasm, echoing with the yowls of dying cats. *Shanty, I need you!*

The air around him grew hotter, buzzing with the drone of insects. Pinestar knew he had to return to his Clan. He had to see Leopardfoot and his kits. He was their father, for StarClan's sake! He could do nothing more for Shanty. But he still had responsibilities toward his Clanmates—and his kin.

He padded back to the ravine, pausing only to roll in ferns to disguise the Twolegplace scent on his pelt. His legs trembled from losing a life, and he wondered if Featherwhisker or Goosefeather would know that he was now on his last. It would be hard to explain how he had lost this one.

His heart sank lower as he followed the path down to the gorse tunnel. Ignoring the mutters as he entered the clearing, he headed for the nursery. Featherwhisker was just slipping through the branches.

"Can I see them?" Pinestar asked.

The medicine cat nodded and stepped aside. "The tom's the weakest," he warned.

A savage burst of hope flared in Pinestar's chest. *Perhaps StarClan will take him before the prophecy can come true.*

Leopardfoot looked up as he entered. "You came," she stated flatly. "I waited for you all night."

Pinestar bowed his head. "I'm sorry. I'm glad you're all right."

The queen bent over the tiny damp shapes squirming at her belly. "I won't be all right until I know my babies are safe," she murmured. "They're so frail. I can't even make them feed!" Her voice rose to a wail as she tried to nudge them closer to the milk that stained her fur.

Pinestar stepped forward and placed one paw on her shoulder. "Calm down," he mewed. "You'll frighten them."

"I just want them to take some milk," Leopardfoot whimpered.

"I'm sure they will," Pinestar meowed. His heart was thudding so loud that he thought Leopardfoot would hear it. He peered down at the three little bodies. "Have . . . have you named them?"

Leopardfoot nodded. "The she-cats are Mistkit and Night-kit, and the tom is Tigerkit." She touched each one with her nose as she spoke, moving with the tenderness of every queen that had ever nursed a kit.

Pinestar stared at the dark brown tom. His eyes were tight shut and his mouth opened and closed silently, too feeble even to mew. He looked smaller and more pitiful than a mouse on the fresh-kill pile. Did this kit really have the power to destroy ThunderClan? It was easier to imagine being threatened by a beetle.

Suddenly the kit opened his eyes and glared up at Pinestar. Amber fire blazed in the depths of his gaze, and for a moment he looked older and more terrifying than any cat Pinestar had seen before. He leaped backward and Leopardfoot let out a hiss.

"Careful, you'll tread on them!"

"Tigerkit looked at me!" Pinestar stammered.

"Don't be mouse-brained. They won't open their eyes for days," Leopardfoot snapped. She placed her tail protectively over her son, whose tiny eyes were tight shut once more. "I think you should go now." She looked up at Pinestar. "Our kits are very sick. Pray to StarClan that they survive."

CHAPTER NINE

❧

Pinestar dreamed he was back in the nursery, watching his kits
nestle into their mother's fur. The she-cats slept peacefully,
but Tigerkit's cold yellow eyes blinked open and he scowled
up at Pinestar. He was growing now, faster and faster until
he covered his sisters and Leopardfoot, filling the nest, filling the nursery, pressing Pinestar against the bramble walls.
And now Pinestar's paws were sinking into the moss—no, not
moss, some kind of liquid, thick and red and lapping at his
belly. Blood! The nursery was drowning in blood!

Pinestar scrabbled desperately at the brambles, trying to
get out. Behind him, Tigerkit's breath was hot on his neck,
and he could hear his son growling from deep in his belly. The
blood rose higher, splashing against Pinestar's muzzle, pulling
him down. . . .

He was lying on icy stone, somewhere high up, with only
the starlit sky above him. Silver-furred cats surrounded him,
their faces obscured by mist. Pinestar tried to sit up but he was
pressed down by invisible paws.

"Your son is evil!" hissed one of the cats; Pinestar couldn't
see which one because the fog was too thick.

"He's only a kit!" Pinestar protested.

"He won't be a kit forever!"

"Your Clan is in danger!"

"What can I do?" Pinestar wailed.

There was a moment of silence, when even the wind dropped. Then a voice murmured, "Kill him."

Pinestar flinched in horror. "No!"

"Kill him."

"Kill him."

"Kill him! It is the only way to save your Clan!"

Pinestar flung off the unseen paws and leaped to his feet. "I cannot kill my own son!"

The mist and the mountaintop vanished. He was standing in his den, shreds of moss clinging to his fur, his flanks heaving. Goosefeather's face appeared in the entrance.

"Having a bad dream, were you?" he rasped. His watery blue eyes seemed to look right through Pinestar and see into his mind.

"It doesn't matter," Pinestar mewed, shaking off the leaf dust and trying to tidy his nest.

"Oh, I think it does," growled Goosefeather, taking a step into the den. "Sweetpaw is dead."

Pinestar blinked. "But . . . but it's been nearly a quarter-moon since she ate that mouse! Bluefur and Rosepaw got better ages ago!"

"And Sweetpaw didn't," Goosefeather snapped. "Another death, and your kits are still so weak. . . ."

"They have nothing to do with Sweetpaw," Pinestar

retorted. He stared bleakly around his den. "I thought the Clan was getting stronger," he murmured. "The fresh-kill pile has been full for days. I thought everything was going to be okay."

"Did you really?" sneered Goosefeather. "Don't be a fool, Pinestar. I think StarClan has told you exactly what is going on."

He turned and limped out of the den. Pinestar took a deep breath. *Sweetpaw's death is not an omen. I will not kill my own son!*

He padded into the clearing. A knot of sad she-cats was gathered around Sweetpaw's little body. Judging by the emptiness of the rest of the clearing, Sunfall must have taken most of the young cats out on patrol. Pinestar was relieved. He wanted to spare them the grief that seemed to shroud the Clan every moon. Out of the corner of his eye, he saw a tiny shape playing with a piece of moss. *Tigerkit!*

The tom had survived, and not just survived but grown swiftly and strong, unlike his sisters, who were still too frail to leave the nursery. With the gaze of his Clanmates burning his pelt, Pinestar forced himself to go over to his son.

Tigerkit looked up at him. "Sweetpaw's dead," he announced.

"I . . . I know," Pinestar mewed.

"Are you really sad?" Tigerkit asked.

"Of course!" Pinestar replied.

The little brown tom tipped his head on one side. "As sad as if I died? I mean, you're my father, so you must love me more than Sweetpaw or any of the other cats."

Pinestar stared at his son in horror. *Why is he talking about dying?* "Y-yes, of course I love you and your sisters the most. But I care for every cat in ThunderClan."

Tigerkit seemed to lose interest in speculating about his death. "Play with me." He pushed the ball of moss toward Pinestar. It rolled against his paw and he looked down at it.

Kill him!

But he is only a kit!

You have to protect your Clan!

"I'm sorry, I can't play with you today," Pinestar meowed. The blood was roaring in his ears and his vision blurred. "I have to go somewhere." He turned and padded quickly across the clearing.

"Tomorrow?" he heard Tigerkit call after him.

Pinestar didn't answer. He pushed his way into the gorse, relishing the way the thorns clutched at his fur and pricked his muzzle. *I cannot be a father to this kit! Oh Shanty, what should I do?*

He blundered through the undergrowth toward Twoleg-place. He had never missed Shanty more, never yearned more strongly that he had told her about the prophecy before she died. He had deliberately kept his dream from her, knowing that she would have no understanding of StarClan and the meaning of omens. But now he wished he had trusted her with everything so that she could give her honest opinion, let him consider all of the possibilities—and dismiss the idea that the only way to save ThunderClan was to kill a helpless kit.

* * *

When he reached the wooden fence, he stopped. He couldn't go to Shanty's home, not when he knew she wouldn't be there. The emptiness would be too heartbreaking. He decided to look for Jake instead. He trotted through the long grass until he reached the edge of Jake's territory. A quick leap over the fence and he was standing behind Jake's Twoleg den. There was no sign of the ginger cat.

"He's with Quince," mewed a high-pitched voice. A strikingly elegant fawn cat with dark brown ears and paws was looking down at Pinestar from a tree on the other side of a wall. "You're the wild cat, aren't you?"

"Er, yes," mewed Pinestar.

The stranger stood up and stretched each long, slender leg in turn. "I'm Tyr," he meowed. "See you around, I expect." He sprang out of the tree and vanished behind the wall.

Pinestar stood on the grass, feeling the sun warm his pelt. The scents of Twolegplace wafted around him, flowers and leaves and the faint hint of monsters. There was no stench of blood here, no hiss of fear or fury as cats fought over who was allowed to walk where. Some kittypets were more bad-tempered than others, Pinestar had learned, but they never fought to the death. *They are better at following the warrior code than we are!*

There was a noise behind him, and Pinestar turned to see Jake's female Twoleg coming out with something in her front paw. It rattled, and Pinestar knew that it was something Jake called his food bowl, containing the brown pellets that Jake ate. He pricked his ears, feeling a worm of curiosity stir in his belly. Was kittypet food really that bad?

The Twoleg saw him and made a soothing sound. She reached out with her empty paw and Pinestar padded close enough for her to touch him. He had done this enough times with this Twoleg to know that he didn't need to be frightened. He meowed in delight when she smoothed his fur from head to tail tip. She made more friendly noises, then put the food bowl onto the white stone path that surrounded the Twoleg den. Pinestar took a step forward and stretched out his neck to sniff the pellets. They didn't smell too awful; there was a hint of rabbit, even. He licked one of the pellets, then jumped back to consider the taste. *Definitely rabbit, and something else, a bit like pigeon. . . .*

The Twoleg murmured and bared her teeth at him. Pinestar knew this wasn't a sign of hostility; quite the opposite. He bent his head and crunched up a mouthful of pellets. The Twoleg ran her paw along his back again, just the way he liked it. He purred, sounding rather muffled around the food.

When the bowl was empty, Pinestar looked up at the Twoleg and pressed himself against her hind legs. "That was delicious!" he mewed. "Is there any more?"

"Pinestar! What are you doing?"

Pinestar felt his belly flip over in horror, and the pellets stuck in his throat. How long had Lionpaw been standing on top of the fence? He ran across the grass, thinking furiously. "You shouldn't be here! What if that kittypet comes back?" He hoped Lionpaw would remember Pinestar telling him about the ferocious kittypet who had been causing trouble, and needed a close watch.

"RiverClan is invading!" the apprentice meowed. "You have to come!"

Another battle! Time seemed to slow down around Pinestar, and his mind whirled. At this very moment, his Clanmates were fighting to defend a few paw steps of territory, a couple of fox-lengths of trees and grass that would provide prey for whichever Clan was prepared to shed the most blood. *I cannot do this any longer.* No matter what he did, brave cats would die. He pictured Shanty's housefolk, bent double with grief over her death, and then the solemn, calm atmosphere in the camp that morning around Sweetpaw's body.

Have we lost the ability to grieve? he wondered. *Do we watch so many cats die that we cannot let ourselves feel true loss? Does any cat's life really matter at all?*

Then he thought of Tigerkit, his own son, innocently play-ing with a bundle of moss with a cruel and terrible destiny hanging over him. StarClan must have known that he would never be able to kill this kit, whatever warnings they gave. If Pinestar could not prevent the threat, perhaps another cat would; a different leader, one who was able to guide Tigerkit's paws to a brighter destiny.

Every leader faces difficult choices, whispered a voice in Pinestar's ear. *And yours will be the most difficult of all.*

Thunderstar! The cat who had given him one of his nine lives. *And here is my choice,* Pinestar thought. *To stay with my Clan, or leave and follow a different path.* He knew there was a place where he belonged, where he would be needed and loved and kept safe in return for a different kind of loyalty and honor.

There was no choice at all, or if there had been, Pinestar had made it already, without even noticing. Still, he could not meet Lionpaw's eye as he spoke. "I can't."

"Why not? Did the kittypet hurt you?"

"There is no kittypet. Only me."

"You're just pretending to be a kittypet," Lionpaw mewed in confusion. "So the Twoleg doesn't chase you away."

Pinestar looked back at Jake's Twoleg. She was holding the food bowl and watching them. "She won't chase me away. She likes me."

"But . . . but you're our Clan leader! You can't be friends with Twolegs!"

Oh, Shanty! This is the hardest thing I have ever done! I wish you were here with me.

Pinestar took a deep breath. "Then I can't be your Clan leader anymore. I'm sorry, Lionpaw. I tried so hard, but I can't keep the Clan safe. I'm too old, too scared of losing any more battles. Sunfall will make a better leader than me. Tell . . . tell ThunderClan that I am dead."

The apprentice narrowed his eyes in anger. "No! I will not lie for you! You might not want to be our leader anymore, but you could at least be brave enough to tell the Clan yourself. They deserve to know the truth, that you are leaving to become a *kittypet*."

Pinestar hung his head. He couldn't blame Lionpaw for his fury. And the apprentice was right: His Clanmates deserved a proper good-bye. They had done nothing wrong; only served him loyally and courageously and to their deaths, like all good warriors. It wasn't their fault that Pinestar couldn't bear it anymore.

Lionpaw was already racing across the grass and hurling himself over the fence. Pinestar followed, his paws suddenly light as he realized that this was the last time he would have to enter the forest, the last time he would have to take responsibility for these cats who were so much braver, so much better able to fight for their survival, than he was.

And so much stronger to deal with Tigerkit.

"Pinestar!" Sunfall's call greeted Pinestar as he entered the clearing.

Pinestar winced as he noticed the fresh blood on his deputy's ear. Adderfang and Stormtail stood behind him, deep claw marks on their fur. *Oh, my Clanmates. I am sorry that I did not fight alongside you today. You deserve more than this, I promise.*

"Where were you?" Sunfall meowed.

Pinestar blinked. "Did you win?"

Sunfall nodded. "We chased those fish-faces back as far as the river. They still have Sunningrocks—that is a battle for another day—but they won't set foot across the border for a while."

One more tiny victory. Until the next battle.

"Good," Pinestar mewed out loud. *It is time. The last time I will summon my Clan. The last time I will call myself a warrior. The last time I will breathe the air in this place that has been my home for so many seasons.*

The smooth gray stone felt familiar beneath his paws as he took his place on Highrock. He looked down at his Clanmates, knowing he would dream about this sight for the rest of his life. "Let all cats old enough to catch their own prey gather to hear what I have to tell you!"

Warriors and queens turned tired, grief-stricken eyes to face him. Pinestar felt a fresh wave of sadness roll in his belly. *I wish I could take you all with me!* he thought for one wild moment.

"Cats of ThunderClan, I can no longer be your leader. From now on, I will leave the Clan and live with housefolk in Twolegplace."

There was a pause of horrified silence, then Stormtail hissed, "You're going to be a *kittypet*?"

Sunfall looked as if a hedgehog had just sprouted wings. "Why?"

"How could you?" wailed Poppydawn from where she crouched beside Sweetpaw's body.

Pinestar bowed his head. *I love you all! Please believe me!* "I have been honored to serve you this long," he explained. "The rest of my life will be spent as a kittypet, where I have no battles to fight, no lives depending on me for food and safety."

"*Coward*," Adderfang snarled.

Pinestar avoided the warrior's gaze. "I have given eight lives to ThunderClan—each of them willingly. But I am not ready to risk my ninth."

"What could be more honorable than to die for your Clan?" rasped Weedwhisker.

"You would live among StarClan," Poppydawn mewed.

"And share tongues with Clanmates you have lost."

Pinestar forced himself to keep still and not run into the welcoming bracken behind him. "I am doing this for ThunderClan, I promise."

"You're doing it for *you*," Stormtail muttered.

Then a small golden-striped shape moved to the front of the cats and turned to face them. Pinestar stared down in surprise. *What was Lionpaw doing now?*

The apprentice raised his head boldly. "Do we really want a leader who no longer wishes to lead?" he demanded.

Thank you, Lionpaw. Pinestar watched his Clanmates' eyes flicker with uncertainty. They shot fleeting, baffled glances at him, light as a butterfly's wings, as if he was a stranger who had blundered into the camp by mistake.

"Sunfall will lead you well, and StarClan will understand," Pinestar promised.

"The other Clans might not," Sunfall suggested. There was a flash of anger in his eyes, and his fur bristled along his spine. "You won't be able to come back to the forest, you know."

Pinestar shrugged. "Oh, I can imagine the names they'll call me. I wouldn't be surprised if one of the leaders suggests an addition to the warrior code, that all true warriors scorn the easy life of a kittypet. But you'll make ThunderClan as strong as it ever was, Sunfall. My last act as leader is to entrust my Clan to you, and I do so with confidence."

Sunfall bowed, though his gaze still burned. "I am honored, Pinestar. I promise I will do my best."

Pinestar jumped down and studied his Clanmates. *Former*

Clanmates? For a moment he wondered if they would treat him as a kittypet from this moment, if he would have to claw his way out of his own home. But Sunfall padded forward and rested his tail against Pinestar's flank.

"You have led us well, Pinestar," he murmured.

Larksong joined him. "We will miss you."

"Sunfall will make a good leader," White-eye insisted, and the cats around her nodded.

"Thank you," Pinestar murmured. He turned to face Lion-paw, and felt a purr rising inside him. ThunderClan was lucky to have this young cat among them. "You were right," Pinestar told him. "I had to tell the Clan myself. It would not have been fair to them, or to you, to do anything else. You have a good spirit, young one. When it is time for you to receive your warrior name, tell Sunfall I would have called you Lionheart."

Lionpaw's eyes glowed, and Pinestar knew he had judged well. *Not everything I have done was a mistake.*

He started toward the gorse tunnel but Leopardfoot blocked his way. "Pinestar, what about our kits?" she pleaded, her voice high with disbelief. "Won't you stay to watch them grow up?" She had brought the kits out of the nursery; Mistkit and Nightkit were huddled on the ground, barely any bigger than the day they had been born, their eyes cloudy and unfocused. Tigerkit loomed beside them, broad and strong, crouching down to pounce on Pinestar's tail.

Pinestar twitched his tail out of harm's way. *This is the hardest part of all. I can never tell this Clan about the warning StarClan gave me. Tigerkit deserves to grow up being treated fairly, given the best chance to succeed. It is not my duty to taint his reputation forever.* "They'll be fine with you, Leopardfoot. I'm not a father they could be proud of, but I will always be proud of them. Especially you, little warrior," he forced himself to add.

Tigerkit stared up at him and let out a tiny growl.

"Be strong, my precious son," Pinestar whispered. "Serve your Clan well." *Prove StarClan wrong, whatever happens.*

There was nothing more to say. It was time to leave. He gazed around the clearing once more, committing every branch, every paw print to memory. Then he pushed his way into the gorse tunnel and left everything behind.

CHAPTER TEN

Pinestar padded through the forest for the last time, keeping to well-trodden paths. It didn't matter if a patrol saw him; he was no longer their leader. No cat would be interested in him now. He had no responsibilities, no need to worry about the fresh-kill pile or border marks or whether the elders' den would leak in the next rainstorm. . . .

As he neared the wooden fence, Pinestar broke into a run. The long grass closed around him as he crouched down and leaped over the border between his old life and his new one. He landed with a thud, his legs suddenly feeling old and tired. He realized he was trembling, and for a heartbeat a sense of dizzying emptiness opened up inside him. All his life he had known what he was: kit, apprentice, warrior, deputy, leader, each role marked out by his name, the way his Clanmates treated him, the boundaries of the territory, and the routine of each day. All that had vanished. What was left?

For a moment, Pinestar wanted to go back. He would no longer be ThunderClan's leader, but he could be an elder, safe, sheltered, well fed, with no responsibilities, not even for his own ticks. But his Clanmates would still be around him. He would still have to watch cats go out to fight, and never return. And he would be just as powerless to change Tigerkit's destiny.

Pinestar kept going. He trotted through several kittypet territories, passing Tyr, who was dozing on a patch of sunbaked stone. Over a wall, along a narrow path, and then he was standing on the edge of the Thunderpath, picturing the very last time he had seen Shanty in the orange glow cast by the strange light-making poles. His paws felt heavy as he crossed the Thunderpath, not letting himself look down at the faint brown stain where she had died. She wasn't there anymore, he told himself. All her pain, all her fear in that terrible moment, was over. Wherever she was, she was safe now.

He paused at the entrance to Shanty's home. He could hear her housefolk talking outside their den, their voices rumbling softly. Was it his imagination, or did they sound sadder than before? *They must miss Shanty even more than I do,* he thought. He took a deep breath. This was it. This was why he had made his choice to leave the Clan. *I can help you. I can never replace Shanty, but I might fill part of the gap she has left. I know you feel it, because I feel it too.*

He walked past the glossy green hedge and into Shanty's territory. The Twolegs stopped talking and stared at him, their brown eyes wide. The male gestured at Pinestar and yowled. He clearly wanted Pinestar to go away.

"It's me!" Pinestar mewed. "Shanty's friend!"

The Twoleg took a step toward him, suddenly looming as tall as a tree and rumbling ominously. Pinestar shrank back in alarm. *What do I do now, Shanty?* This wasn't an enemy he could fight. There was no rule about this in the warrior code. He was nothing more than an intruder here!

But the female Twoleg moved forward and put out her light brown paw on the male's foreleg. Her voice was softer, as if she was asking him something. She pointed at Pinestar and bared her teeth. Pinestar held his breath and waited. After a few moments, the female crouched down and held out her paw toward him. She was making the same noise she had made to Shanty, gentle and encouraging, like an invitation to come closer.

Pinestar took one step forward. He knew Shanty's Twoleg wasn't going to hurt him. The first time she had tried to touch him, he had been nervous. But now he didn't feel brave so much as trusting, relieved, and full of memories of his beloved kittypet friend. It was almost as if Shanty was beside him, wreathing around him in delight. *I knew you two would be friends,* she purred in his ear.

He kept very still as Shanty's Twoleg stroked his ears. Her paw was softer than Jake's Twoleg's, and it tickled. She made another sound that seemed even more welcoming to Pinestar. Fascinated, he moved nearer to her. This time she ran her whole paw along his back, smoothing his fur and dislodging the leaf scraps he had collected on his run through the forest.

The male Twoleg joined her. Even when he was crouched down, he was still huge. Pinestar forced himself to stay still as the male reached out with his huge dark brown paw. But he was as gentle as the female, though his paw felt heavier and rougher. Pinestar rubbed his head against the hairless under-side, letting his scent mingle with the strong, musky scent of the Twoleg.

The female Twoleg straightened up and looked at Pinestar. She beckoned to him with her paw, a gesture that Pinestar had seen from many, many tails. She wanted him to follow her. Pinestar told himself there was nothing to be afraid of; he had seen how Shanty trusted these Twolegs, loved them as much as he loved his Clanmates. But Shanty was not here now, and Pinestar missed her so much he could hardly breathe.

The female stepped inside the den and beckoned to him again. Pinestar paused in the entrance, trembling. This felt more dangerous than any battle with a rival Clan, any con-frontation with a snarling badger or snapping fox. As his eyes adjusted to the dim light, he made out a sharp-edged, white-walled space, much smaller than the outside walls suggested. The floor was hard and shiny, like ice. Pinestar placed one paw cautiously on it. *Not as slippery as it looks, good.* He walked in and looked around. The female Twoleg had crouched down in the corner and seemed to be pointing to something.

But Pinestar couldn't concentrate. Shanty was *everywhere.* Her scent, the things she had played with, the food bowl he had seen her eating from once outside. Most of all, the feeling that she was there with him, only just out of sight, encourag-ing him on. Even if she was not in StarClan, Pinestar felt her presence as strongly as he had ever felt a StarClan cat along-side him. He was not alone here. *I will never be alone.*

He padded carefully across the gleaming floor and sniffed

at the soft, lumpy pelt that the female had pointed to. This was
Shanty's nest, judging by the smell and the shape left behind
by her body. Pinestar felt a pang in his belly. *My nest, now.* If he
wanted it. And he did, very much. He climbed into the middle
of the nest and curled up. The Twoleg made a happy purring noise and bared her teeth at him again. The male Twoleg
appeared and rumbled in a pleased way. He bent down and
patted Pinestar's head, almost making his teeth rattle. *Twolegs
are strong!*

The female Twoleg stood up and put something into the
feed bowl. Pinestar peered at it. This wasn't pellets, like Jake's
food, but chunks of some kind of meat. His belly rumbled, and
he reminded himself that as an elder, he wouldn't be catching
his own prey anyway. Did it matter who caught it for him? He
reached out and took a mouthful. It wasn't bad—in fact, it was
juicier and tastier than anything he'd eaten in leaf-bare. Better than Jake's dry pellets, too. Pinestar cleaned out the bowl
and the Twolegs purred at him.

Feeling restless now his belly was full, Pinestar stepped
out of the nest and headed outside. He looked back to see the
Twolegs watching him anxiously.

"I'll come back," he promised. He felt a warm glow spread
through him at the thought that they might be waiting for
him. *Is this what it was like to be a kittypet? To know that Twolegs would
keep you safe and warm and fed? Why do warriors despise this way of life so
much? It is all we ever want for our kits and elders!*

He trotted across the grass and hopped over a low wall.
Jake was sunning himself on a flat expanse of gray stone next

to the empty Thunderpath. He blinked in surprise when he saw Pinestar.

"Hey! I didn't think you'd come back," he meowed. "You know, after Shanty . . ." He trailed off.

Pinestar nodded. "For a while, I wasn't sure I would," he admitted. "But I think I can do some good here . . . for Shanty's housefolk. More than I can do for my Clan." *Except it's not my Clan any longer. It belongs to Sunfall now.*

Jake flicked the tip of his tail. "What do you mean? Have you left ThunderClan?"

"Yes, I have." *Wow. That makes it feel very real.*

The ginger tom looked impressed. "You'd really give all that up to be a kittypet for Shanty's housefolk?"

"I really would," Pinestar murmured.

Jake's eyes softened. "Shanty would like that, Pinestar." He stood up. "Do you want to go meet some of your new neighbors? You haven't seen Quince yet, have you? She's a sweetheart."

"I should go home," Pinestar meowed. "My . . . my housefolk are expecting me. Oh, and my name isn't Pinestar anymore. It's Pine. Just Pine."

Jake twitched his ears. "It suits you." He turned away, then paused and glanced back. "Welcome home, Pine."

WARRIORS

THUNDERSTAR'S
ECHO

Special thanks to Clarissa Hutton

ALLEGIANGES
THUNDERCLAN

LEADER

THUNDERSTAR—orange tom with big white paws

DEPUTY

LIGHTNING TAIL—black tom

MEDIGINE GAT

CLOUD SPOTS—long-furred black tom with white ears, white chest, and two white paws

HUNTERS

VIOLET DAWN—sleek dark gray she-cat with bits of black around her ears and paws

OWL EYES—gray tom with amber eyes

PINK EYES—white tom with pink eyes

LEAF—black-and-white tom with amber eyes

MILKWEED—splotchy ginger-and-black she-cat with scar on muzzle

CLOVER—ginger-and-white she-cat with yellow eyes

THISTLE—ginger tom with green eyes

GOOSEBERRY—pale yellow tabby she-cat

YEW TAIL—cream-and-brown tom

APPLE BLOSSOM—orange-and-white she-cat

SNAIL SHELL—dappled gray tom

BLUE WHISKER—white she-cat with yellow splotches

APPRENTIGES

HAZEL BURROW—black-and-white tom

MORNING FIRE—dark brown she-cat with amber eyes

SHIVERING ROSE—black she-cat with white splotch on one ear and amber eyes

DEW NOSE—brown splotchy tabby she-cat with white tips on nose and tail, yellow eyes

EAGLE FEATHER—brown tom with yellow eyes, broad shoulders, and striped tail

WILLOW TAIL—pale tabby she-cat with blue eyes

SKYCLAN

LEADER

SKYSTAR—light gray tom with blue eyes

DEPUTY

SPARROW FUR—tortoiseshell she-cat with amber eyes

MEDICINE CAT

ACORN FUR—chestnut-brown she-cat

HUNTERS

STAR FLOWER—she-cat with thick, golden tabby fur

DEW PETAL—silver-and-white she-cat

FLOWER FOOT—she-cat with tan stripes

THORN—splotchy brown tom with bright blue eyes

QUICK WATER—gray-and-white she-cat

NETTLE—gray tom

BIRCH—ginger tom with white circles of fur around his eyes

ALDER—gray, brown, and white she-cat

BLOSSOM—tortoiseshell-and-white she-cat with yellow eyes

RED CLAW—a reddish-brown tom

HONEY PELT—striped yellow tom

RIVERCLAN

LEADER

RIVERSTAR—silver long-furred tom with amber eyes

DEPUTY	**NIGHT**—black she-cat
MEDICINE CAT	**DAPPLED PELT**—delicate tortoiseshell she-cat with golden eyes
HUNTERS	**SHATTERED ICE**—gray-and-white tom with green eyes
	DEW—gray she-cat
	DAWN MIST—orange-and-white she-cat with green eyes
	MOSS TAIL—dark brown tom with golden eyes
	DRIZZLE—gray-and-white she-kit with pale blue eyes
	PINE NEEDLE—black tom-kit with yellow eyes
	SPIDER PAW—white tom

SHADOWCLAN

LEADER	**SHADOWSTAR**—black, thick-furred she-cat with green eyes
DEPUTY	**SUN SHADOW**—black tom with amber eyes
MEDICINE CAT	**PEBBLE HEART**—gray tabby tom with white mark on his chest and amber eyes
HUNTERS	**JUNIPER BRANCH**—long-furred tortoiseshell she-cat with green eyes
	RAVEN PELT—black tom with yellow eyes
	MOUSE EARS—big tabby tom with unusually small ears
	MUD PAWS—pale brown tom with four black paws
	BUBBLING STREAM—white she-cat with yellow splotches

CAT VIEW

SHADOWCLAN CAMP

THUNDERCLAN CAMP

SKYCLAN CAMP

NORTH

WINDOVER FARM

DEVIL'S FINGERS
[disused mine]

NORTH ALLERTON ROAD

DRUID'S HOLLOW

WINDOVER MOOR

DRUID'S LEAP

RIVER CHELL

MORGAN'S FARM CAMPSITE

MORGAN'S FARM

MORGAN'S LANE

NORTH ALLERTON
AMENITY TIP

TWOLEG VIEW

WINDOVER ROAD

WHITE HART WOODS

NORTH

CHAPTER ONE

Thunderstar watched approvingly as Snail Shell scrambled through the bracken at the edge of the forest, moving fast. Tensing his hind legs, the young dappled gray tom gave a flying leap and disappeared from sight. After a few heartbeats, he emerged from the undergrowth with his tail held high, a fat vole dangling from his mouth.

"Nicely done." Thunderstar blinked approvingly at Owl Eyes beside him. "You've trained him well."

Owl Eyes purred. "He was eager to learn."

Snail Shell dropped the vole at Thunderstar's feet. "Did you see how I pounced?" he asked excitedly. "When Owl Eyes started training me, I always landed a little short of the prey, but he told me to try to jump just *in front of* prey, and I'd get my paws right on it."

His sister, Apple Blossom, flicked her tail dismissively. "Lightning Tail didn't have to show me that," she bragged. "My pounces were always good."

Lightning Tail's whiskers twitched with amusement. "But it took a while for you to learn to pick out the scent of your prey. Let's show Thunderstar what you've learned."

The orange-and-white she-cat scented the air. "I can smell . . . mice," she mewed. "And there's a rabbit! In the ferns by that oak tree."

"Very good," Thunderstar told her. "So which should you hunt?"

Apple Blossom gave a thoughtful flick of her tail. "The mice would be easier to catch," she mewed slowly, "but a fat rabbit would feed more of the Clan. The rabbit?"

Thunderstar nodded. "Rabbits can be hard to catch," he told her. "The cats in WindClan eat a lot of rabbit, and they hunt them in pairs to make it easier. Why don't you and Snail Shell hunt this rabbit together?" Apple Blossom hesitated, and Thunderstar twitched his ears at her encouragingly. "You're in charge." If the young cats had trouble catching the rabbit, there would still be plenty of the day left to hunt easier prey.

"Okay." Apple Blossom's eyes lit with excitement, and she turned to her brother. "Snail Shell, go around on the far side of the ferns, and keep upwind. I'll chase it out toward you."

The young she-cat, her tail held low, slunk carefully toward the tall patch of ferns, each paw step silent.

Thunderstar nudged Lightning Tail. "Good stalking form," he whispered, and the black tom nodded, his eyes fixed on his apprentice.

Leaves rustled as the rabbit hopped hesitantly out of the ferns, its ears twitching. It sniffed the air, its bright eyes darting alertly in every direction. Apple Blossom froze for a second and then charged.

With a flip of its white tail, the rabbit bolted away from her, straight through the ferns. Apple Blossom followed. There were the sounds of a struggle and the rabbit's short shriek, then Snail Shell and Apple Blossom pushed their way back through the ferns, Apple Blossom proudly carrying the plump rabbit in her mouth.

"*Very* good," Thunderstar praised them, impressed. "That will fill a lot of hungry bellies."

The cats buried the rabbit and the vole to collect on their way back to camp, and Thunderstar led the hunting patrol toward the river that marked ThunderClan's border with RiverClan.

As the patrol emerged from the treeline onto the riverbank, Thunderstar took a deep, happy breath, letting water-scented air bathe his tongue. Sunlight sparkled off the river, and Thunderstar could scent the rich smells of prey and new growing plants. It had been a mild leaf-bare and his Clan had managed to hunt enough that no cat went hungry. Now that they were well into new-leaf, there was plenty of fat prey running through the forest.

"There's Moss Tail!" Apple Blossom exclaimed excitedly. "Moss Tail! Hello!"

On the other side of the river, the dark brown RiverClan tom flicked his tail in greeting and continued making his way through the reeds at the edge of RiverClan's territory.

"Is it true that RiverClan cats *swim*?" Snail Shell asked curiously, and Owl Eyes purred in amusement.

"Watch and see," he said. The brown tom waded into the

river, looked carefully around, and dived. Snail Shell and Apple Blossom gasped as he disappeared beneath the water, then resurfaced, a silver fish in his mouth.

"I heard that they eat fish," Apple Blossom said. "*Weird.*"

"Fish isn't bad," Lightning Tail told her. "Riverstar's given me some before. Maybe sometime I'll take you to RiverClan's camp and you can taste it yourself."

Apple Blossom's nose wrinkled in disgust. "No, thanks," she said. "I prefer squirrel."

They watched Moss Tail pick his way back to the riverbank and, after nodding his head in farewell, carry the fish toward RiverClan's camp.

As he watched the RiverClan tom, warm contentment spread through Thunderstar's chest. Not long ago, any River-Clan cat would have challenged a ThunderClan cat so close to their border, and certainly Lightning Tail would never have suggested taking a younger cat to visit RiverClan's camp. But the cats of the forest had been at peace for many moons now.

WindClan and SkyClan had briefly fought over their border last new-leaf, but that skirmish had ended quickly. Otherwise, all five Clans had been at peace since they had banded together to drive out the vicious rogue Slash. Cats had died in the forest then—including Gray Wing, Thunderstar's kin, who had raised him like a son—but now, rogues knew to steer clear of their territories. Now young cats like Snail Shell and Apple Blossom could explore the forest without fear.

"So, what prey should we be looking for this close to the

water?" Owl Eyes asked the younger cats, but Snail Shell interrupted.

"We've been hunting all morning," he complained. "I'm tired. Can't we stop and take a break? Just for a little while?" Thunderstar nodded and, with a dramatic huff of breath, Snail Shell sank down to the ground as if he were exhausted. Tucking her tail neatly around her paws, Apple Blossom sat down beside him.

Lightning Tail and Thunderstar exchanged a wry look.

"Tired," Lightning Tail said dryly. "When Thunderstar and I were your age, we walked all the way to the Twolegplace to rescue Owl Eyes, Pebble Heart, and Sparrow Fur. We didn't have time to sit around complaining about being tired from a little hunting."

"Really?" Apple Blossom asked, her eyes wide. "You rescued them from *Twolegs*? Owl Eyes, is that true?"

"It certainly is." The dark gray tom settled down on his haunches beside them. "It was scary. One of the Twolegs picked up Lightning Tail like it was going to take him away, but Thunderstar got it to drop him."

"Before we even made it to the Twolegplace, I fell in the river," Lightning Tail went on. "And that's how we met Riverstar for the first time. If he hadn't pulled me out, I wouldn't be here now."

Owl Eyes purred. "Tell them about the battle with One Eye. Sparrow Fur and I were old enough to fight in that one."

Snail Shell leaned forward, his tail lashing, tiredness

forgotten. "Is that when Skystar got kicked out of SkyClan by *rogues*?"

Thunderstar listened as Lightning Tail began the story. His friend was so good with the apprentices, patient with their training and always knowing just what to say to engage a young cat's interest. Fascinated by his tales of the battle with One Eye, Apple Blossom and Snail Shell looked ready to jump up and begin practicing their fighting skills. There would be no more complaining about being tired today.

Thunderstar sighed in satisfaction. He was sure he had chosen the right deputy. If anything ever happened to Thunderstar, Lightning Tail would protect ThunderClan.

Thunderstar's cheerful mood lasted until they headed back to the ThunderClan camp in the late afternoon, heavily laden with prey. The high-pitched yowls of squabbling cats rose out of the ravine as they approached it, and Thunderstar's heart sank.

There was *always* some cat arguing. And they *always* wanted Thunderstar to settle their arguments for them. It was as if the peace between the Clans had freed the cats to concentrate on all their small disagreements with each other.

As the hunting party scrambled down the side of the sandy ravine toward their camp, the angry voices got clearer.

"You were the one who said these were right!" That was Clover.

"I only did what Cloud Spots wanted!" And that was her brother Thistle.

Followed by the rest of the hunting party, Thunderstar shouldered his way through the gorse tunnel into Thunder-Clan's camp.

"These don't look anything like dock leaves! I don't understand how you two even made this mistake! I'm *supposed* to be practicing how to chew it up and put it on wounds. If some cat gets hurt and we don't have any dock leaves, it'll be your fault!" Shivering Rose, the black-and-white medicine cat apprentice, was hissing with rage, her fur puffed up along her back.

Thistle rolled his eyes. "No cat's hurt. There's no emergency. What, do you think there's going to be some big fight? With who?"

"Foxes, maybe? Badgers?" Blue Whisker tossed in from where she was watching the argument with interest, her tail folded neatly around her. Thunderstar flicked his ears reprovingly as he passed her. Moth Flight, the WindClan medicine cat, had given each Clan one of her own kits to link the Clans together and guarantee peace between them. His foster daughter—Moth Flight's smallest kit—had grown up to be a fine young ThunderClan warrior, but sometimes she made trouble for trouble's sake.

"Yes! Foxes and badgers!" Shivering Rose agreed, her yowl getting shriller. "Rogues! Or a cat could step on a sharp rock, or be scratched by thorns. ThunderClan doesn't have to be fighting another Clan for cats to get hurt!"

Hoping to avoid their argument, Thunderstar dropped the thrush he was carrying onto the prey pile and turned toward his den. Maybe his mate, Violet Dawn, would be there. His spirits lifted, as they always did, at the thought of the beautiful, loving she-cat. If only he could get to their den before—

"Thunderstar!" Clover yowled plaintively. "Tell them it wasn't *my* fault!"

With a sigh, Thunderstar turned back toward the squabbling young cats and tried to look interested. "What's the matter?" Lightning Tail brushed past him with a soft purr of amusement and leaped into the branches of a nearby ash tree. He wasn't leader; he could ignore this kind of thing. For a moment, Thunderstar itched with jealousy.

"Cloud Spots sent them out to gather dock leaves so I could practice how to help my Clanmates who get hurt," Shivering Rose told him. "Instead, they brought back *beech* leaves, so the whole day's wasted."

"They look almost the same," Thistle said defensively, poking the broad, shiny leaves on the ground in front of him with one paw.

Shivering Rose gave a sharp yowl of disbelief, and Thunderstar settled down on his haunches and tried to listen patiently. But as Thistle and Clover each started to argue that their mistake had been the other's fault, Thunderstar's mind wandered.

He was glad to see peace between the five Clans at last. There were no more pitched battles in the forest, no more bristling and insults at the borders. No vicious rogues had bothered them for moons, and the Clans were respected by nearby loners. Prey was running well, and no fires, floods, or harsh storms had broken the forest's peace for a long time.

It was everything Thunderstar had ever wanted for his Clan. They were safe; they were thriving.

And yet . . .

He could remember the thrill of crouching by Gray Wing's side, making a battle plan. Of charging into a fight side by side with Lightning Tail. Of all the times when a hunt or a journey had desperately mattered, because it meant life or death.

He didn't miss it, of course he didn't, Thunderstar thought, ruffling his fur. It was just that, in his memory at least, there hadn't been this constant low-key squabbling all the time. The things they had cared about then—scarce prey and battles and making a home for themselves—had been the big things. The important things.

"At least I'm faster than a tortoise!" Clover snarled indignantly at her brother, and Thunderstar guiltily snapped back to attention.

Thistle sniffed. "But your nose might as well be on your haunches for all the good it did while we were looking for Cloud Spots's beech leaves."

Shivering Rose draped her tail across her eyes, groaning dramatically. "*Dock* leaves! Cloud Spots told you to get dock leaves! You mouse-brain!"

Clover bristled, angrily digging her claws into the earth beneath her paws. "Don't talk to my brother like that!"

Thunderstar stood up, and Shivering Rose bit back her reply and looked up at him expectantly.

"Stop, all of you," he said. "Clover and Thistle, apologize to Cloud Spots and Shivering Rose for bringing back the wrong leaves." He turned to the medicine cat apprentice. "Shivering Rose, go into the forest tomorrow with Clover and Thistle and teach them what dock leaves look like, and what they smell like, so next time they'll get it right."

All three cats opened their mouths to reply, but Thunderstar silenced them with a weary look. "And stop fighting. You're Clanmates, not a litter of kits. Respect each other." The young cats hesitated, then nodded, murmuring agreement.

Thunderstar headed for his den again, only to be brought up short by more angry yowls.

"Prey should go on the prey pile!" Pink Eyes was lashing his tail, glaring at Leaf. "You can't just hunt for your mate, even if she has new kits! Part of being a Clan cat is taking care of every cat, not only your kin."

"I wasn't on a hunting patrol! I just knew Milkweed needed something extra to keep her strength up," Leaf hissed back, his amber eyes angry.

"Milkweed and the new kits are all you think of these days. You have a responsibility to feed the whole Clan!" Pink Eyes spat.

"You're one to talk about feeding the Clan," Leaf mewed sarcastically. "Even if you could see the prey, you'd be out of breath in half a rabbit chase."

Pink Eyes jerked back, looking hurt, and Thunderstar stepped between the two angry toms. "Leaf, that's not fair. Pink Eyes might not be able to hunt anymore, but you know he'll be looking after your kits as soon as they're big enough to come out of the nursery. And Pink Eyes, leave Leaf alone.

If he's not hunting enough for the Clan, Lightning Tail and I will send him out on more patrols." Both cats looked rebellious, and Thunderstar twitched his tail with irritation. "You're both too old to squabble like this. No wonder the younger cats are acting the same way! Set a better example. If you keep fighting, I'll ask Cloud Spots to have you both pick ticks off Gooseberry—she got some on her pelt when she went out to the moor."

Leaf and Pink Eyes dipped their heads submissively as Thunderstar walked away. It had been a long day, and he just wanted to curl up around his mate. Did his Clanmates have to bother him with every little dispute? Thunderstar sighed and stretched. *I guess that's what being a leader means,* he supposed.

Finally, he reached his den in the Highrock, pushing through the lichen that hung over the entrance. But the cave was dark and deserted, and Thunderstar felt a pang of disappointment. He came back to the entrance and looked around the clearing, searching for Violet Dawn.

Morning Fire and Hazel Burrow were play-fighting in the center of the clearing. Gooseberry and Yew Tail were sharing a vole near the warriors' den, and Owl Eyes had joined Lightning Tail in the ash tree. Shivering Rose and Blue Whisker were sharing tongues, while Pink Eyes had settled down to nap in the sunshine. Through the walls of the nursery thornbush, Thunderstar saw black-and-white fur: Leaf had gone to visit Milkweed and their new kits.

He finally glimpsed a familiar dark gray pelt in the fern tunnel that led to the recently built medicine cat's den.

Thunderstar twitched his ears thoughtfully. Why was Violet Dawn visiting Cloud Spots's den? *Is she sick? She seemed fine this morning.*

He crossed the clearing again and ducked to fit himself through the tunnel of fragrant ferns. He found Violet Dawn and Cloud Spots in the den at the end of the tunnel, and both turned to look at him, startled.

"Hi," Thunderstar said, suddenly feeling awkward. He shifted from one paw to another. "Everything okay?"

Cloud Spots glanced at Violet Dawn questioningly, and Thunderstar's heart sped up. What did that look mean? Cloud Spots didn't look upset, exactly . . . more like he knew something he didn't want to say.

"I'll leave you two alone for a moment," the long-furred tom murmured. He slipped past Thunderstar, but Thunderstar didn't watch him go. His attention was fixed on Violet Dawn.

"What is it?" Thunderstar asked, pressing himself against his mate's side and inhaling her sweet scent. She was reassuringly sturdy against him, and she rubbed her cheek affectionately against his.

"It's nothing bad," she said softly, her amber eyes warm. "Quite the opposite, really."

Thunderstar stared at her. Violet Dawn looked away shyly, but her tail stroked against his side. "Do you mean . . ."

Violet Dawn pressed closer to him. "I'm going to have kits."

Thunderstar froze, his mind whirling. A warm glow

sparked in his chest, spreading through his whole body.

He was going to be a *father*.

That night, Thunderstar couldn't sleep.

Violet Dawn was curled against him, breathing slowly and steadily. Her tail twitched slightly as she dreamed. Thunderstar buried his nose in her fur and shut his eyes, then opened them again and flexed his claws irritably. Rolling onto his back, he stared at the rock ceiling above him. Finally, he got to his paws and padded out into the clearing. Maybe if he went for a walk, it would be easier to sleep when he returned.

The camp was quiet. He could hear Pink Eyes's snoring, but no other cat was stirring. Thunderstar slipped across the clearing, his pelt prickling in the cool new-leaf breeze. Lightning Tail was standing guard by the gorse tunnel, heavy-eyed and sleepy-looking, and he flicked his tail in greeting as Thunderstar approached.

"You're up late," he meowed. "What's going on?"

"I can't sleep."

Lightning Tail cocked his head curiously. Thunderstar sighed. "Violet Dawn is going to have kits."

Lightning Tail's eyes lit up. "That's amazing! Congratulations!" Then he looked at Thunderstar more closely. "You're not excited?"

Thunderstar stiffened. "Of course I'm excited," he answered indignantly. "It's just . . ." He scuffed his paws against the earth of the clearing.

"Why don't we go out of camp?" Lightning Tail suggested. "Not every cat here needs their claws in your prey."

Thunderstar followed his friend through the gorse tunnel and out of the ravine. When they emerged into the forest, he breathed deeply. The scents of trees and grass and the rustle of small prey in the dark were soothing.

The two toms faced each other. Lightning Tail waited expectantly.

"I am excited, but I'm worried, too," Thunderstar confessed. "I couldn't sleep, thinking of having my own kits, and how I'll have to protect them."

"This is a good time to have kits," Lightning Tail mewed seriously. His eyes, reflecting the moonlight, gleamed at Thunderstar in the darkness. "The Clans are at peace and the forest is full of prey. By the time your kits are born, it'll be greenleaf. They'll grow up healthy and strong, Thunderstar."

Thunderstar's shoulders slumped. "But what if the Clans turn on each other? What about hawks and foxes? Greencough. Whitecough. Redcough. Remember the fire when we were young and how Moon Shadow died? Remember how Turtle Tail was killed by the Twoleg monster?" Suddenly it was difficult to catch his breath as a wave of panic shot through him. "I'm sure there's so much more I don't even know to worry about yet. How can I protect them from *everything*?"

Sometimes Thunderstar felt like he was barely hanging on by his front claws, trying to keep his Clan united and happy, trying to take care of every cat who depended on him. Was he really ready for kits, too?

Lightning Tail draped his tail across Thunderstar's back reassuringly. "You can't predict what's going to happen. But you'll have a whole Clan looking out for your kits. And you protect all of us already. I know you and Violet Dawn can do this."

Thunderstar's mew caught in his throat. "What if I'm a bad father? Clear Sky—Skystar—didn't even want to look after me when I was a kit. What if I'm like him?"

Lightning Tail's whiskers twitched. "You're worried about becoming a father because of *Skystar*? Skystar might be your father, but Gray Wing raised you. And he was the best father a cat could have. You've already learned everything you need to know from him. You'll see."

Thunderstar thought again of Gray Wing, who had taught him to hunt, fought to protect him, given him a home. Through all the moons of his kithood, wise, gentle Gray Wing had guided him. "Gray Wing was pretty great."

"You will be too," Lightning Tail told him. "And even if you're not, Violet Dawn and I will make sure the kits grow up right. I'm honorary kin as well as their Clanmate, you know."

Thunderstar blinked at his friend fondly, his heart feeling lighter. Maybe Lightning Tail was right. Maybe everything would be fine. "Of course you are. I know I can depend on you."

CHAPTER TWO

"I'm just hungry all the time now," Violet Dawn said wistfully, staring out at the rain from under the thornbush by the warriors' den.

Milkweed purred in amusement. "That's totally natural. In the moon before these kits were born, I didn't want to do a thing except eat. Your body is making sure your kits are big and strong."

Her small ginger-and-black tom-kit, Patch Pelt, threw himself at his pale ginger littermate, Beech Tail, and knocked her over. "I'm the biggest and strongest!"

Scrambling to her feet, Beech Tail bared her tiny teeth at him. "I'm stronger than you! You're no bigger than a vole!"

The kits began to wrestle, and Milkweed swept her tail over them lovingly. "Hush, kits," she said fondly. "You're kicking up mud."

Thunderstar looked at Violet Dawn's swollen sides, a familiar curl of anxiety beginning in his chest. Was she getting enough to eat? It had, as expected, been an easy newleaf, with plenty of prey. But these last few days had been gray and

238

rainy, and prey had been much harder to find. Every cat was hungry.

Owl Eyes, Clover, and Leaf trooped through the gorse tunnel, looking soaked and grumpy. A ragged vole dangled from Owl Eyes's mouth and a skinny shrew from Leaf's. Clover was limping.

"That's all you caught?" Thunderstar mewed as they came closer.

Leaf dropped the shrew and pushed it toward the kits. "It's been raining so long all the prey scents are washed away. We were lucky to find these."

Clover winced. "Cloud Spots, can you look at my leg? I slipped in the mud and I think I might have sprained it." The medicine cat nodded and went over to feel gently along her hind leg.

"You'd better come to my den," he told her. "Shivering Rose, come help me. You can practice treating sprains."

"Can we eat the shrew, Milkweed?" asked Patch Pelt eagerly as the rest of the Clan watched the medicine cats help Clover toward their den.

Milkweed hesitated, glancing at Violet Dawn.

"They can have it," Violet Dawn said firmly. "Kits need to eat."

Thunderstar managed to keep himself from objecting, but it wasn't easy. They needed more prey.

"You should have the vole," Owl Eyes said, dropping it in front of Violet Dawn.

"Thank you," Violet Dawn said, and then nudged Milk-weed. "We'll share it. Your kits need you to be strong as well."

Thunderstar looked around. The rest of the Clan watched, looking a little mournful, as the two she-cats devoured the small vole in just a few bites. He couldn't let them all go hungry. His heart began to beat faster: He was responsible for all of them. And his kits would need a strong Clan.

"I'm taking out another hunting party now," he decided. "We need more prey."

Owl Eyes and Leaf exchanged glances, taken aback. "The hunting's terrible," Owl Eyes said. "The prey's all taken shelter from the weather in their own dens."

"There's just not much out there," Leaf agreed, and Clover nodded.

"Are you arguing with me?" Thunderstar growled. "This isn't enough prey. We have to try harder. Thistle, Apple Blossom, Gooseberry, you're coming with me." He knew that he was being a little unreasonable, but he couldn't let his Clan go hungry another day. Not when the kits would be here soon.

A large drop of cold water splashed down from the branches of the thornbush onto his shoulders. Apple Blossom slowly got to her feet, her tail drooping. The other cats were looking at each other dismally, seeming skinnier than usual with their damp fur plastered to their backs.

"But it's *horrible* out," Thistle objected.

Gooseberry licked her chest fur, avoiding Thunderstar's gaze. "If the others hunted for so long and found so little, are we going to do any better?"

The fur along Thunderstar's spine began to bristle. *Don't they understand how important this is? What kind of cat would let their Clan go hungry?*

Before Thunderstar could let his anger out on his Clan-mates, Lightning Tail hurriedly stepped forward. "It's tough hunting out there," he agreed. "But we're a *Clan*. We protect each other and take care of each other. And we're the best hunters of any Clan in the forest."

"We are!" Hazel Burrow raised his head proudly, and Thunderstar saw Pink Eyes's whiskers twitching with fond amusement at the young cat's declaration.

"Leaf and Clover and Owl Eyes managed to find prey for ThunderClan even in these terrible conditions," Lightning Tail went on, his tail lashing excitedly. "We're all grateful to them. Thunderstar's grateful to them, too. But the rest of us have to try to do just as well. If we don't give up, we can feed every cat!"

Gooseberry, who had looked stiff and resentful when Thunderstar chose her for his hunting party, was now sitting up straight, her eyes bright. Apple Blossom's tail wasn't droop-ing anymore, and Thistle was puffing out his chest proudly.

Thunderstar shot a grateful look at his deputy. Lightning Tail blinked at him cheerfully, and padded closer. "I'll come, too. ThunderClan will always take care of its own," he said.

Thunderstar tasted the air, searching for the scent of prey in the rain-washed forest. Leaf had been right, and there was little to find after three days of this steady drizzle. But they had gotten lucky; Apple Blossom had stumbled across a nest of mice, and the six the cats had managed to catch would go a long way toward feeding ThunderClan.

He couldn't find any trace of prey in the air now, just the heavy scents of wet earth and growing plants. But as Thunderstar began to move on, he heard a slight crackling coming from a nearby clump of bracken. Pricking his ears to listen more closely, he peered beneath the bush. At first, he saw nothing in the shadows, but then he made out the shape of a fat bird.

Thunderstar's mouth watered. He signaled with his tail, and Thistle and Lightning Tail joined him.

"Under the bush," Thunderstar said softly, and Thistle's tail twitched with excitement.

"It can't fly off from under there," Lightning Tail said. "Let's spread out in case it tries to run." He signaled to Gooseberry and Apple Blossom, and the four cats, hunching low, began to approach the bush from different directions.

Thunderstar moved quickly and silently, coming as close to the bush as he could without alerting the bird inside. He could see now that it was a pigeon, hunched against the rain, its feathers fluffed, keeping almost entirely still. He was lucky to have spotted it. It was a fat, large bird, and would feed several of his Clanmates.

The pigeon's head turned, its bright orange eyes catching sight of Thunderstar at last. But he launched himself forward before it could move. Landing squarely on top of the pigeon, he bit down on its neck. Warm blood flooded his mouth, and the bird twitched once and lay still. Thunderstar backed out of the bracken, dragging the pigeon with him.

That was their last catch of the afternoon, but with the mice they had caught earlier, Thunderstar was feeling fairly satisfied by the time the shadows began to grow long and they headed back to camp. Every cat would have something to eat today, even if their bellies would not be completely filled.

The rain had even begun to let up by the time the hunting party pushed their way through the gorse back into camp.

"Yum!" said Clover, hobbling toward them. Her leg was clearly still injured, despite Cloud Spots's treatment, but her eyes were bright. "You had better luck than we did!"

Blue Whisker and Shivering Rose hurried toward them. "Can we share a mouse?"

"Of course you can," Thunderstar said, glancing at the rest of his expectant Clan. "Every cat has to share, but there should be enough for all of us to have something." His gaze met Violet Dawn's warmly admiring one across the camp, and his tail fluffed a little with pride.

But as she came toward the prey pile, Milkweed suddenly froze, one paw extended in the middle of a step, sniffing the air.

"What is it?" Owl Eyes asked.

The ginger-and-black she-cat's eyes were wide with fright. "Do you smell that?" she asked. Thunderstar sniffed, but before he could identify the faint foul scent drifting on the air, a wild chorus of barking erupted outside camp.

Dogs!

CHAPTER THREE

Thunderstar grabbed Patch Pelt, the closest kit, by the scruff of his neck. "Up," he ordered through a mouthful of fur, swinging the tiny ginger-and-black tom-kit partway up the trunk of one of the trees at the edge of the clearing. Wide-eyed, the kit dug in his claws and scrambled up toward the birch's branches. Next to him, Milkweed helped Beech Tail climb the same tree and followed her up, the trunk shaking under their weight.

If the dogs found their way into the camp, the kits would be safe. There were growls and heavy footsteps at the top of the ravine, accompanied by the sound of sniffing. The dogs wouldn't be able to see them through the gorse and brush, so there was still a chance they would pass the ravine by.

Thunderstar climbed a few tail-lengths up the tree and turned to check on the rest of his Clan. Lightning Tail was helping Pink Eyes up a tall ash on the other side of the clearing, coaching the half-blind cat on where to put his paws as he climbed. Blue Whisker had already reached the branches above them.

Cloud Spots and Shivering Rose were just coming out of

the medicine cats' den, their faces sharp with fear as they turned toward another tall tree. Around the camp, the rest of the Clan was also rushing to climb out of the dogs' reach.

Where was Violet Dawn? Thunderstar scanned the clearing for her. He heard a snarl from above, followed by renewed frantic barking. Had the dogs scented the Clan below?

A scattering of stones fell from the ledges above as three huge dogs charged down the sides of the ravine. They were even uglier than most dogs, with flat, broad, short-furred faces and powerful jaws that dripped drool as they charged toward the cats. Where had they come from? He'd never seen dogs like these before.

Thunderstar thought briefly of standing and fighting, but it was too great a risk—if his Clanmates were safe, any harm the dogs could do to their camp was a small price to pay.

Was every cat safe? There was a frightened yowl, and Thunderstar, his heart dropping, saw Violet Dawn, Owl Eyes, and Snail Shell huddled in the middle of the clearing by the warriors' den, Clover leaning against them for support. *Clover's hurt leg must have held them up.*

The dogs had almost made it to the bottom of the ravine. They didn't seem to have noticed the four cats by the den yet; their eyes were fixed on the tree directly across the clearing, in which Lightning Tail, Blue Whisker, and Pink Eyes clung to branches out of the dogs' reach.

I have to save Violet Dawn.

As the dogs' paws touched the bottom of the ravine, Thunderstar flung himself toward them, pushing off the tree's trunk with his powerful hind legs. He hit the ground with a jolt, but he didn't stop, his paws pounding the earth as he ran directly at the dogs.

Oh, StarClan, I hope this works.

He caught a glimpse of long sharp teeth and gaping jaws as he raced toward the big dogs. They seemed surprised to have a cat come right at them, and their momentary hesitation saved him.

He caught a whiff of something foul and acrid—almost like the scent of a Thunderpath—as he dashed directly beneath the nose of the lead dog, and then he ran at top speed in the opposite direction from where the four cats huddled by the den.

I need to give Violet Dawn and the others time to get away. He was sure that his Clanmates were moving as quickly as they could, but Clover's injury would slow them down. Weaving between the trees at the edge of the clearing, Thunderstar thought of Violet Dawn, and of their kits. Both he and his mate needed to survive this. Their kits had to be safely born, and he would not let them be fatherless.

He could feel the hot breath of the dog on his heels. It wasn't snarling now—it was saving its breath for running, just like he was. It was too close. With a thrill of panic, Thunderstar realized that he wouldn't be able to outrun it.

Instead, he swerved and ran straight at an ash tree. There was no time to climb. At the last moment, Thunderstar dodged, slipping past the trunk to one side. The dog couldn't veer away in time. With a satisfying thump, it crashed head-first into the tree. The second dog, following close behind, skidded right into it, and both went down in a chorus of snarls and a tangle of flailing legs.

Thunderstar scrambled up another tree and onto a branch. It was a lower branch than he would have preferred, but it didn't matter—dogs might be fast and strong, but they were terrible climbers. Regaining their feet, the two dogs leaped, barking frantically, but they couldn't reach him.

Panting, Thunderstar looked to see if he had distracted the dogs long enough for Violet Dawn and the others to get to safety.

Clover was halfway up a tree. But Violet Dawn, Snail Shell, and Owl Eyes were still on the ground, positioned protectively between the injured cat and the approaching third dog.

All three cats were backing away, their fur bristling and their tails puffed out, hissing and yowling to try to scare the dog off. But it kept stalking closer, its body low to the ground, its lips drawn back in a snarl. *It's hunting them like we hunt prey,* Thunderstar thought with a shock of fear.

"Violet Dawn!" Thunderstar yowled. He scrambled to the end of his branch and flung himself to the next tree, catching hold of the end of one of its branches and clawing his way to the next. A surge of renewed barking came from below.

Racing to the end of the next branch, he leaped to another tree. Its trunk swayed dizzyingly below him and he almost lost his balance. Steadying himself, Thunderstar looked up in time to see Violet Dawn slash her claws across the angry dog's face, aiming for its eyes. With a yelp, it fell back for a moment, and Violet Dawn shoved Snail Shell into the nearest tree and clawed her way up behind him, moving as fast as Thunderstar had ever seen her despite the clumsy weight of her rounded belly. Owl Eyes leaped after them, barely dodging the dog's snapping jaws. A furious howl came from below.

Thunderstar scanned the clearing: There was no cat on the ground now. He could only hope that the whole Clan had escaped injury.

A few drops spattered onto the leaves around him, and then a heavy downpour picked up again. Thunderstar inched closer to the tree's trunk as cold water streamed down his ears and dribbled off the ends of his whiskers. At least the dogs were getting just as wet as ThunderClan.

The rain kept falling, harder and harder, as the dogs paced the clearing below. Thunderstar shifted miserably on his branch and tried to peer across to the other trees to check on Violet Dawn, and on the rest of his Clanmates, but he could see very little through the sheets of driving rain. Gradually, shadows began to spread through the clearing.

After a long time, as darkness fell and the rain continued, the dogs finally wandered off, after a few last barks up at the unreachable cats. They looked as wet and muddy as he was, and Thunderstar hoped they were even more uncomfortable.

As soon as he could no longer hear them crashing through the undergrowth of the forest, Thunderstar leaped down into the clearing.

"I think it's safe now," he called, and his Clan gradually joined him, some dropping daringly from the branches above, the rest scrambling down tree trunks with varying amounts of caution. Thunderstar looked carefully around: Yes, they were all here, from tiny Patch Pelt and Beech Tail to Pink Eyes, the oldest cat in the Clan.

"Thank StarClan no cat was killed," Milkweed said, her eyes wide.

"They scattered our prey everywhere, though," Yew Tail said, poking disdainfully at a bedraggled shrew. "I don't think we can eat this."

Clover gingerly tested her paw against the ground, sheathing and unsheathing her claws. "Well, if I didn't have a sprained paw before, I definitely have one now."

Thunderstar pressed himself close to Violet Dawn's side, and she leaned against him, nuzzling his shoulder. "We're all okay," she said soothingly. "We made it."

For how long? Thunderstar wondered. *Now those dogs know where we live.*

The rain had cleared overnight, and the sun was shining. Normally, the ThunderClan cats would have stretched out in the sunshine and let it warm their pelts after a quarter moon of rain. But this morning every cat was on edge, scanning the treeline and listening with their ears pricked, wondering if the dogs were coming back.

"I've never seen dogs like that before." The fur on Leaf's shoulders bristled at the memory. "They were so vicious."

"Their muzzles looked big enough to swallow us whole!" Blue Whisker mewed, her green eyes wide.

"I was brave, though, wasn't I?" Snail Shell asked. "As brave as Lightning Tail and Thunderstar were when they saved Owl Eyes from the Twolegplace! I helped Violet Dawn and Owl Eyes protect Clover."

"And I'm very grateful for it," Clover replied warmly. She looked at the long scrapes the dogs' claws had left in the ground beneath the trees and shuddered.

Thunderstar gestured with his tail for Violet Dawn and Lightning Tail to join him by his den.

"We might not be safe here anymore," he announced quietly, and Violet Dawn dipped her head in agreement.

"Now that they know where we live, they could come back at any time," she mewed.

"We can send out extra patrols to watch for them," Lightning Tail suggested. "But dogs sometimes travel far with their Twolegs. They might not even live near here."

"We should send out extra patrols," Thunderstar agreed. "Since there's been peace with the other Clans, we've gotten too complacent." He looked around at his Clanmates, who were already beginning to relax as the warmth of the sunshine and the normal sounds of the forest soothed them. "It's not even just those dogs. There are dangers out there we're not watching for." He looked from the beautiful amber gaze of his mate to the sympathetic green eyes of his deputy. There were so *many* dangers in the forest. How could he protect his Clan from all of them? Or his kits?

His own littermates, who he barely even remembered, had been killed by Twoleg monsters, along with his mother, when they were much smaller than Beech Tail and Patch Pelt. If something like that—if *anything*—happened to his own kits, or to Violet Dawn, Thunderstar didn't think he could survive it.

"There have always been dangers in the forest," Violet Dawn said gently. "We are much safer here than I ever was with Slash, or than you were when the Clans were at war and rogues roamed the forest. All we can do is be careful and alert."

"We should go find them," Thunderstar declared, and Lightning Tail cocked his ears questioningly.

"Go find the *dogs*?" he asked. "Have you gone mouse-brained?"

Thunderstar flicked his tail in irritation. "Maybe you're right and they live with Twolegs far from here and we'll never see them again," he meowed. "But if that's not true, we need to find their camp. If they're too close, we'll have to move ThunderClan."

Lightning Tail's eyes went round. "Move out of the ravine?"

"If we have to. If the dogs hunt near here, the ravine's not safe anymore."

"Is SkyClan safe?" Violet Dawn wondered. "They're not far from us. We should warn them."

Lightning Tail stood up. "We should warn all the Clans. They need to know if they might be in danger. I'll send patrols to tell them to keep a sharp lookout."

"Good idea," Thunderstar agreed. "Send messengers to WindClan, ShadowClan, and RiverClan. But I'll go to

SkyClan myself." He squared his shoulders, feeling resigned. He and Skystar tried to get along, but there was always tension between them. They had too long a history of hurts and betrayals. "I need to pay a visit to my father."

CHAPTER FOUR

❧

As Thunderstar traveled toward SkyClan's territory, he kept his ears cocked and his eyes open, watching for any sign of the dogs that had attacked ThunderClan's camp. Scenting the air, though, he smelled nothing other than the usual musty scents of the forest.

Violet Dawn had wanted him to take a patrol with him, but he couldn't bear to leave the camp with fewer cats to protect it while he was gone. She had made him promise, though, her gaze wide and worried, that he would be on his guard.

As Thunderstar approached the hollow where SkyClan had their camp, he caught a glimpse of silver-and-white fur moving through the bracken.

"Hey!" a voice called, and the silver-and-white cat sped toward him. "Hi! Thunderstar!"

As she burst out of the bracken, he recognized Dew Petal, one of Skystar and Star Flower's kits. She greeted him enthusiastically, her tail high in the air. "It's my brother!" she called, and Honey Pelt, brother of ThunderClan's own Blue Whisker, hurried out of the bracken after her.

Thunderstar blinked, a bit startled to hear Dew Petal call

him brother. Skystar had fathered both of them, of course, but Dew Petal and her sister, Flower Foot, seemed much more like Skystar's kits than Thunderstar ever had. Warmed by their greeting, he touched noses with both Dew Petal and Honey Pelt.

"How're you?" Dew Petal asked. "Is Violet Dawn almost ready to have her kits? How's ThunderClan?"

"I need to talk to Skystar about that, actually," Thunderstar told them. "Are you two out here by yourselves?"

Dew Petal puffed out her chest with pride. "Skystar asked me to help train Honey Pelt to hunt. I'm one of the best hunters in our Clan!"

The dogs must not have come near SkyClan if Skystar is letting his own kits roam the forest alone, Thunderstar thought. Skystar would certainly never put Dew Petal in danger, or Honey Pelt, who he had raised as his own after Moth Flight gave him to SkyClan.

"You'd better come to the hollow with me," he suggested. "Will you take me to Skystar?"

Both cats happily agreed, and they chattered about the latest happenings in SkyClan as they strolled with him toward their camp. Honey Pelt asked about Blue Whisker, and Thunderstar assured him that his sister was thriving in ThunderClan. Dew Petal bragged that Skystar had praised her for managing to catch a fat squirrel yesterday despite the rain.

"Skystar said *I* really helped the Clan yesterday by finding a big patch of tansy for Acorn Fur to have in case any cat gets hurt," Honey Pelt retorted.

"It sounds like you're *both* important to SkyClan,"

Thunderstar mewed cheerfully. But there was a strange pang in his chest as he heard about the encouragement and praise Skystar heaped on these young cats. In the brief time he had spent in SkyClan, his father had been harsh in his treatment of Thunderstar, unforgiving at any sign of disagreement or disobedience. What would it have been like to have the same kind of relationship with Skystar as his younger kits did now?

Thunderstar flicked his ears, wishing the thought away. There was no use in digging up old prey now. Fatherhood didn't come naturally to every tom, and Skystar had improved with time.

Even if it isn't easy at first, I can learn *to be a good father, like Skystar did,* Thunderstar thought. He didn't have to be perfect right away, although he privately vowed that he would at least be better than Skystar had been to him.

As they reached the edge of the hollow, Honey Pelt ran ahead, calling for Skystar. Dew Petal paused by Thunderstar's side.

"Can I come and see the kits when they're born?" she asked eagerly. "They'll be my kin, too."

Touched by the request, Thunderstar blinked at her fondly. "Of course you can," he said.

Skystar strode out of his den toward them, and Dew Petal slipped away to join Honey Pelt at the prey pile, waving her tail to Thunderstar in farewell. Skystar looked a little thinner than he used to, Thunderstar thought, and age had dulled some of the shine of his thick gray fur, but his shoulders were still broad and his gaze as sharp as ever.

"Thunderstar," he said, sounding pleased. "It's good to see you outside of a full-moon Gathering. How is everything in ThunderClan?" Thunderstar hesitated, and a gleam of anxiety came into Skystar's eyes. "Is Violet Dawn all right? No problems with the kits?"

"No, no, Violet Dawn's fine," Thunderstar said. "But we had some trouble yesterday." He told Skystar about the dogs' attack on the ThunderClan camp. "We wanted to warn you that they may still be nearby," he finished. "I've never seen such vicious dogs. We were lucky no cat was killed."

Skystar was looking away from Thunderstar, and his tail flicked indecisively, as if he was wondering whether to tell Thunderstar something. Thunderstar narrowed his gaze, struck by an unpleasant suspicion. "Did you already know these dogs were in the forest?" he asked.

Skystar was still avoiding Thunderstar's gaze. "We've been scenting dogs here and there lately, but never too close to our camp, so we haven't been worried."

Thunderstar lashed his tail angrily. "Close to ThunderClan's borders, I suppose? You're never worried about anything unless it threatens your own Clan. You could have warned us."

There was a genuine look of regret in Skystar's eyes when he finally raised them to meet Thunderstar's. "Believe me, Thunderstar, I would have told you if I'd thought your Clan was in danger. The scent seemed to have been carried here on the wind from far away. I didn't think the dogs I smelled were a threat to any of us."

"Well, they are," Thunderstar said, his fur still ruffled. "We're all going to have to be alert if we want to keep our Clanmates safe."

"Their scent was very different from the scents of the forest," Skystar said thoughtfully. "Almost as acrid as the scent of the Thunderpath. We would have noticed an animal that smelled that strange if they had been here before."

Thunderstar's pelt prickled with anxiety. "So they must have come a long way. If they're brave enough to roam that far while they're hunting, they won't think anything of raiding our camps. Perhaps we should find where they live and teach them a lesson so they won't dare to come near us again."

Skystar stared at him doubtfully, and Thunderstar went on, thinking hard. "If we could get the other Clans and all attack them together. . . ."

Skystar cut him off, flicking his ears dismissively. "That sounds like trying to get ourselves killed. SkyClan isn't going to attack a pack of fierce dogs on their own territory."

Thunderstar's tail drooped. "I wouldn't have thought you'd back away from a fight, Skystar," he said. "But maybe you're right. Even all the Clan cats together might struggle to defeat these dogs. And what if there are more of them?"

"I can show you where I last caught their scent," Skystar offered. "Maybe we can figure out where they came from." He glanced back at the cats sunning themselves and sharing prey in the SkyClan camp. "Tell Star Flower I went with Thunderstar and I'll be back soon," he called to Quick Water, and the gray-and-white she-cat twitched her whiskers in acknowledgment.

Skystar led Thunderstar back through the forest. When they reached the border with ThunderClan, he hesitated. "It was around here that I scented strange dogs," he said, turning his face to the wind.

Thunderstar sniffed, too, and caught a whiff of the acrid dog-scent. It was weak, noticeable only on the odd burst of air, and he had to admit that if this was the only hint of the dogs he had gotten, he wouldn't have been worried enough to alert the other Clans either.

He told Skystar this, and the older cat brightened. "Let's try to follow the scent," he said.

Stopping and sniffing the breeze, following each hint of dog-scent, Thunderstar and Skystar passed through ThunderClan's territory as far as the Thunderpath that marked their border with ShadowClan. Thunderstar pressed his paws against the Thunderpath, feeling for the vibration that would mean monsters were approaching, and then they quickly crossed.

Skystar was as fast as ever, Thunderstar noted. His long legs still moved surely and steadily, covering as much territory with each stride as Thunderstar's could. His father wasn't really getting old, not yet.

Skirting ShadowClan's territory, Thunderstar wrinkled his nose in disgust as they passed the foul-smelling Carrionplace. "I can't smell anything here except the usual stench," he said.

"This way, I think," Skystar said.

They walked a long way, the sun climbing to sunhigh and then beginning its descent on the other side of the sky. They had passed out of Clan territory, and out of anywhere Thunderstar had traveled before. Thunderstar's paw pads were beginning to ache, but the dog-scent was getting stronger.

As they topped a hill, the valley below came into view and both cats froze.

"I've never seen anything like this before," Thunderstar murmured, and Skystar nodded.

Below them, a vast stretch of land, made of the same black stuff as the Thunderpaths, spread out behind a glittering silver fence. All over it, as still as if they were sleeping, were Twoleg monsters. Not normal monsters, though.

"They're *dying*," Thunderstar whispered. "Or already dead." These monsters would never race down a Thunderpath again. No Twoleg would ride inside them. The eyes of one of the great beasts were broken into pieces. Another gaped open, the top of what must have been its mouth torn off completely. Others were missing their round black feet or were only strangely shining bones.

This was the source of the strange acrid smell Thunderstar had not been able to identify, the smell the dogs had carried with them that was almost like the scent of the Thunderpath, but not quite. Mixed in with it came the stench of dogs and, in the distance, a faint, fierce barking.

"This is it," Thunderstar meowed. "This is where they come from."

Chapter Five

"I never thought that Twoleg monsters could die," Violet Dawn mewed, twitching her tail thoughtfully. Thunderstar had pulled her and Lightning Tail aside as soon as he returned to camp, and now all three were sitting outside Thunderstar's den and discussing his and Skystar's discovery.

"So we've found where the dogs live, but now what?" Lightning Tail asked. "Do you really think we should move ThunderClan's camp? If that's what we're going to do, we should do it soon so we have all of greenleaf to settle into a new camp."

Thunderstar shook his head. "I don't want to move until it's clear we don't have any other choice. There's no other place in ThunderClan's territory that would make as good a camp as the ravine." He hesitated. Violet Dawn wasn't going to like what he was going to say next, but he was sure it was the right thing to do. "Before we think about moving, I want to learn more about these dogs. If I go into that Twolegplace where they live, maybe I can find out more about them."

Lightning Tail cocked his head curiously. "You're going to

walk all that way just to look at a bunch of dogs? What good will that do?"

"I don't know," Thunderstar said. "I'm not sure anything will come of it, but it's better than just sitting here waiting for them to come back. Or moving the whole Clan when we don't know if a new camp would be any safer."

Violet Dawn twitched her ears. "Are you hoping a good idea will just suggest itself once you're there?"

Thunderstar hunched his shoulders, feeling stubborn. "I want to do *something*. The more I learn about these dogs, the easier it will be to figure out the best way to fight them."

Violet Dawn stroked her tail along Thunderstar's side, looking worried. "I'm afraid you're going to get hurt. Those dogs are so dangerous."

"If you're going, you're not going alone," Lightning Tail said fiercely. "The two of us will be stronger together. I'm your deputy; I should be with you, supporting you."

It would be so much better to have Lightning Tail with me, Thunderstar thought. From their kithood adventures to the fiercest battles of carving out the Clans' territory, Thunderstar had always fought better, climbed higher, thought more quickly, with Lightning Tail by his side. But when he looked at Violet Dawn, her sides rounded with his kits, he knew he had to refuse. "I need you to look after Violet Dawn," he said. "You're the only one I trust to make sure she's safe. You're right, you are my deputy—so you're the one who has to keep the Clan safe when I'm not there."

"I can keep the Clan safest by going with you to where the

danger is. Owl Eyes can watch out for the Clan, and Cloud Spots will make sure Violet Dawn's healthy," Lightning Tail argued. "She doesn't need me."

Thunderstar shook his head. "They're good cats, but I'll feel better if you're in charge. Cloud Spots isn't a fighter, and Owl Eyes isn't as experienced as you are. I need Violet Dawn to be safe."

"Do I get a say in this?" Violet Dawn huffed. "I'm having kits, not *becoming* one."

Thunderstar licked at his chest, embarrassed. Violet Dawn had fought off one of the dogs herself so that she, Snail Shell, and Owl Eyes could escape. She wasn't fragile or helpless. "You're right," he agreed. "I'm sorry. I'm just worried about you, and I'll feel better if Lightning Tail is here."

"Well, I'm worried about you, too," Violet Dawn mewed, the end of her tail twitching. "You're walking into some kind of weird Twoleg camp. All we know is that a pack of vicious dogs lives there. And *I* will feel much better if Lightning Tail is with *you*." She looked at him pleadingly. "You're my Clan leader as well as my mate, and I respect you, but please don't walk into this alone. I want you to come home."

Thunderstar hated to leave Violet Dawn without the very best protection she could have in his absence, but he had to admit to himself that she was right.

Leaping lightly to the top of the Highrock, he called out to his Clan. "All cats gather here beneath the Highrock! I have something to tell you." He saw Beech Tail and Patch Pelt, about to be bundled into the nursery, turn toward him with sleepy faces, and amended, "I mean, all cats old enough to catch their own prey, gather here beneath the Highrock."

He waited as his Clan, ears perked with interest, gathered in the clearing below him.

"Tomorrow morning, Lightning Tail and I are going to travel out of the forest for a couple of days," he announced when they had all settled down and given him their full attention. "We're going to figure out what to do about the dogs that attacked our camp. While we're gone, Violet Dawn will be in charge." He found Owl Eyes in the crowd and continued, "Owl Eyes will act as her deputy, and you should listen to him just like you'd listen to Lightning Tail. And Cloud Spots will advise them just like he would us." Cloud Spots nodded to him across the clearing while Owl Eyes sat up straight, proudly holding his head high.

"Good luck, Thunderstar," Apple Blossom called enthusiastically, and there were yowls of agreement from the crowd of cats.

"Thank you," Thunderstar meowed, and leaped down from the Highrock. His eyes met Lightning Tail's and he knew he and his deputy were thinking the same thing: They were definitely going to need that luck.

The next day, the two cats passed the Carrionplace as the sun was climbing the sky. The sun was warm, but a cool breeze ruffled Thunderstar's fur. It was a good day for walking.

Lightning Tail stopped and sniffed the breeze. "Do you smell that?"

"The Carrionplace?" Thunderstar asked, his face wrinkling in disgust. "Sure, my nose isn't broken."

"No, not that." Lightning Tail sniffed again. "It smells like those dogs. But something else. . . ."

Thunderstar could smell it now, too, and he shuddered. "Strange cats. And blood. A lot of blood."

Lightning Tail shifted nervously. "Maybe we should go another way."

"No." Thunderstar scented the air carefully. "It's old scent. They're not here anymore, not the cats or the dogs. We should see what happened."

Following the stale scents, Thunderstar and Lightning Tail crossed a long stretch of open land until they came to a small dip in the ground.

"This was some kind of camp," Lightning Tail said softly. There were the remains of several nests tucked beneath a barberry bush, but they had been torn apart, and the scent of the dogs was heavy in the air. A group of rogues must have lived here. Cat fear-scent was heavy, too, and Thunderstar's pelt prickled uneasily.

"I hope they got away," he said, but Lightning Tail was staring at a ragged bundle of brown fur on the other side of the bush.

"They didn't. Not all of them," he said.

They approached cautiously. Close up, they could see that the bundle of fur was a small brown she-cat, her face fixed in an expression of terror. She was dead. The scent of the dogs around her and the bloody toothmarks in her pelt made it all too clear how she had been killed. Thunderstar shuddered. It must have been a terrible way to die. And Violet Dawn could have died the same way, or any of the cats in ThunderClan, if they hadn't been able to get to the trees in time.

"The other cats ran away and left her," Lightning Tail mewed indignantly. "Fox-hearted rogues."

"They were scared," Thunderstar replied. "You've seen what these dogs are like."

"If they were Clan cats, they would have fought to save their Clanmate," Lightning Tail argued staunchly.

He was right. Thunderstar couldn't imagine abandoning a Clanmate to this fate: He would have fought beside her, and, if there was no way to save her, he would never have left her body to lie outside the camp like crow-food. But he couldn't blame the rogues for their terror.

"We should bury her," he murmured. "We can at least give her that."

Sunhigh passed as the two cats dug the rogue's grave. They didn't talk much as they dug, and dirt caked uncomfortably beneath Thunderstar's claws. His heart felt as heavy as a stone: The rogue's death made it clearer than ever how dangerous these dogs were, and how unlikely it was that Thunderstar and his Clanmates would be able to fight against them. Where would ThunderClan go, if they had to leave their comfortable camp in the ravine? And what if the dogs found them again after that?

The rogue's body was light as they tumbled her into her grave, and Thunderstar's chest ached with sorrow at how small she seemed. He bowed his head. "StarClan," he said, "I don't know who this cat was. She wasn't a Clan cat, and so maybe she won't be able to walk among you. But please help her to find her own hunting grounds."

The shadows were getting longer and their steps were heavy by the time they reached the hill overlooking the strange Twolegplace. This time, the strangeness of the dead monsters seemed less important. The dogs were walking among them, weaving their way between the monsters and around the Twoleg dwelling they surrounded.

They were even bigger than Thunderstar remembered, and their stench wafted up to the cats so clearly that Thunderstar wanted to cover his nose and turn away. Their shoulders were broad, and bulging muscles moved under their short fur—they looked very strong.

"There are four of them now," Lightning Tail muttered, and Thunderstar realized he was right—there was one more dog than there had been in the attack on ThunderClan's camp. The new dog was even larger than the other three and, as the cats watched, he growled and snapped at one of his packmates. The smaller dog snarled back, and soon the two were rolling in the dirt, struggling and yelping as the other dogs barked.

"They don't even like each other," Thunderstar noted.

Suddenly, the door of the Twoleg dwelling slammed open with a bang and a pair of Twolegs burst out. They were jabbering loudly and angrily, and one grabbed a piece broken off from one of the monster skeletons and used it to hit the fighting dogs. With a howl of pain, the dogs separated, and the Twolegs each grabbed one by the collar, continuing to jabber at each other.

"Is that what Twolegs are like?" Lightning Tail asked, shocked. "Why would *any* cat want to be a kittypet?"

"I don't think all Twolegs are like this," Thunderstar mewed uneasily. He hated those dogs, but he still couldn't be glad to see them treated so cruelly.

The Twolegs began dragging the two dogs inside their dwelling, calling crossly to the other two, who followed. As the door closed behind them, Thunderstar's heart began to pound faster. "They're all inside. This is our chance to check things out."

Signaling for Lightning Tail to follow, Thunderstar crept down the hill toward the Twoleg dwelling. He tried to keep a wary eye on both the door to the den and the dead monsters around it, but nothing stirred. The two cats halted by the fence of glittering silver strands that surrounded the whole Twolegplace.

Lightning Tail put out a tentative paw to touch one of the strands and immediately pulled it back. "Ouch," he muttered. The silver was twisted into sharp knots at intervals. "How're those dogs getting out? I couldn't get through that, and they're a lot bigger than I am."

"Maybe the Twolegs let them out?" Thunderstar suggested, but Lightning Tail shook his head.

"I doubt it. Remember when dogs have come to the forest before?" he asked. "There are always Twolegs somewhere behind them, calling and whistling for them to come back. Why would these Twolegs let their dogs run free? They don't seem like they want the dogs to be happy."

"Yeah," Thunderstar mewed thoughtfully. "I bet they're supposed to patrol around here and guard the Twoleg den."

The two cats began to walk alongside the silver strands, inspecting them carefully. They were far too high to jump. Dogs were good diggers, but the ground here was hard, and there was no sign of a tunnel.

They turned a corner, and Thunderstar spotted a bush growing close up beside the fence, long creepers climbing up and twining themselves among the silver strands. The strands were fully concealed behind the overgrown bush, so Thunderstar pushed his way through the branches for a closer look.

Low down, hidden by the bush, the silver strands were torn and hanging, leaving a hole big enough for even the largest of the dogs.

"Lightning Tail," he called. "Over here."

Thunderstar and Lightning Tail gazed at the opening. Now that they had found it, how could they prevent the dogs from coming through again?

"We can't mend the strands," Lightning Tail mewed at last. "What if we blocked the hole with something?"

"But what?" Thunderstar asked. He thought wildly of rolling a fallen tree across it to shut the dogs in, but they had no fallen tree and, if they had, he couldn't imagine being able to move one with only the two of them.

"Rocks?" Lightning Tail asked dubiously. "Big ones?"

"But the dogs are stronger than we are," Thunderstar objected. "Anything we can move, they can move." He thought. "Maybe a whole heap of rocks? If we could pile enough together, the dogs might not be able to get through."

Lightning Tail flexed his claws. "I don't know if it'll work, but I can't think of anything better. And we need to get moving before the dogs come back."

"Maybe the Twolegs will keep them shut in until tomorrow," Thunderstar suggested hopefully.

Finding stones heavy enough to make a difference but light enough for Thunderstar and Lightning Tail to roll or push up to the fence was difficult, tedious work. Soon, both cats' fur was heavy with dirt and their paws were sore from prying stones out of the ground.

"This won't work," Lightning Tail finally declared, eyeing the small heap of stones they had managed to gather. He shoved one of the larger stones to lie more securely against the edge of the hole, and another stone fell, rattling down the side of the heap and landing beside them with a thump. Thunderstar sighed and rolled it to a new position.

"Even if all it does is slow the dogs down a little, it'll be better than nothing," he mewed. But he felt dispirited. They had been working for a long time, and the pile of stones was nowhere close to blocking the hole. They needed a new plan. His eye fell upon a tangle of brambles growing farther along, close to the fence.

"What about this?" Thunderstar carefully bit off one of the brambles close to its root and carried it to the hole. Pushing the end of the bramble through a gap between the silver strands above the hole, he strung it across, weaving the other end through another gap in the strands near the bottom. "If they run into this, it'll scratch their eyes. With enough of these here, they may decide it's not worth it."

Lightning Tail cocked his head and looked at the brambles. "It's a good idea," he said. "A scratch on the eye will make them think twice." He bit off a stem and followed Thunderstar's example, draping the bramble carefully across the hole.

They had both collected more brambles and were heading for the hole again when they heard a sudden bang. Thunderstar froze, the fur on his shoulders bristling with fear. The dogs burst out of the Twoleg den, barking loudly.

As the cats watched, the largest dog raised his head, sniffing the air. *There aren't enough brambles,* Thunderstar thought, his heart sinking. Past the silver strands, through the hole, the dog's eyes met Thunderstar's.

With a snarl, he charged.

Thunderstar dropped the bramble. "Run!" he yowled.

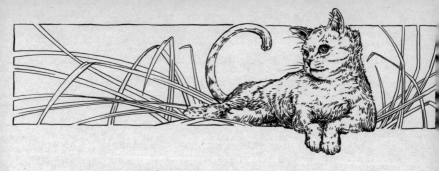

CHAPTER SIX

Thunderstar ran, Lightning Tail beside him. His heart was pounding and his sore paws ached as he pushed himself harder. The land here was flat and open, with no trees to climb, but if they could make it back up the hill toward home, they would be able to climb out of the dogs' reach. It seemed so far, though. Thunderstar stretched his legs, panting, willing himself to run faster.

A dog cut him off, growling. Thunderstar swerved and tried to run past it, and saw Lightning Tail dodge after him. But there was another dog blocking their path. Thunderstar doubled back, only to see yet another dog behind him. The four dogs were approaching from four different directions, drool dripping from their mouths as they herded the cats closer together.

We're trapped between them like rabbits, Thunderstar thought, panicked. The gaps between the dogs weren't large enough for them to run through. He and Lightning Tail had worked together to fight dogs in the past, but all their practiced maneuvers assumed there'd only be one dog after them, or at most two.

"What do we do?" Lightning Tail asked, his eyes wide. Yowling a challenge, he swiped his claws at one of the dogs. It fell back for a moment, but another dog darted in from the side immediately, its jaws open wide.

"Dogs are dumb, right?" Thunderstar panted. "Let's see if we can trick them. When I run, you run the other way, up the hill."

"Okay," Lightning Tail agreed, and both cats hesitated for a moment, back to back. The dogs moved in closer still, baring their huge teeth.

Thunderstar bolted forward. The dogs, barking, surged toward him. *I hope Lightning Tail makes it,* he thought. He just needed to get the dogs to move toward him, so he and Lightning Tail would be able to get through the gap they left behind. The next part of Thunderstar's plan would be trickier.

Twisting himself so quickly that his front paws left the ground, Thunderstar doubled back. With luck, he'd be able to follow Lightning Tail's path before the dogs could close the gap and catch up with him.

Lightning Tail had made it out of the circle of dogs, Thunderstar saw with relief. His deputy was streaking toward the hill, already some distance away. Thunderstar put on speed, rushing past the dogs as they charged at him.

I'm going to make it! Thunderstar was getting closer to the hill.

A sharp pain shot through his tail, and he was jerked suddenly backward, his paws scrabbling against the earth. His feint had cost him too much time, he realized, and now the lead dog had an agonizing grip on his tail.

He struggled, trying to turn and swipe at the dog's eyes, but he was yanked off his paws and fell heavily to the ground.

Another dog closed in and a second set of teeth pierced his pelt, tearing into Thunderstar's shoulder. Dark spots floated across his vision. Weakly, he struggled. *I have to get free! I have to get home, to Violet Dawn and my kits.*

Dimly, he saw a black shape racing toward him. Lightning Tail. *No,* he thought. *Save yourself! Don't come back for me.*

But Lightning Tail was already there. In a flurry of claws, he flew at the muzzle of the larger dog biting Thunderstar. The dog dropped Thunderstar to the ground and turned to face the new threat.

With a fresh burst of energy, Thunderstar struggled to his paws and fought beside his deputy, slashing at the dogs' eyes and noses. A dog gnawed at his leg, snarling, shaking him. Thunderstar pulled away, feeling his flesh tear, and spotted an opening between the dogs. "Run," he gasped. "Lightning Tail, run!"

Together, they sped through the gap and ran and ran and ran. Thunderstar felt like his paws were barely touching the ground. He had never run so fast, without even paying attention to where he was going. The only thing he cared about was getting far away from those terrible dogs.

Finally, Thunderstar and Lightning Tail halted at the foot of a huge oak. They were among trees again, and the dogs had been left behind or had given up.

As soon as he stopped running, Thunderstar began to shake. Black spots filled his vision again, and he blinked them away. He had forgotten his pain in the surge of panic as they ran, but now every bit of his body hurt. He sank to the ground, and Lightning Tail collapsed beside him.

"Thank you," Thunderstar said hoarsely. "You saved me. You shouldn't have come back for me, but I'm grateful." He licked his friend's shoulder.

"I couldn't leave you. That's not what a Clan cat does." Lightning Tail's green eyes were distant and half closed, and Thunderstar realized he was wounded, blood welling from his side. Lightning Tail had been bitten, too.

There's too much blood. It's coming too fast, Thunderstar thought. It was a distant thought, as if he were drifting away, but he felt terribly, terribly sorry. Why should Lightning Tail get hurt helping *him*? Thunderstar was the leader. It was his duty to protect all the cats of his Clan.

He tried to shift closer to Lightning Tail, so that he could curl around him and try to stop the steady gush of blood, but he couldn't move. Thunderstar became aware that warm liquid was running down his own legs, that it must be his own blood drenching the ground below them, too.

It was a great effort to speak. "Are we dying?" he whispered.

It felt like a long time before Lightning Tail answered, and his voice was weak and strained. "StarClan gave you nine lives, remember? You'll go on, for the Clan."

Thunderstar remembered now. He had been told that Windstar had been hurt, badly. Her medicine cat, her daughter Moth Flight, had taken her to the Moonstone. There, StarClan had healed her and given her nine lives, so that she could lead and protect her Clan. He had traveled to the Moonstone himself, with Cloud Spots, and cats from StarClan—dead cats he had known and loved, including his almost-forgotten mother and his beloved mentor Gray Wing—had appeared and each given him a life.

But he had not seen Windstar die and come back to life. He had believed what StarClan told him, but he had never *seen* a cat come back from the dead.

"I don't know if it's true," he mumbled. "I hope it is, but I don't know for sure." His heart ached. "If I die and I don't come back, Violet Dawn will be alone." *I'll never meet my kits.*

He felt his deputy's tail fall across his back. "I believe it's true," Lightning Tail said quietly. "You've been the best leader I could have asked for, the strongest cat I know. StarClan will save you."

The world was growing dim before Thunderstar's eyes. "If I was a good leader," he whispered, "it's only because I had you to rely on. I could never have formed ThunderClan without you."

There was no answer from Lightning Tail. The world was being eaten up by a thick gray nothingness, like fog. Thunderstar blinked slowly, and shadows crept in, the gray replaced by darkness.

When Thunderstar blinked his eyes open again, he found himself in a sunny clearing. Birds were singing overhead, and the air was rich with prey-scent. Leaves rustled in the trees around him. He struggled to his feet and stretched experimentally. Nothing hurt.

Fur brushed against his, and he realized Lightning Tail was beside him. The two cats looked at each other, their eyes wide.

"How did we get here?" Thunderstar wondered. "Where are we?"

"I don't know, but it's nice, isn't it?" Lightning Tail said. He flicked his tail and turned around, sniffing the air. "No dogs."

"We have to figure out how to get to ThunderClan from here," Thunderstar said, then hesitated. "No, we still need to get rid of those dogs. We'll have to go back." His heart sank at the idea.

"Yes, Thunderstar, you have to go back," a quiet voice mewed from behind them.

Thunderstar spun around. A sleek dark gray tom had emerged from the forest and was watching them with calm golden eyes.

"Gray Wing!" Thunderstar gasped. Joy shot through his pelt. It was his foster father, the cat who had raised him. And he was no misty silver spirit cat, but as solid and real as he had ever been. Thunderstar rushed toward him and rubbed his cheek against Gray Wing's. Lightning Tail, who had known Gray Wing all his life, who had been taught to hunt by the older cat when he was just a kit, ran toward him, too, touching his nose to Gray Wing's in greeting.

"What's going on?" Thunderstar said. "Where *are* we?"

Gray Wing flicked his tail. "Don't you know?"

An idea occurred to Thunderstar, but he pushed it away. It wasn't possible.

But Gray Wing was dead. Thunderstar had seen him die, gasping for breath as the illness he had fought for so long finally claimed him.

"You seem well," he said tentatively, ignoring Gray Wing's question for now. "You're not sick anymore?"

Gray Wing's whiskers twitched in amusement. "No cat is sick here," he said. "And prey never runs short, and there are no dangers to guard against."

Lightning Tail sat down abruptly, as if his legs had given out under him. "We're in StarClan? We're dead, then."

Gray Wing tilted his head thoughtfully. "Yes," he said. "And no. Lightning Tail, you can join StarClan now. Hunt with us, walk with your friends in a forest where there is nothing to fear. Your parents, Jackdaw's Cry and Hawk Swoop, are here, and they will be so glad to see you."

Lightning Tail's eyes glistened with emotion. Thunderstar knew how Lightning Tail had mourned his parents, killed in the first battle between the cats before the Clans were formed.

Gray Wing went on. "But Thunderstar, you have to go back. Your next life is about to begin."

"What?" Thunderstar burst out. "I get to be alive again, and Lightning Tail has to stay dead? That's not fair! He only died because he saved me." A new thought struck him. "And he didn't have to, did he? I would have come back to life?"

Gray Wing shook his head. "If you hadn't escaped those dogs, they could have killed you again and again. Lightning

Tail truly did save you." He looked at the black cat proudly. "And there is nothing more important than protecting the cats you love."

Lightning Tail stepped toward Thunderstar, his green eyes shining. "StarClan gave you nine lives for a reason. Thunder-Clan needs its leader. You *must* go on. You'll be a good father to your kits and keep looking after your Clan."

"But I can't do it without you," Thunderstar pleaded. Lightning Tail had been beside him every step of the way, since they were kits together. "You're my deputy. You're the only one I can trust to help me lead."

"I expect I'll be watching over you from StarClan," Lightning Tail replied, glancing at Gray Wing, who nodded. "And you'll find the right cat to be your new deputy. But I will always be right beside you, Thunderstar."

Thunderstar opened his mouth to protest again, but it was too late. He felt as if he was rushing forward, even though he wasn't moving. The pleasant sunny clearing whirled dizzy-ingly around him, and then everything went dark.

Thunderstar blinked his eyes open. He felt groggy, as if he was waking from a deep sleep, and refreshed, as if it had been the best sleep of his life. It was almost dark, evening sliding into night. Where was he?

Memories began to come back to him: the dogs, the chase. He climbed to his feet. Nothing hurt now. Had he died? Had StarClan brought him back? As soon as he thought it, he knew, with a deep certainty, that it was true. He almost purred with excitement.

Then the last of his memories fell into place, and he froze, horrified. *The dogs caught us both. Lightning Tail. Where is Lightning Tail?*

Looking around, he saw Lightning Tail on the ground to his right, a bit farther away than he remembered. *Is he alive?* He whispered his friend's name, approaching slowly.

Lightning Tail wasn't breathing. Thunderstar nosed gently at his face, but he was cold and stiff. Already, he smelled *wrong*.

A great pain shot through Thunderstar's chest. It wasn't fair. He was alive but brave Lightning Tail was dead.

Night had fallen, and it was dark, except for the light of the half-moon above them. Thunderstar lay down beside the body of his deputy, their fur touching. Tonight, he would not sleep. He would not leave Lightning Tail alone, not yet. He would keep his Clanmate company for one last night. He would hold vigil and watch over his friend.

CHAPTER SEVEN

As the sun rose, Thunderstar got to his feet, stretching wearily. He had spent the night lying close beside Lightning Tail, remembering his deputy. They had always been together; when they were kits, the older cats had joked that they were a storm in the making. It seemed so unfair that Lightning Tail was dead and Thunderstar alive.

Thunderstar looked down at Lightning Tail's body. He looked peaceful at least, his bright green eyes closed and his strong body at rest. Thunderstar, too, felt more at peace than he had the night before. Spending the night watching over his friend one more time had been the right thing to do.

But now it was time to bury Lightning Tail and return home. He would have to carry the news to ThunderClan that their much-loved deputy was dead.

"No," Thunderstar said, realizing. He couldn't go home, not yet. Lightning Tail had died trying to protect their Clan, and their job wasn't finished. Thunderstar was going to have to find a way to stop the dogs before they invaded Thunder-Clan's territory again. He couldn't let them hurt any more of his Clanmates.

The sun was climbing higher every moment that he hesitated. The more time that passed, the more likely it was that the dogs would escape through that hole again.

Lightning Tail needed to be buried, but he would have wanted Thunderstar to wait until their mission had been accomplished. Thunderstar couldn't bear to leave him exposed, though—he knew there were birds that fed on the dead.

Clumps of long grass grew nearby, and Thunderstar bit through some stalks and spread them over Lightning Tail's body, concealing it. There. That would have to do for now.

"I'll be back," he said softly, and turned toward the strange Twolegplace once more.

He would take a different route this time, he decided, just in case the dogs were tracking them. Skirting the open stretch of land they had run over yesterday, Thunderstar walked up a gradual incline, until he was looking down on the field of dead monsters from a hill above them. There was a good-sized rock perched at the top of the hill, and Thunderstar leaped onto it to get a better look.

As he watched, the door of the Twoleg dwelling opened and the four dogs raced out, barking and yelping. Thunderstar stiffened: He could see the place where the hole in the silver strands was from here. Would the dogs come through it? Would they see him? He shuddered.

But there was an angry shout from inside the dwelling and the dogs hesitated, then turned to cluster around the door. One of the Twolegs came out, shoving the dogs out of the way before dropping something in front of them. They rushed forward and appeared to be eating—their Twoleg must have given them food.

What could Thunderstar do? The problem was the hole. If it wasn't there, the dogs would never be able to venture back to the forest. But blocking it with stones and brambles clearly wouldn't have worked, even if they had finished. The dogs had broken through their pile of rocks so easily.... They hadn't had the time, or the strength, to make a real barrier. And without Lightning Tail, everything would be twice as hard and take twice as long.

What if I had one really big stone, one big enough to cover the hole? Thunderstar's tail twitched with excitement. He and Lightning Tail hadn't been strong enough to move a stone that big. But he was sitting on one—and it was on a hill, directly upslope from the hole. What if he could roll it down? He jumped off the stone so he could inspect it more clearly.

Looking at the base of the stone, Thunderstar felt hopeful for the first time since he had lain down by Lightning Tail's body. The earth below the stone was wet and muddy, soft from the days of rain. He scooped away some earth from in front of the stone with his paw: It wasn't set too deeply. He could feel the stone's edge just a few paw-lengths below.

He quickly dug more dirt from in front of the stone. After a bit of digging, the stone tilted dangerously forward. Thunderstar jumped back quickly, but the stone stilled again.

He ran around behind it. The edge of the stone was sticking up from the earth. *If I can get something underneath on this side, maybe I can get it to start rolling.* Thunderstar looked around. *A stick, maybe.*

He found a thick, long branch beneath a nearby tree and wedged one end beneath the stone. *This would be easier if I wasn't alone,* he thought, with a pang of sorrow. Would he miss Lightning Tail at every turn from now on? Thunderstar threw his weight against the far end of the branch. Gradually, the stone tipped farther and farther forward.

At last it fell, leaving a gaping muddy pit behind, and began to roll down the hill. Excited, Thunderstar jumped over the pit to watch the stone's progress. The hill was steep here, and the stone picked up speed as it rolled toward the Twoleg dwelling.

It was working! Thunderstar began to run after the stone as it tumbled. Could it be this easy?

But the stone must have hit a branch or rock, because it veered off course suddenly. Wobbling, it rolled a bit farther, then fell over with a thump.

No! Thunderstar ran to the stone. It had fallen on its side, its muddy edge now up in the air. There was no space to get a stick under it here, and even if he could start it rolling again, its path would no longer take it toward the hole in the fence. He put his paws on the stone, testing its weight, but he couldn't shift it at all, not even with all his strength.

I have to think of something else. Keeping low, Thunderstar approached the strange Twolegplace from downwind. With luck, the dogs wouldn't see him coming.

They weren't eating anymore. They were sprawled in the

sunshine between the dead monsters. Thunderstar looked at them with fear and hatred. The largest one's eyes were closed, while one of the others was beating its stubby tail in a steady rhythm against the ground. They were peaceful now, enjoying the sun's warmth while Lightning Tail was dead. Thunderstar shut his eyes for a moment as another wave of sorrow washed over him.

A Twoleg yowled something, sharp and angry, and Thunderstar's eyes shot open. Had it spotted him? No, he could see that the door to the Twoleg den was open, but the Twolegs must be inside. There was no sign of them among the monsters.

They were unpleasant Twolegs, Thunderstar thought, and he was almost sure they had no idea the dogs could sneak out through the fence whenever they wanted. If the dogs were supposed to guard the dead monsters, the Twolegs wouldn't want them wandering off.

If the Twolegs had patrolled their territory properly, they would have seen the hole, but Thunderstar had always heard that Twolegs were lazy and unobservant. But what if he could *show* the Twolegs the hole?

Thunderstar realized what he would have to do. Standing up, he swallowed hard and began to walk closer to the Twolegplace. His paws were heavy and reluctant. These dogs had already killed him once.

Stopping outside the barrier, Thunderstar put a paw against the silver strands. They had sharp barbs on them like thorns, but he saw that he could clamber up the fence without touching those, if he was careful. What if the dogs saw him before he'd done what he had to do? He would have to be fast.

He walked to another part of the fence, closer to the door of the Twoleg den. The closer he was to the Twolegs when he started, the better. As he slipped one paw onto a strand, he was already looking for another smooth spot. He climbed, at first hesitantly, then more quickly as he realized the silver thorns appeared in a pattern, each the same distance away from the others. He kept his ears pricked: Surely the dogs would bark if they spotted him.

Thunderstar reached the top and balanced for a moment on the topmost strand, which swayed beneath his feet. The door to the Twoleg den was straight ahead of him. The dogs were farther away, and the bodies of several monsters lay between them and Thunderstar. This might work. He took a deep breath and leaped down into the place of the dead monsters.

Landing lightly just in front of the open Twoleg door, Thunderstar wrinkled his nose in disgust at the scents that surrounded him: the strange smell of Twolegs, the rank smell of the dogs. And over everything, the reek of Thunderpaths. It must come from the dead monsters, he thought, and it was so strong here that the dogs carried the scent with them wherever they went.

He could hear the Twolegs moving about inside their den. Bracing himself, Thunderstar opened his mouth and let out the loudest yowl he could. He had to get their attention.

There was a crash as something fell inside the Twoleg

place, then a startled voice. Almost at the same time, there was a chorus of angry barks. Still yowling, Thunderstar took off, running away from the dogs, around the Twoleg den.

Please let the Twolegs come out to see what's happening. Please let them care what the dogs do.

He could hear Twoleg footsteps and excited voices. They must be coming out. But he could hear the snarling dogs much closer, their paw steps getting louder. Thunderstar whipped around another corner of the Twoleg dwelling and leaped up onto a dead monster.

It was hard and surprisingly hot under his paws. *What if it's not dead?* But no, it was completely still beneath him; the body must simply have soaked up the warmth of the sun.

Paws scrabbled against one end of the dead monster as the largest dog tried to haul himself up onto it. Thunderstar risked a glance over his shoulder. The Twolegs were running around the corner, not far away. Now was his chance. Thunderstar leaped from the back of the monster and shot toward the hole in the fence.

It was wide enough for him to pass through easily, but as he sped through it, something scratched his shoulder. *One of the brambles Lightning Tail and I put there,* he realized with another pang of sorrow. He kept running, expecting at every moment to feel fangs ripping through his pelt.

But as he streaked up the hill, he realized that he couldn't hear the dogs behind him. And he was only a few tail-lengths from the safety of the trees now. He was going to make it. With a long leap, he dug his claws into the trunk of a tall ash tree and scrambled up to the highest branch that would support his weight.

His heart was pounding in his chest and he was gasping for breath, but he was safe for now. Climbing farther out onto the branch, he looked back at the Twolegplace.

The dogs had not chased him through the hole. Instead, the Twolegs were each holding on to two dogs' collars as they spoke, pointing at the hole. After a while, one of the Twolegs spoke sternly to the dogs until they were all sitting; then he went into the Twoleg den and came back out with a new length of silver strands. With many harsh noises, he began to fit it across the hole.

It worked, Thunderstar thought, dizzy with relief. The Twolegs hadn't known the dogs were getting out through the hole in the fence, and now that Thunderstar had shown them, they were fixing the hole.

If this had happened yesterday, he would have been happy about it, but right now he could only feel surprise at his success and a sort of grim satisfaction. He had done what he and Lightning Tail had set out to do. Thunder Clan would be safe.

Jumping down from the tree, Thunderstar padded back toward where his friend was waiting for him.

Nothing had disturbed the place where Lightning Tail lay. Thunderstar brushed the long grass away from his friend's body and looked down at him.

"It's done," he said softly. "We protected our Clan."

There was a spot near the roots of an oak tree where sun

shone through the branches and warmed the ground. Lightning Tail had always liked to bask in the sun. Thunderstar began to dig.

His paws ached and the earth was heavy. Digging was much harder alone than it had been when he and Lightning Tail dug the rogue's grave together. But Lightning Tail deserved to be laid in the earth the right way. The thought gave Thunderstar new strength, and the strain of his muscles was almost comforting: He was doing this for Lightning Tail.

As he dug, he thought about Violet Dawn and his kits again. Lightning Tail had believed Thunderstar would be a good father. But how could he look after tiny, helpless kits properly when he hadn't managed to protect his best friend, a powerful warrior?

He would have to try to trust in himself, and trust in Violet Dawn. Maybe Lightning Tail would watch over the kits from StarClan. Lightning Tail had always loved kits.

Finally, the hole was deep enough, and Thunderstar gently pushed Lightning Tail's body into the grave.

When it was covered again, he laid some grass across it so that the earth wouldn't look too freshly disturbed—and no predator would dig to find what was buried below.

It was very quiet here. Thunderstar bowed his head and spoke. "I'll miss you so much, Lightning Tail. You were brave and clever and loyal, and you always helped any cat who needed you. You died saving me, and there's no way I can thank you properly for that." Thunderstar took a deep breath, his mouth dry. "Good-bye, Lightning Tail. I'll never forget you."

The shadows were lengthening again. It was time to go back to camp, time to tell ThunderClan that their deputy would not be returning. Thunderstar turned away from his friend's grave and began the long walk home.

Chapter Eight

It was dark by the time Thunderstar, sore-pawed and exhausted, reached the ThunderClan camp. He slipped through the gorse tunnel, nodding at Leaf, who was standing guard, but said nothing. The camp was quiet, the cats asleep.

Violet Dawn was sleeping, too, in the mossy nest they shared in their den. In just the two days that he'd been gone, she seemed to have grown even more round. He lay down beside her and felt a kit squirm inside her belly, tiny paws kicking at him through her side. Warmth spread through him at this proof that the kits were alive and growing.

In a moment, though, his joy dimmed. How could he be happy so soon after Lightning Tail's death? In the morning, he would have to tell the Clan what had happened. His chest felt tight at the thought. No matter how gently he tried to tell them, they would suffer. Every cat in the Clan had loved Lightning Tail. And would they blame Thunderstar? He had been given nine lives so he could protect his Clan, but instead, Lightning Tail had died protecting him.

Thunderstar rolled over onto his back, gazing up at the rock at the top of his den. He was so tired, but his mind was spinning. He shifted again, accidentally bumping Violet Dawn's side.

"Hmm?" she murmured softly, and her eyes blinked open. "Thunderstar," she mewed sleepily. "I missed you."

He nuzzled his cheek against hers. "I missed you, too. How are you feeling?" Her voice sounded weak, he thought.

Violet Dawn shrugged. "I'm okay. The kits have been really lively at night, so I haven't been sleeping well."

"You aren't sleeping?" Thunderstar asked, alarmed.

Violet Dawn purred. "Don't worry so much," she told him. "Cloud Spots says I'm fine, and it's completely normal for the kits to be keeping me up this close to when they'll be born. Milkweed says the same thing, and she's had kits three times. The only problem was that I was feeling too tired to lead the Clan while you were gone. But Owl Eyes has been doing great," she added quickly. "He's kept everything running smoothly and even sent out extra hunting patrols to take advantage of the good weather." She gave a little huff of amusement. "If Lightning Tail doesn't watch out, Owl Eyes will be deputy before he knows it."

Thunderstar stiffened. Violet Dawn, sensitive to his moods as always, sat up. "What is it?" she asked, concerned. "Did you find the dogs? Are we going to have to move camp?"

"No," Thunderstar answered sadly. "We're not going to have to move. Lightning Tail and I took care of the dogs." He felt his whiskers drooping. "Lightning Tail was really brave," he added.

"Well, that's good, isn't it?" Violet Dawn sounded puzzled. "But what's wrong?"

I shouldn't upset her when she's carrying kits, Thunderstar thought. But how could he pretend that nothing had happened? Every cat would be wondering where Lightning Tail was in the morning.

And Violet Dawn had never flinched from facing the truth.

"Lightning Tail fought valiantly," Thunderstar told her. "But the dogs were too fast and too strong for us. They killed him. They killed me, too, but Star Clan gave me nine lives, so I came back again."

In the darkness he could see the glint of Violet Dawn's wide eyes staring at him. She sat absolutely still for a few heartbeats, and then gave out a wail of grief. "*No!* Oh, no!" Her cry echoed around the clearing.

From out in the camp came sleepy exclamations as cats began to stir.

"What's going on?"

"Are we under attack?"

"The dogs! The dogs!"

Violet Dawn wailed again. Thunderstar curled against her, licking her fur, trying to comfort her.

"It's Violet Dawn!"

"Are the kits coming?"

Violet Dawn took a deep, shuddering breath. Pressing her face against Thunderstar's shoulder for a moment, she sobbed once and then pulled back, calming herself. "They need to know what happened. Let's go out," she meowed.

Thunderstar shook his head. "You're more important right now. You need to rest."

"No." She got to her feet, her heavy body dignified. "I will be fine. Come on." She led him out of their den, her head held high.

Out in the clearing, the whole Clan was milling around, their faces worried. At Thunderstar's appearance, they surged forward.

"Thunderstar, you're back!" Milkweed mewed, Beech Tail and Patch Pelt staggering sleepily behind her.

"Why is it so *loud*?" Beech Tail asked crossly, her little tail switching. "Why is every cat awake?"

"What happened?" Pink Eyes blinked nearsightedly at Thunderstar. "We heard a terrible yowl."

"Is some cat hurt?" Shivering Rose and Blue Whisker were huddled close together.

Thunderstar looked around. Every cat's face was turned toward him—anxious, concerned, expecting him to put everything right.

"I—" He paused and leaped up onto the Highrock so that every cat could see him. "I have bad news," he began.

He expected them to erupt in a babble of speculation, but instead the clearing was silent, every cat's face turned toward him.

He swallowed hard. "We found the dogs, and they won't be coming back. But Lightning Tail was killed. He . . . he died saving my life." Thunderstar didn't add that he had died, too, or that StarClan had fulfilled their promise and brought him back. He couldn't bear to, not when Lightning Tail was gone.

Cries of mourning rose all around him.

They would blame him, now that he had admitted that Lightning Tail had died protecting him, Thunderstar thought. But looking around, he saw that he had underestimated his Clan. The faces below him were contorted with grief, but there was no anger or hatred. As their cries gradually fell silent, he saw nothing but love in their faces.

Apple Blossom stood up, her head high. "Lightning Tail was a good deputy and a fine cat. He taught me to hunt and to fight. He was never impatient with me, and when I was discouraged, he always had an exciting story to tell me to make me feel strong again."

"Lightning Tail saved me from Twolegs when I was a kit," Owl Eyes said, standing next to the younger warrior. "There was no cat braver than him. He died the way he would have wanted—saving a Clanmate."

"Lightning Tail was one of the first cats to welcome me and my kits to ThunderClan," Milkweed said. "He was always willing to play with kits, and they loved him."

"When my eyes got too bad to hunt, Lightning Tail always made sure I was fed," Pink Eyes said. "He was a generous cat."

All the cats were murmuring agreement, remembering kind things Lightning Tail had done or the way he had shown his bravery in battle and in protecting his Clan.

"We'll never forget Lightning Tail," Violet Dawn meowed finally. "He was brave and strong and good, and we were lucky to have him."

* * *

The next two days were quiet and somber as ThunderClan mourned Lightning Tail.

Thunderstar and Violet Dawn sat in the mouth of their den, watching their Clanmates. Clover lay in the shade, picking sadly at a vole. Cloud Spots came out of the medicine den and passed the prey pile by, his tail drooping sadly. Everywhere cats were moving slowly, not speaking to each other, wrapped in their separate grief.

"This has to stop," Violet Dawn mewed, eyeing them. "Lightning Tail wouldn't have wanted the Clan to act like this, especially not because of him."

Thunderstar wrapped his tail around his paws, feeling cold. "No, but what can we do? I can't tell them to stop being sad."

"Maybe you should pick a new deputy," Violet Dawn suggested. "You need to have one, and it will help things get back to normal. It will give the Clan something new to think about, too."

"A new deputy?" Thunderstar replied doubtfully. He couldn't imagine any cat being able to support him the way Lightning Tail had. *How can I replace my best friend?*

"Owl Eyes was an excellent deputy while you and Lightning Tail were gone," Violet Dawn told him. "Leaf and Gooseberry got into an argument about the nests in the warriors' den, and Owl Eyes figured out a solution every cat could live with. He managed so well that I didn't even know there was an argument until it was over."

Thunderstar hesitated. The idea of another deputy—*any*

deputy—taking Lightning Tail's place beside him made him ache inside. But Owl Eyes was smart and hardworking. Every cat liked him. He was brave and strong and sensible.

Thunderstar wasn't ready.

But the Clan needed a new deputy.

Sitting up straight, he made up his mind. Thunderstar opened his mouth to agree with Violet Dawn—Owl Eyes was the right cat for the job—when Violet Dawn suddenly gasped.

"What is it?" Thunderstar asked, Owl Eyes forgotten. Violet Dawn swayed and Thunderstar instinctively moved to support her.

"It's the kits," Violet Dawn told him, her eyes wide and glassy with pain. "They're coming!"

CHAPTER NINE
❧

"Cloud Spots! Come quickly!" Thunderstar yowled. Violet Dawn, gasping, leaned against him suddenly and he staggered under her weight.

Cloud Spots hurried across the clearing, followed by Shivering Rose.

"It's time, isn't it?" the long-furred medicine cat asked calmly. He pressed a paw to Violet Dawn's side. "Take a deep breath. Deeper."

Violet Dawn made a visible effort to slow her shallow panting, and Cloud Spots nodded approvingly.

Some of the other cats were crowding behind Cloud Spots and Shivering Rose, looking on with interest and excitement. Violet Dawn gave a low moan, her tail drooping, and Thunderstar licked her ear. "It's okay," he whispered. *Is this normal?*

Violet Dawn was shaking. *Surely she shouldn't be in this much pain,* Thunderstar thought.

"Let's get her into the nursery where she'll be more comfortable," Cloud Spots ordered. "All of you need to back off and give her some room," he added, shooting a glare around at the onlookers.

"It *hurts*," Violet Dawn mewed.

"Wait for the wave of pain to stop for a heartbeat, and then we'll move," Cloud Spots told her, taking Violet Dawn's weight from Thunderstar. He gestured to Shivering Rose with his tail and she went to Violet Dawn's other side, so that they could support her between them.

After a moment, Violet Dawn mewed, her voice calmer, "Okay, I can move now." The three cats started forward, crossing the clearing toward the nursery. Milkweed had already bundled Beech Tail and Patch Pelt out of the den, leaving more space for Violet Dawn and the medicine cats.

Thunderstar followed them to the nursery, his stomach churning with excitement and worry. He hovered in the doorway, looking in at the fresh nest Shivering Rose had made for Violet Dawn a few days ago, padded with clean, soft moss.

"Get some chervil from the medicine den and chew it up," Cloud Spots told Shivering Rose. "The juice will help with her kitting."

"Yes, Cloud Spots." Shivering Rose obediently made for the door of the nursery and stopped. "Excuse me, Thunderstar."

Thunderstar blinked in surprise and realized he was blocking the door. "Oh, sorry," he muttered, and moved aside. He felt embarrassed and useless. Usually, he knew how to help the cats in his Clan. But what could he do now? He didn't know anything about having kits.

He shifted his paws miserably. What kind of father was he going to be? *If I can't even help Violet Dawn bring them* into *the world, how will I look after them once they're here?*

Another pelt brushed his, and Thunderstar looked up to find Owl Eyes regarding him sympathetically.

"You look worried," Owl Eyes mewed. "Cloud Spots says that Violet Dawn's in perfect health and he expects the kits to be fine, you know."

"I know," Thunderstar answered, hunching his shoulders. "But she's in pain and I don't know how to help her." He heard Violet Dawn moan again inside the den, and glared down at his own paws. "I'm just out here, and I don't know . . ." His great fear forced itself up and out of his mouth. "I didn't have a father of my own when I was a kit. What kind of father am I going to be? How will I know how to take care of them?"

He licked at his chest, too embarrassed to look up at Owl Eyes. Why was he telling the younger cat any of this? He'd never confided his fears to any cat in the Clan except Violet Dawn and Lightning Tail—his Clanmates needed to believe in Thunderstar's strength to feel safe. *I'm falling apart,* he realized.

A soft purr made him snap his head back up to look at Owl Eyes. The sleek dark gray tom's eyes were shining with warmth. "How can you say that?" he asked. "Thunderstar, you look after the whole Clan. Being a father will be easy compared to that."

"I'm not so sure," Thunderstar muttered. But his spirits rose a little, and he brushed his tail against Owl Eyes's side gratefully. At least some cat believed in him, even if he didn't believe in himself.

Shivering Rose returned to the nursery, carrying a mouthful of chewed pulp.

"The chervil, good," Cloud Spots mewed inside the nursery. "Now try to take a little of this, Violet Dawn."

"Okay," Thunderstar heard Violet Dawn answer in a shaky mew, and then she gasped again in pain. He shuddered at the sound. Should he go in? Or would he only be in the way?

"It's perfectly normal for it to hurt," Cloud Spots told her soothingly. "You're doing very well."

Violet Dawn yowled sharply, and then moaned. "Thunderstar. Where's Thunderstar? I can't do this without him!"

Thunderstar bolted into the den. Cloud Spots glanced at him sharply. "Sometimes it's better for the father to wait outside."

"No, I *need* him," Violet Dawn insisted.

Shivering Rose, her paws on Violet Dawn's side, mewed, "I think they're almost here." Violet Dawn yowled again, pain in her voice.

Thunderstar lay beside her, curling his body around hers. "It's all right," he murmured into her ear. "Just think how beautiful our kits will be. They'll finally be able to kick you from the outside instead of the inside."

Violet Dawn gave a short *mrrow* of laughter, which turned into another gasp.

"The first one's coming," Cloud Spots announced.

"Take a deep breath and push," Shivering Rose mewed. "Not long now."

There was a commotion of movement from the medicine

cats down at the other end of Violet Dawn's body, but Thunderstar's attention was focused on his mate's face, her amber eyes locked on his as she shook and panted. "You're doing so well," he mewed softly to her. "You're so brave and strong."

"A tom," Cloud Spots announced, his voice warm, and a tiny wet kit was placed next to Violet Dawn's belly. "Lick him warm."

Thunderstar bent his head toward the little tom, whose coat was the same bright ginger as Thunderstar's own. As he began to lick, he was flooded with wonder and love. Why had no cat told him this was how it would feel? Of course he would protect and teach this little one. The path seemed clear at last: He would love his kits. Everything else would follow.

By the time the sun had almost set, it was all over.

"Four healthy kits," Thunderstar purred with satisfaction. He looked around the nursery. Milkweed was nursing Patch Pelt and Beech Tail in their nest on the other side of the den, and her two kits, who had seemed small to Thunderstar just that morning, now looked enormous in contrast to his tiny, beautiful kits.

"They're quite nice, aren't they?" Violet Dawn mewed, gently licking the head of the last to be born, a gray tom even smaller than his brothers and sisters.

"I used to think it was silly when cats called their kits perfect," Thunderstar confessed. "But now I know what they mean. *Our* kits are absolutely perfect. All four of them."

"This one is going to be the strongest, I think." Violet Dawn nosed gently at one of the she-kits, a ginger-striped tabby. "See how hard she's kneading at my side already. And look." She gently nudged the kit over onto her back. "See that?"

The little she-kit had a white stripe zigzagging across her belly. It looked just like a bolt of lightning.

A twinge of grief broke into Thunderstar's happiness. Lightning Tail would have laughed at the echo of his own name and made a special favorite out of the kit. He would have been so happy to watch over and play with all four of the kits. But Lightning Tail would never see them. *I'll tell them all about brave Lightning Tail,* Thunderstar vowed silently. *The cat who saved me.*

CHAPTER TEN

❧

A breeze blew through the high branches of Fourtrees, and a full moon floated high in the sky overhead. Thunderstar leaped up onto the Great Rock beside Skystar and Windstar, leaving his Clanmates to mingle with the other cats of SkyClan and WindClan.

"Where are the others?" he asked.

"ShadowClan's just coming now," Windstar replied, nodding toward the edge of the hollow, where a slender black she-cat was leading a stream of cats into the clearing.

"I can hear RiverClan," Skystar mewed. "And smell fish." All three cats purred with amusement—Riverstar was a wise and generous leader, but his Clan's diet left them all with a very identifiable odor.

In just a few heartbeats, the other two leaders had joined them on the Great Rock, and Windstar called the cats in the hollow below them to order.

"What news?" she asked, looking around at the other leaders.

"I'll go first, if you don't mind," Thunderstar mewed. "We have a lot of news in ThunderClan."

"Starting with your new kits, I assume?" Shadowstar asked with a purr. There were meows of excitement and congratulation from the cats of all five Clans.

"Yes," Thunderstar said, warmth creeping through his pelt. "Violet Dawn and I welcomed four healthy kits, two toms and two she-cats. They're all doing really well, and so is Violet Dawn."

"I'm very happy for you, and I know all of RiverClan is, too," Riverstar mewed, and Windstar and Shadowstar chimed in with their own congratulations.

"Give Violet Dawn all our best wishes," Windstar added. "Maybe in a few moons she'll come to a Gathering again."

"I can't wait to meet the kits." Skystar's blue eyes were shining. "My own kit with kits." He draped his tail across Thunderstar's. "I only wish Gray Wing was here. He would have been so proud of you."

Thunderstar felt unexpectedly touched by the sincere happiness in Skystar's voice. *Part of me still wants Skystar's approval,* he realized. And it would be good for the kits to have kin in his father's Clan, if they ever needed SkyClan's help.

"I have sad news, too." Thunderstar waited for the Clans to quiet, every face turned up to him attentively. "We sent word that the dogs were no longer a threat, but I didn't tell you that we paid a terrible price. Lightning Tail was killed fighting the dogs."

There were murmurs of dismay from every Clan. Every cat had liked and respected Lightning Tail.

Windstar bowed her head in sorrow. Lightning Tail had

been born and grown up in her group on the moor, and she knew him well. "WindClan will mourn Lightning Tail," she mewed, and the other leaders agreed.

"I kept vigil over his body through the night after he died," Thunderstar added. "It gave me a chance to remember him, and to say good-bye."

"Did it give you peace?" Riverstar asked solemnly.

"It did," Thunderstar mewed. "And it felt right. It felt like a way to honor all he'd done for me."

Riverstar nodded. "It's a good idea to show respect to our dead," he said.

The other leaders agreed, murmuring thoughtfully.

"Perhaps we can all honor our warriors by spending a last night with them before they pass on to StarClan," Shadowstar added solemnly.

"Have you chosen your new deputy?" Skystar asked. "You can't leave your Clan without one. What if something happened to you?"

Shadowstar agreed. "And you need a cat to help you run the everyday life of the Clan."

Thunderstar looked around the hollow. His gaze sought out Skystar's deputy Sparrow Fur; Windstar's mate and deputy, Gorse Fur; Riverstar's deputy, Night; Shadowstar's deputy, Sun Shadow. All cats who were absolutely trusted by their leaders, who had proved themselves good friends and wise advisors. They were all admired and respected by their Clans.

Thunderstar looked over his own Clan: generous Pink

Eyes, brave Snail Shell, clever Blue Whisker, strong hunter Leaf. They were all fine cats. None of them were Lightning Tail. No cat was.

A breeze ran through his pelt, almost like the brush of a tail across his back, and for a moment Thunderstar almost thought he heard the purr of his oldest friend.

If Lightning Tail were here, he would tell me not to be a mouse-brain, he thought. *The Clan needs a deputy, and there's one cat who's right for the job. I decided the night the kits were born; I just haven't been able to bring myself to tell the Clan.*

"Thunder Clan's new deputy will be Owl Eyes," he announced. His mew felt rusty and stiff to him at first, but his voice rose and got more confident as he went on. "He's proved himself more than deserving."

"Hooray!" Apple Blossom burst out from the crowd below, and there were *mrrows* of laughter from all around her. "Sorry, Thunderstar."

All the ThunderClan cats looked pleased, and the cats of the other Clans were nodding in approval. Thunderstar caught sight of Owl Eyes himself, looking stunned and happy, near the base of the Great Rock.

He's the obvious choice, Thunderstar thought. *Now I just have to be fair to him. He'll be a great deputy and I can't hold it against him that he's not Lightning Tail.*

After the meeting, Thunderstar caught up to Owl Eyes. "I'm sorry to spring that on you," he mewed. "I hope you *do* want to be deputy. I've been thinking about it for a while, and I think you'll be great."

"I do. I do want to be deputy," Owl Eyes answered quickly, tripping over his words. His round amber eyes were shining with emotion and excitement. "I just—I won't let you down, Thunderstar."

"I know you won't." Thunderstar was surprised to find that he meant it.

Owl Eyes suddenly looked solemn. "I don't know if I'll ever be as good a deputy as Lightning Tail was. He always knew what to do. But I'll honor him by trying my best every day, I promise."

Thunderstar purred. "You know, even Lightning Tail didn't always know what he was doing. Remember when he was playing with Clover and Thistle when they were kits and he slipped and sent the whole prey pile flying?"

Owl Eyes twitched his whiskers in amusement. "I had forgotten that."

"Lightning Tail made mistakes sometimes," Thunderstar told him. "Every cat does. But he tried his best to take care of his Clan, and that's all I can ask of you."

Talking about Lightning Tail made Thunderstar's heart lighter. He pressed his flank against Owl Eyes's. "I know you're going to be a great deputy."

Back in camp, Thunderstar went into the nursery to check on Violet Dawn and the kits. "I made Owl Eyes deputy," he told her, lying down next to her and sweeping up the smallest of the kits to cuddle into his side.

"About time," she replied sleepily. "I told you he was the right choice."

"Remember that your mother is always right," Thunderstar instructed the kit, and the kit looked up at him with sleepy blue eyes and yawned, showing sharp white kit-teeth.

"Of course I am," Violet Dawn mewed contently. "I am also right that you need to name that kit and his sister. I already named Shell Claw and Feather Ear. I can't go on calling the other two the gray one and the tabby one, especially not now that their eyes are open. They need names."

"I know," Thunderstar nuzzled her cheek. "I will before we sleep tonight, I promise."

He got up and wandered to the door of the nursery, looking out at the camp and watching his Clan settle down to sleep. He saw Owl Eyes bring Milkweed a piece of prey, then distract her kits so she had a moment to eat it. All was well.

In the nursery, there was a tiny mew behind him, and he turned around, feeling the pleasant swell that filled his chest whenever he thought of his kits. Three of the kits were sleeping, nestled against Violet Dawn's side. But the third, the tabby she-kit, stared up at him with amber eyes that blazed like fire. She was only a quarter-moon old, but he could already see intelligence and courage in her eyes. She was going to be something special; he knew it.

The she-kit rolled over and stretched, showing the

lightning-shaped splash of white on her belly. *Of course,* Thunderstar thought, *something special.*

"What do you think about Lightning Stripe for her name?" he asked Violet Dawn, and she purred in approval.

"It's perfect," she said.

"And the gray one should be Sleek Fur," Thunderstar said, looking down at the sleeping tom affectionately. "He has the softest fur I've ever felt."

"Wonderful," Violet Dawn said. "Thank StarClan they have names now. I wouldn't want them getting jealous of their littermates."

A cool breeze ruffled Thunderstar's fur, and he glanced back out of the nursery into the clearing outside. Clouds were gathering overhead; it looked like a storm was brewing. A flash of lightning lit up the sky for a moment, followed by a rumble of thunder that echoed around the camp.

Thunderstar purred. Lightning and thunder together, just like he and Lightning Tail had always been.

He knew that, from now on, whenever he saw lightning in the sky, he would remember the best friend he had ever had. And his own kit, beautiful, spirited Lightning Stripe, would remind him of his first deputy every day.

It was all right to be happy again, to look forward to his kits' growing up, to accept his new deputy. He hadn't lost Lightning Tail, not forever.

Lightning Tail will always be with me . . . and with all of ThunderClan.

ERIN HUNTER

is inspired by a love of cats and a fascination with the ferocity of the natural world. As well as having great respect for nature in all its forms, Erin enjoys creating rich mythical explanations for animal behavior. She is also the author of the Seekers, Survivors, and Bravelands series.

Download the free Warriors app at www.warriorcats.com.

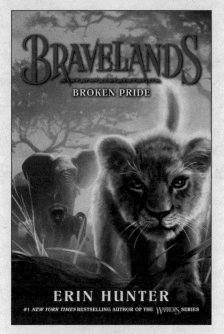

FOLLOW THE ADVENTURES!

WARRIORS: THE PROPHECIES BEGIN

1

2

3

4

5

6

In the first series, sinister perils threaten the four warrior Clans.
Into the midst of this turmoil comes Rusty, an ordinary housecat,
who may just be the bravest of them all.

HARPER
An Imprint of HarperCollinsPublishers

www.warriorcats.com

WARRIORS: THE NEW PROPHECY

1

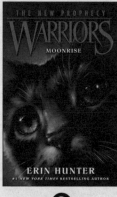

2

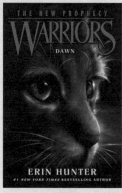

3

4

5

6

In the second series, follow the next generation of heroic cats as they set off on a quest to save the Clans from destruction.

HARPER
An Imprint of HarperCollinsPublishers

www.warriorcats.com

WARRIORS: POWER OF THREE

1

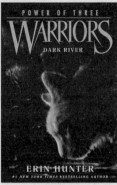

2

3

4

5

6

In the third series, Firestar's grandchildren begin their training as warrior cats. Prophecy foretells that they will hold more power than any cats before them.

HARPER
An Imprint of HarperCollinsPublishers

www.warriorcats.com

WARRIORS: OMEN OF THE STARS

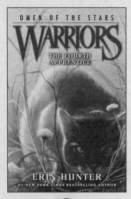

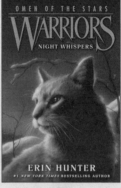

In the fourth series, find out which ThunderClan apprentice will complete the prophecy.

HARPER
An Imprint of HarperCollinsPublishers

www.warriorcats.com

WARRIORS: DAWN OF THE CLANS

1

2

3

4

5

6

In this prequel series,
discover how the warrior Clans came to be.

HARPER
An Imprint of HarperCollinsPublishers

www.warriorcats.com

WARRIORS: SUPER EDITIONS

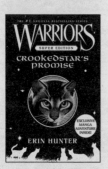

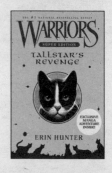

These extra-long, stand-alone adventures will take you deep inside each of the Clans with thrilling tales featuring the most legendary warrior cats.

HARPER
An Imprint of HarperCollinsPublishers

www.warriorcats.com

WARRIORS: BONUS STORIES

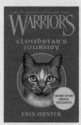

Discover the untold stories of the warrior cats and Clans
when you download the separate ebook novellas—or read
them in four paperback bind-ups!

HARPER
An Imprint of HarperCollinsPublishers

www.warriorcats.com

WARRIORS: FIELD GUIDES

Delve deeper into the Clans with these Warriors field guides.

HARPER
An Imprint of HarperCollinsPublishers

www.warriorcats.com

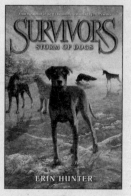